1/13/11
#6.50

PRAISE FOR AWARD-WINNING AUTHOR OCTAVIA E. BUTLER

"Butler is among the best SF writers, blessed with a mind capable of conceiving complicated futuristic situations that shed considerable light on our current affairs."

—*Houston Post*

"Butler's spare, vivid prose style invites comparison with the likes of Kate Wilhelm and Ursula Le Guin."

—*Kirkus Reviews* (starred review)

"What 'cyberpunk' author William Gibson does for [white readers], Octavia Butler does for people of color. She gives us a future."

—*Vibe*

"Butler brings Toni Morrison to mind."

—*Publishers Weekly*

"Butler's books are exceptional. . . . Butler is a realist, writing the most detailed social criticism and creating some of the most fascinating female characters in the genre. . . . The hard edge of cruelty, violence and domination is described in stark detail . . . real women caught in impossible situations."

—*Village Voice*

"She is one of those rare authors who pay serious attention to the way human beings actually work together and against each other, and she does so with extraordinary plausibility."

—*Locus*

more . . .

Books by Octavia E. Butler

Adulthood Rites
Clay's Ark
Dawn
Imago
Mind of My Mind
Parable of the Sower
Patternmaster
Wild Seed

Available from
Warner Aspect

OCTAVIA E. BUTLER

ADULTHOOD RITES

ASPECT®

WARNER BOOKS

A Time Warner Company

To Lynn—
write!

WARNER BOOKS EDITION

Aspect® is a registered trademark of Warner Books, Inc.

Cover design by Don Puckey
Cover illustration by John Jude Palencar

Warner Books, Inc.
1271 Avenue of the Americas
New York, NY 10020

Ⓦ A Time Warner Company

Visit our Web site at
http://pathfinder.com/twep

Printed in the United States of America

ISBN 10:   0-446-60378-3
ISBN 13: 978-0-446-60378-2

Originally published in hardcover by Warner Books.
First Printed in Paperback: May, 1989
Reissued: April, 1997
10 9 8

LO

1

He remembered much of his stay in the womb.

While there, he began to be aware of sounds and tastes. They meant nothing to him, but he remembered them. When they recurred, he noticed.

When something touched him, he knew it to be a new thing—a new experience. The touch was first startling, then comforting. It penetrated his flesh painlessly and calmed him. When it withdrew, he felt bereft, alone for the first time. When it returned, he was pleased—another new sensation. When he had experienced a few of these withdrawals and returns, he learned anticipation.

He did not learn pain until it was time for him to be born.

He could feel and taste changes happening around him— the slow turning of his body, then later the sudden headfirst thrust, the compression first of his head, then gradually along the length of his body. He hurt in a dull, distant way.

Yet he was not afraid. The changes were right. It was time for them. His body was ready. He was propelled along in regular pulses and comforted from time to time by the touch of his familiar companion.

There was light!

Vision was first a blaze of shock and pain. He could not

3

escape the light. It grew brighter and more painful, reached its maximum as the compression ended. No part of his body was free of the sharp, raw brilliance. Later, he would recall it as heat, as burning.

It cooled abruptly.

Something muted the light. He could still see, but seeing was no longer painful. His body was rubbed gently as he lay submerged in something soft and comforting. He did not like the rubbing. It made the light seem to jerk and vanish, then leap back to visibility. But it was the familiar presence that touched him, held him. It stayed with him and helped him endure the rubbing without fear.

He was wrapped in something that touched him every- where except his face. He did not like the heavy feel of it, but it shut out the light and did not hurt him.

Something touched the side of his face, and he turned, mouth open, to take it. His body knew what to do. He sucked and was rewarded by food and by the taste of flesh as familiar as his own. For a time, he assumed it was his own. It had always been with him.

He could hear voices, could even distinguish individual sounds, though he understood none of them. They captured his attention, his curiosity. He would remember these, too, when he was older and able to understand them. But he liked the soft voices even without knowing what they were.

"He's beautiful," one voice said. "He looks completely Human."

"Some of his features are only cosmetic, Lilith. Even now his senses are more dispersed over his body than yours are. He is . . . less Human than your daughters."

"I'd guessed he would be. I know your people still worry about Human-born males."

"They were an unsolved problem. I believe we've solved it now."

"His senses are all right, though?"

"Of course."

"That's all I can expect, I guess." A sigh. "Shall I thank you for making him look this way—for making him seem Human so I can love him? . . . for a while."

"You've never thanked me before."

"... no."

"And I think you go on loving them even when they change."

"They can't help what they are ... what they become. You're sure everything else is all right, too? All the mismatched bits of him fit together as best they can?"

"Nothing in him is mismatched. He's very healthy. He'll have a long life and be strong enough to endure what he must endure."

of another person and recognize himself as the cause of that pain.

Now he perceived, through the tendril of flesh he had extended into Lilith, expanses of living cells. He focused on a few cells, on a single cell, on the parts of that cell, on its nucleus, on chromosomes within the nucleus, on genes along the chromosomes. He investigated the DNA that made up the genes, the nucleotides of the DNA. There was something beyond the nucleotides that he could not perceive—a world of smaller particles that he could not cross into. He did not understand why he could not make this final crossing—if it were the final one. It frustrated him that anything was beyond his perception. He knew of it only through shadowy ungraspable feelings. When he was older he came to think of it as a horizon, always receding when he approached it.

He shifted his attention from the frustration of what he could not perceive to the fascination of what he could. Lilith's flesh was much more exciting than the flesh of Nikanj, Ahajas, and Dichaan. There was something wrong with hers—something he did not understand. It was both frightening and seductive. It told him Lilith was dangerous, though she was also essential. Nikanj was interesting but not dangerous. Ahajas and Dichaan were so alike he had to struggle to perceive differences between them. In some ways Joseph had been like Lilith. Deadly and compelling. But he had not been as much like Lilith as Ahajas was like Dichaan. In fact, though he had clearly been Human and native to this place, this *Earth*, like Lilith, he had not been Lilith's relative. Ahajas and Dichaan were brother and sister, like most Oankali male and female mates. Joseph was unrelated, like Nikanj—but although Nikanj was Oankali, it was also ooloi, not male or female. Ooloi were supposed to be unrelated to their male and female mates so that they could focus their attention on their mates' genetic differences and construct children without making dangerous mistakes of overfamiliarity and overconfidence.

"Be careful," he heard Nikanj say. "He's studying you again."

"I know," Lilith answered. "Sometimes I wish he'd just nurse like Human babies."

Lilith rubbed Akin's back, and the flickering of light

between and around her fingers broke his concentration. He withdrew his flesh from hers, then released her nipple and looked at her. She closed clothing over her breast but went on holding him on her lap. He was always glad when people held him and talked to each other, allowing him to listen. He had already learned more words from them than he had yet had occasion to use. He collected words and gradually assembled them into questions. When his questions were answered, he remembered everything he was told. His picture of the world grew.

"At least he isn't any stronger or faster in physical development than other babies," Lilith said. "Except for his teeth."

"There have been babies born with teeth before," Nikanj said. "Physically, he'll look his Human age until his metamorphosis. He'll have to think his way out of any problems his precocity causes."

"That won't do him much good with some Humans. They'll resent him for not being completely Human and for looking more Human than their kids. They'll hate him for looking much younger than he sounds. They'll hate him because they haven't been allowed to have sons. Your people have made Human-looking male babies a very valuable commodity."

"We'll allow more of them now. Everyone feels more secure about mixing them. Before now, too many ooloi could not perceive the necessary mixture. They could have made mistakes and their mistakes could be monsters."

"Most Humans think that's what they've been doing."

"Do you still?"

Silence.

"Be content, Lilith. One group of us believed it would be best to dispense with Human-born males altogether. We could construct female children for Human females and male children for Oankali females. We've done that until now."

"And cheated everyone. Ahajas wants daughters, and I want sons. Other people feel the same way."

"I know. And we control children in ways we should not to make them mature as Oankali-born males and Human-born females. We control inclinations that should be left to individual children. Even the group that suggested we go on this way knows we shouldn't. But they were afraid. A male who's

Human enough to be born to a Human female could be a danger to us all. We must try though. We'll learn from Akin."

Akin felt himself held closer to Lilith. "Why is he such an experiment?" she demanded. "And why should Human-born men be such a problem? I know most prewar men don't like you. They feel you're displacing them and forcing them to do something perverted. From their point of view, they're right. But you could teach the next generation to love you, no matter who their mothers are. All you'd have to do is start early. Indoctrinate them before they're old enough to develop other opinions."

"But..." Nikanj hesitated. "But if we had to work that blindly, that clumsily, we couldn't have trade. We would have to take your children from you soon after they were born. We wouldn't dare trust you to raise them. You would be kept only for breeding—like nonsentient animals."

Silence. A sigh. "You say such godawful things in such a gentle voice. No, hush, I know it's the only voice you've got. Nika, will Akin survive the Human males who will hate him?"

"They won't hate him."

"They will! He isn't Human. Un-Human women are offensive to them, but they don't usually try to hurt them, and they do sleep with them—like a racist sleeping with racially different women. But Akin... They'll see him as a threat. Hell, he *is* a threat. He's one of their replacements."

"Lilith, they will not hate him." Akin felt himself lifted from Lilith's arms and held close to Nikanj's body. He gasped at the lovely shock of contact with Nikanj's sensory tentacles, many of which held him while others burrowed painlessly into his flesh. It was so easy to connect with Nikanj and to learn. "They will see him as beautiful and like themselves," Nikanj said. "By the time he's old enough for his body to reveal what he actually is, he'll be an adult and able to hold his own."

"Able to fight?"

"Only to save his life. He'll tend to avoid fighting. He'll be like Oankali-born males now—a solitary wanderer when he's not mated."

"He won't settle down with anyone?"

"No. Most Human males aren't particularly monogamous. No construct males will be."

"But—"

"Families will change, Lilith—are changing. A complete construct family will be a female, an ooloi, and children. Males will come and go as they wish and as they find welcome."

"But they'll have no homes."

"A home like this would be a prison to them. They'll have what they want, what they need."

"The ability to be fathers to their kids?"

Nikanj paused. "They might choose to keep contact with their children. They won't live with them permanently—and no construct, male or female, young or old, will feel that as a deprivation. It will be normal to them, and purposeful, since there will always be many more females and ooloi than males." It rustled its head and body tentacles. "Trade means change. Bodies change. Ways of living must change. Did you think your children would only *look* different?"

3

Akin spent some part of the
day with each of his parents. Lilith fed him and taught him.
The others only taught him, but he went to them all eagerly.
Ahajas usually held him after Lilith.

Ahajas was tall and broad. She carried him without seeming to notice his weight. He had never felt weariness in her.
And he knew she enjoyed carrying him. He could feel pleasure
the moment she sank filaments of her sensory tentacles into
him. She was the first person to be able to reach him this way
with more than simple emotions. She was the first to give him
multisensory images and signaling pressures and to help him
understand that she was speaking to him without words. As he
grew, he realized that Nikanj and Dichaan also did this. Nikanj
had done it even before he was born, but he had not understood. Ahajas had reached him and taught him quickly. Through
the images she created for him, he learned about the child
growing within her. She gave him images of it and even
managed to give it images of him. It had several presences: all
its parents except Lilith. And it had him. Sibling.

He knew he would be male when he grew up. He
understood male, female, and ooloi. And he knew that because
he would be male, the unborn child who would begin its life
seeming much less Human than he did would eventually

12

become female. There was a balance, a naturalness to this that pleased him. He should have a sister to grow up with—a sister but not an ooloi sibling. Why? He wondered whether the child inside Ahajas would become ooloi, but Ahajas and Nikanj both assured him it would not. And they would not tell him how they knew. So this sibling should become a sister. It would take years to develop sexually, but he already thought of it as "she."

Dichaan usually took him once Ahajas had returned him to Lilith and Lilith had fed him. Dichaan taught him about strangers.

First there were his older siblings, some born to Ahajas and becoming more Human, and some born to Lilith and becoming more Oankali. There were also children of older siblings, and finally, frighteningly, unrelated people. Akin could not understand why some of the unrelated ones were more like Lilith than Joseph had been. And none of them were like Joseph.

Dichaan read Akin's unspoken confusion.

"The differences you perceive between Humans—between groups of Humans—are the result of isolation and inbreeding, mutation, and adaptation to different Earth environments," he said, illustrating each concept with quick multiple images. "Joseph and Lilith were born in very different parts of this world—born to long separated peoples. Do you understand?"

"Where are Joseph's kind?" Akin asked aloud.

"Now there are villages of them to the southwest. They're called Chinese."

"I want to see them."

"You will. You can travel to them when you're older." He ignored Akin's rush of frustration. "And someday I'll take you to the ship. You'll be able to see Oankali differences, too." He gave Akin an image of the ship—a vast sphere made up of huge, still-growing, many-sided plates like the shell of a turtle. In fact, it was the outer shell of a living being. "There," Dichaan said, "you'll see Oankali who will never come to Earth or trade with Humans. For now, they tend the ship in ways that require a different physical form." He gave Akin an image, and Akin thought it resembled a huge caterpillar.

Akin projected silent questioning.

"Speak aloud," Dichaan told him.

"Is it a child?" Akin asked, thinking of the changes caterpillars underwent.

"No. It's adult. It's larger than I am."

"Can it talk?"

"In images, in tactile, bioelectric, and bioluminescent signals, in pheromones, and in gestures. It can gesture with ten limbs at once. But its throat and mouth parts won't produce speech. And it is deaf. It must live in places where there is a great deal of noise. My parents' parents had that shape."

This seemed terrible to Akin—Oankali forced to live in an ugly form that did not even allow them to hear or speak.

"What they are is as natural to them as what you are is to you," Dichaan told him. "And they are much closer to the ship than we can be. They're companions to it, knowing its body better than you know your own. When I was a little older than you are now, I wanted to be one of them. They let me taste a little of their relationship with the ship."

"Show me."

"Not yet. It's a very powerful thing. I'll show you when you're a little older."

Everything was to happen when he was older. He must wait! He must always wait! In frustration, Akin had stopped speaking. He could not help hearing and remembering all that Dichaan told him, but he would not speak to Dichaan again for days.

Yet it was Dichaan who began leaving him in the care of his older sisters, letting him begin to investigate them—while they thoroughly investigated him. His favorite among them was Margit. She was six years old—too small to carry him long, but he was content to ride on her back or sit on her lap for as long as she could handle him comfortably. She did not have sensory tentacles like his Oankali-born sisters, but she had clusters of sensitive nodules that would probably be tentacles when she grew up. She could match some of these to the smooth, invisible sensory patches on his skin, and the two of them could exchange images and emotions as well as words. She could teach him.

"You should be careful," she said as she took him to shelter in their family house, away from a hard afternoon rain. "Your eyes don't track a lot of the time. Can you see with them?"

He thought about this. "I can," he said, "but I don't always. Sometimes it's easier to see things from other parts of my body."

"When you're older, you'll be expected to turn your face and body toward people when you talk to them. Even now, you should look at Humans with your eyes. If you don't, they yell at you or repeat things because they're not sure they have your attention. Or they start to ignore you because they think you're ignoring them."

"No one's done that to me."

"They will. Just wait until you get past the stage when they try to talk stupid to you."

"Baby talk, you mean?"

"Human talk!"

Silence.

"Don't worry," she said after a while. "It's them I'm mad at, not you."

"Why?"

"They blame me for not looking like them. They can't help doing it, and I can't help resenting it. I don't know which is worse—the ones who cringe if I touch them or the ones who pretend it's all right while they cringe inside."

"What does Lilith feel?" Akin asked only because he already knew the answer.

"For her, I might as well look the way you do. I remember when I was about your age, she would wonder how I would find a mate, but Nikanj told her there would be plenty of males like me by the time I grew up. She never said anything after that. She tells me to stick with the constructs. I do, mostly."

"Humans like me," he said. "I guess because I look like them."

"Just remember to look at them with your eyes when they talk to you or you talk to them. And be careful about tasting them. You won't be able to get away with that for much longer. Besides, your tongue doesn't look Human."

"Humans say it shouldn't be gray, but they don't realize how different it really is."

"Don't let them guess. They can be dangerous, Akin. Don't show them everything you can do. But ... hang around them when you can. Study their behavior. Maybe you can collect things about them that we can't. It would be wrong if anything that they are is lost."

"Your legs are going to sleep," Akin observed. "You're tired. You should take me to Lilith."

"In a little while."

She did not want to give him up, he realized. He did not mind. She was, Humans said, gray and warty—more different than most Human-born children. And she could hear as well as any construct. She caught every whisper whether she wanted to or not, and if she were near Humans, they soon began to talk about her. "If she looks this bad now, what will she look like after metamorphosis?" they would begin. Then they would speculate or pity her or condemn her or laugh at her. Better a few more minutes of peace alone with him.

Her full Human name was Margita Iyapo Domonkos Kaalnikanjlo. Margit. She had all four of his living parents in common with him. Her Human father, though, was Vidor Domonkos, not the dead Joseph. Vidor—some people called him Victor—had moved to a village several miles upriver when he and Lilith tired of one another. He came back two or three times a year to see Margit. He did not like the way she looked, yet he loved her. She had seen that he did, and Akin was certain she had read his emotion correctly. He had never met Vidor himself. He had been too young for contact with strangers during the man's last visit.

"Will you tell Vidor to let me touch him when he comes to see you again?" Akin asked.

"Father? Why?"

"I want to find you in him."

She laughed. "He and I have a lot in common. He doesn't like having anyone explore him, though. Says he doesn't need anything burrowing through his skin." She hesitated. "He means that. He only let me do it once. Just talk to him if you meet him, Akin. In some ways he can be just as dangerous as any other Human."

"Your father?"

"Akin... *All of them!* Haven't you explored any of them? Can't you feel it?" She gave him a complex image. He understood it only because he had explored a few Humans himself. Humans were a compelling, seductive, deadly contradiction.

He felt drawn to them, yet warned against them. To touch a Human deeply—to taste one—was to feel this.

"I know," he said. "But I don't understand."

"Talk to Ooan. It knows and understands. Talk to Mother, too. She knows more than she likes to admit."

"She's Human. You don't think she's dangerous, too, do you?"

"Not to us." She stood up with him. "You're getting heavier. I'll be glad when you learn to walk."

"Me, too. How old were you when you walked?"

"Just over a year. You're almost there."

"Nine months."

"Yes. It's too bad you couldn't learn walking as easily as you learned talking." She returned him to Lilith, who fed him and promised to take him into the forest with her.

Lilith gave him bits of solid food now, but he still took great comfort in nursing. It frightened him to realize that someday she would not let him nurse. He did not want to grow that old.

4

Lilith put him on her back in a cloth sack and took him to one of the village gardens. This particular garden was some distance upriver from the village, and Akin enjoyed the long walk through the forest. There were new sounds, smells, and sights on each trip. Lilith would often stop to let him touch or taste new things or to let him view and memorize deadly things. He had discovered that his fingers were sensitive enough to taste which plants were harmful—if his sense of smell did not warn him before he touched.

"That's a good talent," Lilith said when he told her. "At least you're not likely to poison yourself. Be careful how you touch things, though. Some plants do damage on contact."

"Show me those," Akin said.

"I will. We clear them out of the area when we see them, but they always find their way back. I'll take you with me next time we decide to cull them."

"Does cull mean the same as clear?"

"Cull means to clear selectively. We only take out the plants with contact poisons."

"I see." He paused, trying to understand the new scent he had detected. "There's someone between us and the river," he whispered suddenly.

"All right." They had reached the garden. She bent over a

cassava plant and pretended to find it hard to pull up so that she could move casually around to face the river. They could not see the water from where they were. There was plenty of ground between themselves and the river—and plenty of cover.

"I can't see them," she said. "Can you?" She had only her eyes to look with, but her senses were sharper than those of other Humans—somewhere between Human and construct.

"It's a man," Akin said. "He's hidden. He's Human and a stranger." Akin breathed in the adrenaline bite of the man's scent. "He's excited. Maybe afraid."

"Not afraid," she said softly. "Not of a woman pulling cassavas and carrying a baby. I hear him now, moving around near the big Brazil nut tree."

"Yes, I hear!" Akin said excitedly.

"Keep quiet! And hold on. I might have to move fast."

The man had stopped moving. Suddenly, he stepped into view, and Akin saw that he had something in his hands.

"Shit!" Lilith whispered. "Bow and arrow. He's a resister."

"You mean those sticks he's holding?"

"Yes. They're weapons."

"Don't turn that way. I can't see him."

"And he can't see you. Keep your head down!"

He realized then that he was in danger. Resisters were Humans who had decided to live without the Oankali—and thus without children. Akin had heard that they sometimes stole construct children, the most Human-looking construct children they could find. But that was stupid because they had no idea what the child might be like after metamorphosis. Oankali never let them keep the children anyway.

"Do you speak English?" Lilith called, and Akin, straining to look over her shoulder, saw the man lower his bow and arrow.

"English is the only Human language spoken here," Lilith said. It comforted Akin that she neither sounded nor smelled frightened. His own fear diminished.

"I heard you talking to someone," the man said in slightly accented English.

"Hold tight," Lilith whispered.

Akin grasped the material of the cloth sack in which she

carried him. He held on with hands and legs, wishing he were stronger.

"My village isn't far from here," she said to the man. "You'll be welcome there. Food. Shelter. It's going to rain soon."

"*Who were you talking to!*" the man demanded, coming nearer.

"My son." She gestured toward Akin.

"What? The baby?"

"Yes."

The man came closer, peering at Akin. Akin peered back over Lilith's shoulder, curiosity overwhelming the last of his fear. The man was shirtless, black-haired, clean-shaven, and stocky. His hair was long and hung down his back. He had cut it off in a straight line across his forehead. Something about him reminded Akin of the picture he had seen of Joseph. This man's eyes were narrow like Joseph's, but his skin was almost as brown as Lilith's.

"The kid looks good," he said. "What's wrong with him?"

She stared at him. "Nothing," she said flatly.

The man frowned. "I don't mean to offend you. I just . . . Is he really as healthy as he looks?"

"Yes."

"I haven't seen a baby since back before the war."

"I'd guessed that. Will you come back to the village with us? It isn't far."

"How is it you were allowed to have a boy?"

"How is it your mother was allowed to have a boy?"

The man took a final step toward Lilith and was abruptly too close. He stood very straight and tried to intimidate her with his stiff, angry posture and his staring eyes. Akin had seen Humans do that to one another before. It never worked with constructs. Akin had never seen it work with Lilith. She did not move.

"I'm Human," the man said. "You can see that. I was born before the war. There's nothing Oankali about me. I have two parents, both Human, and no one told them when and whether they could have kids and what the sex of those kids would be. *Now, how is it you were allowed to have a boy?*"

"I asked for one." Lilith reached out, snatched the man's

bow, and broke it over her knee before the man was fully aware of what had happened. Her move had been almost too swift for him to follow even if he had been expecting it.

"You're welcome to food and shelter for as long as you like," she said, "but we don't allow weapons."

The man stumbled back from her. "I mistook you for Human," he said. "My god, you look Human."

"I was born twenty-six years before the war," she said. "I'm Human enough. But I have other children in that village. You won't take weapons among them."

He looked at the machete hanging from her belt.

"It's a tool," she said. "We don't use them on each other."

He shook his head. "I don't care what you say. That was a heavy bow. No Human woman should have been able to take it from me and break it that way."

She walked away from him, unsheathed her machete, and cut a pineapple. She picked it up carefully, slashed off most of its spiky top, and cut two more.

Akin watched the man while Lilith put her cassavas and pineapples into her basket. She cut a stalk of bananas, and once she was certain they were free of snakes and dangerous insects, she handed them to the man. He took a quick step back from her.

"Carry these," she said. "They're all right. I'm glad you happened along. The two of us will be able to carry more." She cut several dozen ribbons of quat—an Oankali vegetable that Akin loved—and tied it into a bundle with thin lianas. She also cut fat stalks of scigee, which the Oankali had made from some war-mutated Earth plant. Humans said it had the taste and texture of the flesh of an extinct animal—the pig.

Lilith bound the scigee stalks and fastened the bundle behind her just above her hips. She swung Akin to one side and carried her full basket on the other.

"Can you watch him without using your eyes?" she whispered to Akin.

"Yes," Akin answered.

"Do it." And she called to the man, "Come. This way." She walked away down the path to the village, not waiting to see whether the man would follow. It seemed for a while that the man would stay behind. The narrow path curved around a huge

tree, and Akin lost sight of him. There was no sound of his
following. Then there was a burst of sound—hurrying feet,
heavy breathing.

"Wait!" the man called.

Lilith stopped and waited for him to catch up. He was,
Akin noticed, still carrying the stalk of bananas. He had thrown
it over his left shoulder.

"Watch him!" Lilith whispered to Akin.

The man came close, then stopped and stared at her,
frowning.

"What's the matter?" she asked.

He shook his head. "I just don't know what to make of
you," he said.

Akin felt her relax a little. "This is your first visit to a
trading village, isn't it?" she said.

"Trading village? So that's what you call them."

"Yes. And I don't want to know what you call us. But
spend some time with us. Maybe you'll accept our definition of
ourselves. You came to find out about us, didn't you?"

He sighed. "I guess so. I was a kid when the war started. I
still remember cars, TV, computers...I do remember. But
those things aren't real to me anymore. My parents...All they
want to do is go back to the prewar days. They know as well as
I do that that's impossible, but it's what they talk about and
dream about. I left them to find out what else there might be
to do."

"Both your parents survived?"

"Yeah. They're still alive. Hell, they don't look any older
than I do now. They could still join a...one of your villages and
have more kids. They won't though."

"And you?"

"I don't know." He looked at Akin. "I haven't seen enough
to decide yet."

She reached out to touch his arm in a gesture of sympathy.

He grabbed her hand and held it at first as though he
thought she would try to pull away. She did not. He held her
wrist and examined the hand. After a time he let her go.

"Human," he whispered. "I always heard you could tell by
the hands—that the...the others would have too many fingers
or fingers that bend in un-Human ways."

"Or you could just ask," she said. "People will tell you; they don't mind. It's not the kind of thing anyone bothers to lie about. Hands aren't as reliable as you think."

"Can I look at the baby's?"

"No more than you are now."

He drew a long breath. "I wouldn't hurt a kid. Even one that wasn't quite Human."

"Akin isn't quite Human," she said.

"What's wrong with him?"

"Not a thing."

"I mean . . . What's different about him?"

"Internal differences. Rapid mental development. Perceptual differences. At metamorphosis, he'll begin to look different, though I don't know how different."

"Can he talk?"

"All the time. Come on."

He followed her along the path, and Akin watched him through light-sensitive patches on the skin of his shoulder and arm.

"Baby?" the man said peering at him.

Akin, remembering what Margit had told him, turned his head so that he faced the man. "Akin," he said. "What's your name?"

The man let his mouth fall open. "How old are you?" he demanded.

Akin stared at him silently.

"Don't you understand me?" the man asked. He had a jagged scar on one of his shoulders, and Akin wondered what had made it.

The man slapped at a mosquito with his free hand and spoke to Lilith. "How old is. he?"

"Tell him your name," she said.

"What?"

She said nothing more.

The man's smallest toe was missing from his right foot, Akin noticed. And there were other marks on his body—scars, paler than the rest of his skin. He must have hurt himself often and had no ooloi to help him heal. Nikanj would never have left so many scars.

"Okay," the man said. "I give up. My name is Augustino Leal. Everybody calls me Tino."

"Shall I call you that?" Akin asked.

"Sure, why not? Now, how the hell old are you?"

"Nine months."

"Can you walk?"

"No. I can stand up if there's something for me to hold on to, but I'm not very good at it yet. Why did you stay away from the villages for so long? Don't you like kids?"

"I . . . don't know."

"They aren't all like me. Most of them can't talk until they're older."

The man reached out and touched his face. Akin grasped one of the man's fingers and drew it to his mouth. He tasted it quickly with a snakelike flick of his tongue and a penetration too swift, too slight to notice. He collected a few living cells for later study.

"At least you put things in your mouth the way babies used to," he said.

"Akin," Lilith said, cautioning.

Suppressing his frustration, he let the man's finger go. He would have preferred to investigate further, to understand more of how the genetic information he read had been expressed and to see what nongenetic factors he could discover. He wanted to try to read the man's emotions and to find the marks the Oankali had left in him when they collected him from postwar Earth, when they repaired him and stored him away in suspended animation.

Perhaps later he would have the chance.

"If the kid is this smart now, what's he going to be like as an adult?" Tino asked.

"I don't know," Lilith told him. "The only adult male constructs we have so far are Oankali-born—born to Oankali mothers. If Akin is like them, he'll be bright enough, but his interests will be so diverse and, in some cases, so just plain un-Human that he'll wind up keeping to himself a lot."

"Doesn't that bother you?"

"There's nothing I can do about it."

"But . . . you didn't have to have kids."

"As it happens, I did have to. I had two construct kids by

the time they brought me down from the ship. I never had a chance to run off and pine for the good old days!"

The man said nothing. If he stayed long, he would learn that Lilith had these flares of bitterness sometimes. They never seemed to affect her behavior, though often they frightened people. Margit had said, "It's as though there's something in her trying to get out. Something terrible." Whenever the something seemed on the verge of surfacing, Lilith went alone into the forest and stayed away for days. Akin's oldest sisters said they used to worry that she would leave and not come back.

"They forced you to have kids?" the man asked.

"One of them surprised me," she said. "It made me pregnant, then told me about it. Said it was giving me what I wanted but would never come out and ask for."

"Was it?"

"Yes." She shook her head from side to side. "Oh, yes. But if I had the strength not to ask, it should have had the strength to let me alone."

5

The rain had begun by the time they reached the village, and Akin enjoyed the first few warm drops that made their way through the forest canopy. Then they were indoors—followed by everyone who had seen Lilith arrive with a stranger.

"They'll want your life story," Lilith told him softly. "They want to hear about your village, your travels; anything you know may be news to us. We don't get that many travelers. And later, when you've eaten and talked and whatever, they'll try to drag you off to their beds. Do what you like. If you're too tired for any of this now, say so, and we'll save your party until tomorrow."

"You didn't tell me I would have to entertain," he said, staring at the inpouring of Humans, constructs, and Oankali.

"You don't have to. Do what you like."

"But . . ." He looked around helplessly, cringed away from an Oankali-born unsexed construct child who touched him with one of the sensory tentacles growing from its head.

"Don't scare him," Akin told it from Lilith's back. He spoke in Oankali. "There aren't any of us where he comes from."

"Resister?" the child asked.

26

"Yes. But I don't think he means any harm. He didn't try to hurt us."

"What does the kid want?" Tino asked.

"It's just curious about you," Lilith told him. "Do you want to talk to these people while I put together a meal?"

"I guess so. I'm not a good storyteller, though."

Lilith turned to the still gathering crowd. "All right," she said loudly. And when they had quieted: "His name is Augustino Leal. He comes from a long way away, and he says he feels like talking."

People cheered.

"If anyone wants to go home to get something to eat or drink, we'll wait."

Several Humans and constructs left, ordering her not to let anything begin without them. An Oankali took Akin from her back. Dichaan. Akin flattened against him happily, sharing what he had learned of the new Human.

"You like him?" Dichaan asked by way of tactile signals shaded with sensory images.

"Yes. He's a little afraid and dangerous. Mother had to take his weapon. But he's mostly curious. He's so curious he feels like one of us."

Dichaan projected amusement. Maintaining his sensory link with Akin, he watched Lilith give Tino something to drink. The man tasted the drink and smiled. People had gathered around him, sitting on the floor. Most of them were children, and this seemed to put him at ease in one way—he was no longer afraid—and excite him in another. His eyes focused on one child after another, examining the wide variety of them.

"Will he try to steal someone?" Akin asked silently.

"If he did, Eka, it would probably be you." Dichaan softened the statement with amusement, but there was a seriousness beneath it that Akin did not miss. The man probably meant no harm, was probably not a child thief. But Akin should be careful, should not allow himself to be alone with Tino.

People brought food, shared it among themselves and with Lilith as they accepted what she offered. They fed their own children and each other's children as usual. A child who could walk could get bits of food anywhere.

Lilith prepared Tino and her younger children dishes of flat cassava bread layered with hot scigee and quat alongside hot, spicy beans. There were slices of pineapple and papaya for dessert. She fed Akin small amounts of quat mixed with cassava. She did not let him nurse until she had settled down with everyone else to talk and listen to Tino.

"They named our village Phoenix before my parents reached it," Tino told them. "We weren't original settlers. We came in half-dead from the forest—we'd eaten something bad, some kind of palm fruit. It was edible, all right, but only if you cooked it—and we hadn't. Anyway, we stumbled in, and the people of Phoenix took care of us. I was the only child they had—the only Human child they'd seen since before the war. The whole village sort of adopted me because . . ." He stopped, glanced at a cluster of Oankali. "Well, you know. They wanted to find a little girl. They thought maybe the few kids who hadn't gone through puberty before they were set free might be fertile together when they grew up." He stared at the nearest Oankali, who happened to be Nikanj. "True or false?" he asked.

"False," Nikanj said softly. "We told them it was false. They chose not to believe."

Tino stared at Nikanj—gave it a look that Akin did not understand. The look was not threatening, but Nikanj drew its body tentacles up slightly into the beginnings of a prestrike threat gesture. Humans called it knotting up or getting knotty. They knew it meant getting angry or otherwise upset. Few of them realized it was also a reflexive, potentially lethal gesture. Every sensory tentacle could sting. The ooloi could also sting with their sensory arms. But at least they could sting without killing. Male and female Oankali and constructs could only kill. Akin could kill with his tongue. This was one of the first things Nikanj had taught him not to do. Let alone, he might have discovered his ability by accident and killed Lilith or some other Human. The thought of this had frightened him at first, but he no longer worried about it. He had never seen anyone sting anyone.

Even now, Nikanj's body language indicated only mild upset. But why should Tino upset it at all? Akin began to watch Nikanj instead of Tino. As Tino spoke, all of Nikanj's long head tentacles swung around to focus on him. Nikanj was intensely interested in this newcomer. After a moment, it got up and made its way over to Lilith. It took Akin from her arms.

Akin had finished nursing and now flattened obligingly against Nikanj, giving what he knew Nikanj wanted: genetic information about Tino. In trade, he demanded to have explained the feelings Nikanj had expressed with its indrawn sensory tentacles.

In silent, vivid images and signals, Nikanj explained. "That one wanted to stay with us when he was a child. We couldn't agree to keep him, but we hoped he would come to us when he was older."

"You knew him then?"

"I handled his conditioning. He spoke only Spanish then. Spanish is one of my Human languages. He was only eight years old and not afraid of me. I didn't want to let him go. Everyone knew his parents would run when we released them. They would become resisters and perhaps die in the forest. But I couldn't get a consensus. We aren't good at raising Human children, so no one wanted to break up the family. And even I didn't want to force them all to stay with us. We had prints of them. If they died or kept resisting we could fashion genetic copies of them to be born to trader Humans. They wouldn't be lost to the gene pool. We decided that might have to be enough."

"Tino recognized you?"

"Yes, but in a very Human way, I think. I don't believe he understands why I caught his attention. He doesn't have complete access to memory."

"I don't understand that."

"It's a Human thing. Most Humans lose access to old memories as they acquire new ones. They know how to speak, for instance, but they don't recall learning to speak. They keep what experience has taught them—usually—but lose the experience itself. We can retrieve it for them—enable them to recall everything—but for many of them, that would only create confusion. They would remember so much that their memories would distract them from the present."

Akin received an impression of a dazed Human whose mind so overflowed with the past that every new experience

He faced her angrily. "My people never had a chance! They didn't make the war. They didn't make the Oankali. And they didn't make themselves sterile! But you can be damn sure that everything they did make was good and it worked and they put their hearts into it. Hey, I thought, 'If we made a town, the . . . traders . . . must have made a city!' And what do I find? A village of huts with primitive gardens. This place is hardly even a clearing!" His voice had risen again. He looked around with disapproval. "You've got kids to plan for and provide for, and you're going to let them slide right back to being cavemen!"

A Human woman named Leah spoke up. "Our kids will be okay," she said. "But I wish we could get more of your people to come here. They're as close to immortal as a Human being has ever been, and all they can think of to do is build useless houses and kill one another."

"It's time we offered the resisters a way back to us," Ahajas said. "I think we've been too comfortable here."

Several Oankali made silent gestures of agreement.

"Leave them alone," Tino said. "You've done enough to them! I'm not going to tell you where they are!"

Nikanj, still holding Akin, got up and moved through the seated people until it could sit with no one between itself and Tino. "None of the resister villages are hidden from us," it said softly. "We wouldn't have asked you where Phoenix was. And we don't mean to focus on Phoenix. It's time for us to approach all the resister villages and invite them to join us. It's only to remind them that they don't have to live sterile, pointless lives. We won't force them to come to us, but we will let them know they're still welcome. We let them go originally because we didn't want to hold prisoners."

Tino laughed bitterly. "So everyone here is here of their own free will, huh?"

"Everyone here is free to leave."

Tino gave Nikanj another of his unreadable looks and turned deliberately so that he faced Lilith. "How many men are there here?" he asked.

Lilith looked around, found Wray Ordway who kept the small guest house stocked with food and other supplies. This was where newly arrived men lived until they paired off with one of the village women. It was the only house in the village that had been built of cut trees and palm thatch. Tino might sleep there tonight. Wray kept the guest house because he had chosen not to wander. He had paired with Leah and apparently never tired of her. The two of them with their three Oankali mates had nine Human-born daughters and eleven Oankali-born children.

"How many men have we got now, Wray?" Lilith asked.

"Five," he said. "None in the guest house, though. Tino can have it all to himself if he wants."

"Five men." Tino shook his head. "No wonder you haven't built anything."

"We build ourselves," Wray said. "We're building a new way of life here. You don't know anything about us. Why don't you ask questions instead of shooting off your mouth!"

"What is there to ask? Except for your garden—which barely looks like a garden—you don't grow anything. Except for your shacks, you haven't built anything! And as for building yourselves, the Oankali are doing that. You're their clay, that's all!"

"They change us and we change them," Lilith said. "The whole next generation is made up of genetically engineered people, Tino—constructs, whether they're born to Oankali or to Human mothers." She sighed. "I don't like what they're doing, and I've never made any secret of it. But they're in this with us. When the ships leave, they're stuck here. And with their own biology driving them, they can't not blend with us. But some of what makes us Human will survive, just as some of what makes them Oankali will survive." She paused, looked around the large room. "Look at the children here, Tino. Look at the construct adults. You can't tell who was born to whom. But you can see some Human features on every one of them. And as for the way we live . . . well, we're not as primitive as you think—and not as advanced as we could be. It was all a matter of how much like the ship we wanted our homes to be. The Oankali made us learn to live here without them so that if we did resist, we could survive. So that people like your parents would have a choice."

"Some choice," Tino muttered.

"Better than being a prisoner or a slave," she said. "They

should have been ready for the forest. I'm surprised they ate the palm fruit that made them sick."

"We were city people, and we were hungry. My father didn't believe something could be poison raw but okay to eat cooked."

Lilith shook her head. "I was a city person, too, but there were some things I was willing not to learn from experience." She returned to her original subject. "Anyway, once we had learned to live in the forest on our own, the Oankali told us we didn't have to. They meant to live in homes as comfortable as the ones they had on the ship, and we were free to do the same. We accepted their offer. Believe me, weaving thatch and tying logs together with lianas doesn't hold any more fascination for me than it does for you—and I've done my share of it."

"This place has a thatched roof," Tino argued. "In fact, it looks freshly thatched."

"Because the leaves are green? Hell, they're green because they're alive. We didn't build this house, Tino, we grew it. Nikanj provided the seed; we cleared the land; everyone who was going to live here trained the walls and made them aware of us."

Tino frowned. "What do you mean, 'aware' of you? I thought you were telling me it was a plant."

"It's an Oankali construct. Actually, it's a kind of larval version of the ship. A neotenic larva. It can reproduce without growing up. It can also get a lot bigger without maturing sexually. This one will have to do that for a while. We don't need more than one."

"But you've got more than one. You've got—"

"Only one in this village. And a lot of that one is underground. What you see of it appears to be houses, grasses, shrubs, nearby trees, and, to some extent, riverbank. It allows some erosion, traps some newly arrived silt. Its inclination, though, is to become a closed system. A ship. We can't let it do that here. We still have a lot of growing to do ourselves."

Tino shook his head. He looked around at the large room, at the people watching, eating, feeding children, some small children stretched out asleep with their heads on adults' laps.

"Look up, Tino."

Tino jumped at the sound of Nikanj's soft voice so close to

him. He seemed about to move away, shrink away. He had probably not been this close to an Oankali since he was a child. Somehow, he managed to keep still.

"Look up," Nikanj repeated.

Tino looked up into the soft yellow glow of the ceiling.

"Didn't you even wonder where the light was coming from?" Nikanj asked. "Is that the ceiling of a primitive dwelling?"

"It wasn't like that when I came in," Tino said.

"No. It wasn't as much needed when you came in. There was plenty of light from outside. Look at the smooth walls. Look at the floor. Feel the floor. I don't think a floor of dead wood would be as comfortable. You'll have a chance to make comparisons if you choose to stay in the guest house. It really is the rough wood and thatch building you thought this was. It has to be. Strangers wouldn't be able to control the walls of the true houses here."

Wray Ordway said mildly, "Nika, if that man sleeps in the guest house tonight, I'll lose all faith in you."

Nikanj's body went helplessly smooth, and everyone laughed. The glass-smooth flattening of head and body tentacles normally indicated humor or pleasure, Akin knew, but what Nikanj was feeling now was neither of those emotions. It was more like a huge, consuming hunger, barely under control. If Nikanj had been Human, it would have been trembling. After a moment it managed to return its appearance to normal. It focused a cone of head tentacles on Lilith, appealing to her. She had not laughed, though she was smiling.

"You people are not nice," she said, keeping her smile. "You should be ashamed. Go home now, all of you. Have interesting dreams."

= 6 =

Tino watched in confusion as people began to leave. Some of them were still laughing—at a joke Tino was not sure he understood, not sure he wanted to understand. Some stopped to talk to the woman who had brought him into the village. Lilith her name was. Lilith. Unusual name loaded with bad connotations. She should have changed it. Almost anything would have been better.

Three Oankali and several children clustered around her, talking to the departing guests. Much of the conversation was in some other language—almost certainly Oankali, since Lilith had said the villagers had no other Human languages in common.

The group, family and guests, was a menagerie, Tino thought. Human; nearly Human with a few visible sensory tentacles; half-Human, gray with strangely jointed limbs and some sensory tentacles; Oankali with Human features contrasting jarringly with their alienness; Oankali who might possibly be part Human; and Oankali like the ooloi who had spoken to him, who obviously had no Humanity at all.

Lilith amid the menagerie. He had liked her looks when he spotted her in the garden. She was an amazon of a woman, tall and strong, but with no look of hardness to her. Fine, dark skin. Breasts high in spite of all the children—breasts full of

36

milk. He had never before seen a woman nursing a child. He had almost had to turn his back on her to stop himself from staring as Lilith fed Akin. The woman was not beautiful. Her broad, smooth face was usually set in an expression of solemnity, even sadness. It made her look—and Tino winced at the thought—it made her look saintly. A mother. Very much a mother. And something else.

And she had no man, apparently. She had said Akin's father was long dead. Was she looking for someone? Was that what all the laughter was about? After all, if he stayed with Lilith, he would also be staying with her Oankali family, with the ooloi whose reaction had provoked so much laughter. Especially with that ooloi. And what would that mean?

He was looking at it when the man Lilith had called Wray came up to him.

"I'm Wray Ordway," he said. "I live here permanently. Come around when you can. Anyone here can head you toward my house." He was a small, blond man with nearly colorless eyes that caught Tino's attention. Could anyone really see out of such eyes? "Do you know Nikanj?" the man asked.

"Who?" Tino asked, though he thought he knew.

"The ooloi who spoke to you. The one you're watching."

Tino stared at him with the beginnings of dislike.

"I think it recognized you," Wray said. "It's an interesting creature. Lilith thinks very highly of it."

"Is it her mate?" Of course it was.

"It's one of her mates. She hasn't had a man stay with her for a long time, though."

Was this Nikanj the mate who had forced pregnancy on her? It was an ugly creature with too many head tentacles and not enough of anything that could be called a face. Yet there was something compelling about it. Perhaps he had seen it before. Perhaps it was the last ooloi he had seen before he and his parents had been set down on Earth and let go. That ooloi . . . ?

A very Human-looking young woman brushed past Tino on her way out. Tino's attention was drawn to her, and he stared as she walked away. He saw her join another very similar young woman, and the two both turned to look at him, smile at him. They were completely alike, pretty, but so startling in their similarity that he was distracted from their beauty. He found himself searching his memory for a word he had had no occasion to use since childhood.

"Twins?" he asked Wray.

"Those two? No." Wray smiled. "They were born within a day of one another, though. One of them should have been a boy."

Tino stared at the well-shaped young women. "Neither of them is in any way like a boy."

"Do you like them?"

Tino glanced at him and smiled.

"They're my daughters."

Tino froze, then shifted his gaze from the girls uneasily. "Both?" he asked after a moment.

"Human mother, Oankali mother. Believe me, they weren't identical when they were born. I think they are now because Tehkorahs wanted to make a point—that the nine children Leah and I have produced are true siblings of the children of our Oankali mates."

"Nine children?" Tino whispered. "Nine?" He had lived since childhood among people who would almost have given their lives to produce one child.

"Nine," Wray confirmed. "And listen." He stopped, waited until Tino's eyes focused on him. "Listen, I wouldn't want you to get the wrong idea. Those girls wear more clothing than most constructs because they have concealable differences. Neither of them is as Human as she looks. Let them alone if you can't accept that."

Tino looked into the pale, blind-seeming eyes. "What if I can accept it?"

Wray looked at the two girls, his expression gentling. "That's between you and them." The girls were exchanging words with Nikanj. Another ooloi came up to them, and as the exchange continued, it put one strength arm around each girl.

"That's Tehkorahs," Wray said, "my ooloi mate. That's Tehkorahs being protective, I think. And Nikanj . . . being impatient if anyone can believe that."

Tino watched the two ooloi and the two girls with interest. They did not seem to be arguing. In fact, they had ceased to speak at all—or ceased to speak aloud. Tino suspected they were still communicating somehow. There had always been a rumor that Oankali could read minds. He had never believed it, but clearly something was happening.

"One thing," Wray said softly. "Listen."

Tino faced him questioningly.

"You can do as you please here. As long as you don't hurt anyone, you can stay or go as you like; you can choose your own friends, your own lovers. No one has the right to demand anything from you that you don't want to give." He turned and walked away before Tino could ask what this really meant when it came to the Oankali.

Wray joined his daughters and Tehkorahs and led them out of the house. Tino found himself watching the young women's hips. He did not realize until they were gone that Nikanj and Lilith had come over to him.

"We'd like you to stay with us," Lilith said softly. "At least for the night."

He looked at her lineless face, her cap of dark hair, her breasts, now concealed beneath a simple gray shirt. He had had only a glimpse of them as she had settled herself to nurse Akin.

She took his hand, and he remembered seizing her hand to examine it. She had large, strong, calloused hands, warm and Human. Almost unconsciously, he had turned his back to Nikanj. What did it want? Or rather, how did it go about getting what it wanted? What did the ooloi actually do to Humans? What would it want of him? And did he really want Lilith badly enough to find out?

But why had he left Phoenix if not for this?

But so quickly? Now?

"Sit with us," Lilith said. "Let's talk for a while." She drew him toward a wall—toward the place they had sat when he spoke to the people. They sat cross-legged—or the two Humans crossed their legs—their bodies forming a tight triangle. Tino watched the other two Oankali in the room as they herded the children away. Akin and the small gray child who now held him clearly wanted to stay. Tino could see that, though neither child was speaking English. The larger of the two Oankali lifted both children easily and managed to interest them in something else. All three vanished with the

others through a doorway that seemed to grow shut behind
them—the way doorways had closed so long ago aboard the
ship. The room was sealed and empty except for Tino, Lilith,
and Nikanj.

Tino made himself look at Nikanj. It had folded its legs
under it the way the Oankali did. Many of its head tentacles
were trained on him, seeming almost to be straining toward
him. He suppressed a shudder—not a response of fear or
disgust. Those feelings would not have surprised him. He
felt. . . He did not know what he felt about this ooloi.

"It was you, wasn't it?" he asked suddenly.

"Yes," Nikanj admitted. "You're unusual. I've never known
a Human to remember before."

"To remember his conditioning?"

Silence.

"To remember his conditioner," Tino said nodding. "I
don't think anyone could forget his conditioning. But. . . I don't
know how I recognized you. I met you so long ago, and . . . well,
I don't mean to offend you, but I still can't tell your people
apart."

"You can. You just don't realize it yet. That's unusual, too.
Some Humans never learn to recognize individuals among us."

"What did you do to me back then?" he demanded. "I've
never. . . never felt anything like that before or since."

"I told you then. I checked you for disease and injury,
strengthened you against infection, got rid of any problems I
found, programmed your body to slow its aging processes after
a certain point, and did whatever else I could to improve your
chances of surviving your reintroduction to Earth. Those are
the things all conditioners did. And we all took prints of
you—read all that your bodies could tell us about themselves
and created a kind of blueprint. I could make a physical copy of
you even if you hadn't survived."

"A baby?"

"Yes, eventually. But we prefer you to any copy. We need
cultural as well as genetic diversity for a good trade."

"Trade!" Tino said scornfully. "I don't know what I'd call
what you're doing to us, but it isn't trade. Trade is when two
people agree to an exchange."

"Yes."

"It doesn't involve coercion."

"We have something you need. You have something we need."

"We didn't need anything before you got here!"

"You were dying."

Tino said nothing for a moment. He looked away. The war was an insanity he had never understood, and no one in Phoenix had been able to explain it to him. At least, no one had been able to give him a reason why people who had excellent reasons to suppose they would destroy themselves if they did a certain thing chose to do that thing anyway. He thought he understood anger, hatred, humiliation, even the desire to kill a man. He had felt all those things. But to kill everyone... almost to kill the Earth... There were times when he wondered if somehow the Oankali had not caused the war for their own purposes. How could sane people like the ones he had left behind in Phoenix do such a thing—or, how could they let insane people gain control of devices that could do so much harm? If you knew a man was out of his mind, you restrained him. You didn't give him power.

"I don't know about the war," Tino admitted. "It's never made sense to me. But... maybe you should have left us alone. Maybe some of us would have survived."

"Nothing would have survived except bacteria, a few small land plants and animals, and some sea creatures. Most of the life that you see around you we reseeded from prints, from collected specimens from our own creations, and from altered remnants of things that had undergone benign changes before we found them. The war damaged your ozone layer. Do you know what that is?"

"No."

"It shielded life on Earth from the sun's ultraviolet rays. Without its protection, above-ground life on Earth would not have been possible. If we had left you on Earth, you would have been blinded. You would have been burned—if you hadn't already been killed by other expanding effects of the war—and you would have died a terrible death. Most animals did die, and most plants, and some of us. We're hard to kill, but your people had made their world utterly hostile to life. If we had not helped it, it couldn't have restored itself so quickly. Once it was restored, we knew we couldn't carry on a normal trade. We couldn't let you breed alongside us, coming to us only when you saw the value of what we offered. Stabilizing a trade that way takes too many generations. We needed to free you—the least dangerous of you anyway. But we couldn't let your numbers grow. We couldn't let you begin to become what you were."

"You believe we would have had another war?"

"You would have had many others—against each other, against us. Some of the southern resister groups are already making guns."

Tino digested that silently. He had known about the guns of the southerners, had assumed they were to be used against the Oankali. He had not believed people from the stars would be stopped by a few crude firearms, and he had said so, making himself unpopular with those of his people who wanted to believe—needed to believe. Several of these had left Phoenix to join the southerners.

"What will you do about the guns?" he asked.

"Nothing, except to those who actually do try to shoot us. Those go back to the ship permanently. They lose Earth. We've told them that. So far, none of them have shot us. A few have shot one another, though."

Lilith looked startled. "You're letting them do that?"

Nikanj focused a cone of tentacles on her. "Could we stop them, Lilith, really?"

"You used to try!"

"Aboard the ship, here in Lo, and in the other trade villages. Nowhere else. We control the resisters only if we cage them, drug them, and allow them to live in an unreal world of drug-stimulated imaginings. We've done that to a few violent Humans. Shall we do it to more?"

Lilith only stared at it, her expression unreadable.

"You won't do that?" Tino asked.

"We won't. We have prints of all of you. We would be sorry to lose you, but at least we would save something. We will be inviting your people to join us again. If any are injured or crippled or even sick in spite of our efforts, we'll offer them our help. They're free to accept our help yet stay in their villages. Or they can come to us." It aimed a sharp cone of

head tentacles at Tino. "You've known since I sent you back to
your parents years ago that you could choose to come to us."

Tino shook his head, spoke softly. "I seem to remember
that I didn't want to go back to my parents. I asked to stay with
you. To this day, I don't know why."

"I wanted to keep you. If you'd been a little older. . . But
we've been told and shown that we aren't good at raising fully
Human children." It shifted its attention for a moment to
Lilith, but she looked away. "You had to be left with your
parents to grow up. I thought I wouldn't see you again."

Tino caught himself staring at the ooloi's long, gray sensory arms. Both arms seemed relaxed against the ooloi's sides,
their ends coiled, spiraling upward so that they did not touch
the floor.

"They always look a little like elephants' trunks to me,"
Lilith said.

Tino glanced at her and saw that she was smiling—a sad
smile that became her somehow. For a moment, she was
beautiful. He did not know what he wanted from the ooloi—if
he wanted anything. But he knew what he wanted from the
woman. He wished the ooloi were not there. And as soon as
the thought occurred to him, he rejected it. Lilith and Nikanj
were a pair somehow. Without Nikanj, she would not have
been as desirable. He did not understand this, but he accepted
it.

They would have to show him what was to happen. He
would not ask. They had made it clear they wanted something
from him. Let *them* ask.

"I was thinking," Tino said, referring to the sensory arms,
"that I don't know what they are."

Nikanj's body tentacles seemed to tremble, then solidify
into discolored lumps. They sank into themselves the way the
soft bodies of slugs seemed to when they drew themselves up
to rest.

Tino drew back a little in revulsion. God, the Oankali
were ugly creatures. How had Human beings come to tolerate
them so easily, to touch them and allow them to. . .

Lilith took the ooloi's right sensory arm between her
hands and held it even when Nikanj seemed to try to pull away.
She stared at it, and Tino knew there must be some communi-

cation. Did the Oankali share mind-reading abilities with their pet Humans? Or was it mind reading? Lilith spoke aloud.

"Slow," she whispered. "Give him a moment. Give me a moment. Don't defeat your own purpose by hurrying."

For a moment, Nikanj's lumps looked worse—like some grotesque disease. Then the lumps resolved themselves again into slender gray body tentacles no more grotesque than usual. Nikanj drew its sensory arm from Lilith's hands, then stood up and went to a far corner of the room. There it sat down and seemed almost to turn itself off. Like something carved from gray marble, it became utterly still. Even its head and body tentacles ceased to move.

"What was all that?" Tino demanded.

Lilith smiled broadly. "For the first time in my life, I had to tell it to be patient. If it were Human, I would say it was infatuated with you."

"You're joking!"

"I am," she said. "This is worse than infatuation. I'm glad you feel something for it, too, even though you don't yet know what."

"Why has it gone to sit in that corner?"

"Because it can't quite bring itself to leave the room, though it knows it should—to let the two of us be Human for a little while. Anyway, I don't think you really want it to leave."

"Can it read minds? Can you?"

She did not laugh. At least she did not laugh. "I've never met anyone, Oankali or Human, who could read minds. It can stimulate sensations and send your thoughts off in all sorts of directions, but it can't read those thoughts. It can only share the new sensations they produce. In effect, it can give you the most realistic and the most pleasurable dreams you've ever experienced. Nothing you've known before can match it—except perhaps your conditioning. And that should tell you why you're here, why you were bound to seek out a trade village sooner or later. Nikanj touched you when you were too young to have any defenses. And what it gave you, you won't ever quite forget—or quite remember, unless you feel it again. You want it again. Don't you."

It was not a question. Tino swallowed and did not bother with an answer. "I remember drugs," he said, staring at nothing. "I never took any. I was too young before the war. I remember other people taking them and maybe going crazy for a little while or maybe just being high. I remember that they got addicted, that they got hurt sometimes or killed..."

"This isn't just a drug."

"What then?"

"Direct stimulation of the brain and nervous system." She held up her hand to stop him from speaking. "There's no pain. They hate pain more than we do, because they're more sensitive to it. If they hurt us, they hurt themselves. And there are no harmful side effects. Just the opposite. They automatically fix any problems they find. They get real pleasure from healing or regenerating, and they share that pleasure with us. They weren't as good at repairs before they found us. Regeneration was limited to wound healing. Now they can grow you a new leg if you lose one. They can even regenerate brain and nervous tissue. They learned that from us, believe it or not. We had the ability, and they knew how to use it. They learned by studying our cancers, of all things. It was cancer that made Humanity such a valuable trade partner."

Tino shook his head, not believing. "I saw cancer kill both my grandfathers. It's nothing but a filthy disease."

Lilith touched his shoulder, let her hand slide down his arm in a caress. "So that's it. That's why Nikanj is so attracted to you. Cancer killed three close relatives of mine, including my mother. I'm told it would have killed me if the Oankali hadn't done some work on me. It's a filthy disease to us, but to the Oankali, it's the tool they've been looking for for generations."

"What will it do to me that has to do with cancer?"

"Nothing. It just finds you a lot more attractive than it does most Humans. What can you do with a beautiful woman that you can't do with an ugly one? Nothing. It's just a matter of preference. Nikanj and every other Oankali already have all the information they need to use that they've learned from us. Even the constructs can use it once they're mature. But people like you and me are still attractive to them."

"I don't understand that."

"Don't worry about it. I'm told our children will understand them, but we won't."

"Our children will be them."

"You accept that?"

It took him a moment to realize what he had said. "No! I don't know. Yes, but—" He closed his eyes. "I don't know."

She moved closer to him, rested warm, calloused hands on his forearms. He could smell her. Crushed plants—the way a fresh-cut lawn used to smell. Food, pepper and sweet. Woman. He reached out to her, touched the large breasts. He could not help himself. He had wanted to touch them since he had first seen them. She lay down on her side, drawing him down facing her. It occurred to him a moment later that Nikanj was behind him. That she had deliberately positioned him so that Nikanj would be behind him.

He sat up abruptly, turned to look at the ooloi. It had not moved. It gave no sign that it was even alive.

"Lie here with me for a while," she said.

"But—"

"We'll go to Nikanj in a little while. Won't we."

"I don't know." He lay down again, now glad to keep his back to it. "I still don't understand what it does. I mean, so it gives me good dreams. How? And what else will it do? Will it use me to make you pregnant?"

"Not now. Akin is too young. It . . . might collect some sperm from you. You won't be aware of it. When they have the chance, they stimulate a woman to ovulate several eggs. They collect the eggs, store them, collect sperm, store it. They can keep sperm and eggs viable and separate in their bodies for decades. Akin is the child of a man who died nearly thirty years ago."

"I had heard there was a time limit—that they could only keep sperm and eggs alive for a few months."

"Progress. Before I left the ship, someone came up with a new method of preservation. Nikanj was one of the first to learn it."

Tino looked at her closely, searched her smooth, broad face. "So you're what? In your fifties?"

"Fifty-five."

He sighed, shook his head against the arm he had rested it on. "You look younger than I do. I've at least got a few gray hairs. I remember I used to worry that I really was the Human the Oankali had failed with, fertile and aging normally, and that all I'd really get out of it was old."

"Nikanj wouldn't have failed with you."

She was so close to him that he couldn't help touching her, moving his fingers over the fine skin. He drew back, though, when she mentioned the ooloi's name.

"Can't it go?" he whispered. "Just for a while."

"It chooses not to," she said in a normal voice. "And don't bother whispering. It can hear your heartbeat from where it's sitting. It can hear your subvocalizations—the things you . . . say to yourself in words but not quite out loud. That may be why you thought it could read minds. And it obviously will not go away."

"Can we?"

"No." She hesitated. "It isn't Human, Tino. This isn't like having another man or woman in the room."

"It's worse."

She smiled wearily, leaned over him, and kissed him. Then she sat up. "I understand," she said. "I felt the way you do once. Maybe it's just as well." She hugged herself and looked at him almost angrily. Frustration? How long had it been for her? Well, the damned ooloi could not *always* be there. *Why* wouldn't it go away, wait its turn? Failing that, why was he so shy of it? Its presence did bother him more than another Human's would have. Much more.

"We'll join Nikanj, Tino, once I've told you one more thing," she said. "That is, we'll join it if you decide you still want anything to do with me."

"With you? But it wasn't you I was having trouble with. I mean—"

"I know. This is something else—something I'd rather never mention to you. But if I don't, someone else will." She drew a deep breath. "Didn't you wonder about me? About my name?"

"I thought you should have changed it. It isn't a very popular name."

"I know. And changing it wouldn't do much good. Too many people know me. I'm not just someone stuck with an unpopular name, Tino. I'm the one who made it unpopular. I'm Lilith Iyapo."

He frowned, began to shake his head, then stopped. "You're not the one who . . . who . . ."

"I awakened the first three groups of Humans to be sent back to Earth. I told them what their situation was, what their options were, and they decided I was responsible for it all. I helped teach them to live in the forest, and they decided it was my fault they had to give up civilized life. Sort of like blaming me for the goddamn war! Anyway, they decided I had betrayed them to the Oankali, and the nicest thing some of them called me was Judas. Is that the way you were taught to think of me?"

"I . . . Yes."

She shook her head. "The Oankali either seduced them or terrified them, or both. I, on the other hand, was nobody. It was easy for them to blame me. And it was safe.

"So now and then when we get exresisters traveling through Lo and they hear my name, they assume I have horns. Some of the younger ones have been taught to blame me for everything— as though I were a second Satan or Satan's wife or some such idiocy. Now and then one of them will try to kill me. That's one of the reasons I'm so touchy about weapons here."

He stared at her for a while. He had watched her closely as she spoke, trying to see guilt in her, trying to see the devil in her. In Phoenix, people had said things like that—that she was possessed of the devil, that she had sold first herself, then Humanity, that she was the first to go willingly to an Oankali bed to become their whore and to seduce other Humans . . .

"What do your people say about me?" she asked.

He hesitated, glanced at Nikanj. "That you sold us."

"For what currency?"

There had always been some debate about that. "For the right to stay on the ship and for . . . powers. They say you were born Human, but the Oankali made you like a construct."

She made a sound that she may have intended as a laugh. "I begged to go to Earth with the first group I awakened. I was supposed to have gone. But when the time came, Nika wouldn't let me. It said the people would kill me once they got me away from the Oankali. They probably would have. And they would have felt virtuous and avenged."

"But . . . you are different. You're very strong, fast . . ."

"Yes. That wasn't the Oankali way of paying me off. It was their way of giving me some protection. If they hadn't changed me a little, someone in the first group would have killed me while I was still awakening people. I'm somewhere between Human and construct in ability. I'm stronger and faster than most Humans, but not as strong or as fast as most constructs. I heal faster than you could, and I'd recover from wounds that would kill you. And of course I can control walls and raise platforms here in Lo. All Humans who settle here are given that ability. That's all. Nikanj changed me to save my life, and it succeeded. Instead of killing me, the first group I awakened killed Akin's father, the man I had paired with . . . might still be with. One of them killed him. The others watched, then went on following that one."

There was a long silence. Finally Tino said, "Maybe they were afraid."

"Is that what you were told?"

"No. I didn't know about that part at all. I even heard . . . that . . . perhaps you didn't like men at all."

She threw back her head in startling, terrible laughter. "Oh, god. Which of my first group is in Phoenix?"

"A guy named Rinaldi."

"Gabe? Gabe and Tate. Are they still together?"

"Yes. I didn't realize . . . Tate never said anything about being with him then. I thought they had gotten together here on Earth."

"I awoke them both. They were my best friends for a while. Their ooloi was Kahguyaht—ooan Nikanj."

"What Nikanj?"

"Nikanj's ooloi parent. It stayed aboard the ship with its mates and raised another trio of children. Nikanj told it Gabe and Tate wouldn't be leaving the resisters any time soon. It was finally willing to acknowledge Nikanj's talent, and it couldn't bring itself to accept other Humans."

Tino looked at Nikanj. After a while, he got up and went over to it, sat down opposite it. "What is your talent?" he asked.

Nikanj did not speak or acknowledge his presence.

"Talk to me!" he demanded. "I know you hear."

The ooloi seemed to come to life slowly. "I hear."

"What is your talent!"

It leaned toward him and took his hands in its strength hands, keeping its sensory arms coiled. Oddly, the gesture reminded him of Lilith, was much like what Lilith tended to do. He did not mind, somehow, that now hard, cool gray hands held his.

"I have a talent for Humans," it said in its soft voice. "I was bred to work with you, taught to work with you, and given one of you as a companion during one of my most formative periods." It focused for a moment on Lilith. "I know your bodies, and sometimes I can anticipate your thinking. I knew that Gabe Rinaldi couldn't accept a union with us when Kahguyaht wanted him. Tate could have, but she would not leave Gabe for an ooloi—no matter how badly she wanted to. And Kahguyaht would not simply keep her with it when the others were sent to Earth. That surprised me. It always said there was no point in paying attention to what Humans said. It knew Tate would eventually have accepted it, but it listened to her and let her go. And it wasn't raised as I was in contact with Humans. I think your people affect us more than we realize."

"I think," Lilith said quietly, "that you may be better at understanding us than you are at understanding your own people."

It focused on her, its body tentacles smoothed to invisibility against its flesh. That meant it was pleased, Tino remembered. Pleased or even happy. "Ahajas says that," it told her. "I don't think it's true, but it may be."

Tino turned toward Lilith but spoke to Nikanj. "Did you make her pregnant against her will?"

"Against one part of her will, yes," Nikanj admitted. "She had wanted a child with Joseph, but he was dead. She was...more alone than you could imagine. She thought I didn't understand."

"It's your fault she was alone!"

"It was a shared fault." Nikanj's head and body tentacles hung limp. "We believed we had to ·use her as we did. Otherwise we would have had to drug newly awakened Humans much more than was good for them because we would have had to teach them everything ourselves. We did that later because we saw...that we were damaging Lilith and the others we tried to use.

"In the first children, I gave Lilith what she wanted but could not ask for. I let her blame me instead of herself. For a while, I became for her a little of what she was for the Humans she had taught and guided. Betrayer. Destroyer of treasured things. Tyrant. She needed to hate me for a while so that she could stop hating herself. And she needed the children I mixed for her."

Tino stared at the ooloi, needing to look at it to remind himself that he was hearing an utterly un-Human creature. Finally, he looked at Lilith.

She looked back, smiling a bitter, humorless smile. "I told you it was talented," she said.

"How much of that is true?" he asked.

"How should I know!" She swallowed. "All of it might be. Nikanj usually tells the truth. On the other hand, reasons and justifications can sound just as good when they're made up as an afterthought. Have your fun, then come up with a wonderful-sounding reason why it was the right thing for you to do."

Tino pulled away from the ooloi and went to Lilith. "Do you hate it?" he asked.

She shook her head. "I have to leave it to hate it. Sometimes I go away for a while—explore, visit other villages, and hate it. But after a while, I start to miss my children. And, heaven help me, I start to miss it. I stay away until staying away hurts more than the thought of coming...home."

He thought she should be crying. His mother would never have contained that much passion without tears—would never have tried. He took her by the arms, found her stiff and resistant. Her eyes rejected any comfort before he could offer it.

"What shall I do?" he asked. "What do you want me to do?"

She hugged him suddenly, holding him hard against her. "Will you stay?" she said into his ear.

"Shall I?"

"Yes."

"All right." She was not Lilith Iyapo. She was a quiet, expressive, broad face. She was dark, smooth skin and warm, work-calloused hands. She was breasts full of milk. He wondered how he had resisted her earlier.

And what about Nikanj? He did not look at it, but he imagined he felt its attention on him.

"If you decide to leave," Lilith said, "I'll help you."

He could not imagine wanting to leave her.

Something cool and rough and hard attached itself to his upper arm. He froze, not having to look to know it was one of the ooloi's sensory arms.

It stood close to him, one sensory arm on him and one on Lilith. They *were* like elephants' trunks, those arms. He felt Lilith release him, felt Nikanj drawing him to the floor. He let himself be pulled down only because Lilith lay down with them. He let Nikanj position his body alongside its own. Then he saw Lilith sit up on Nikanj's opposite side and watch the two of them solemnly.

He did not understand why she watched, why she did not take part. Before he could ask, the ooloi slipped its sensory arm around him and pressed the back of his neck in a way that made him shudder, then go limp.

He was not unconscious. He knew when the ooloi drew closer to him, seemed to grasp him in some way he did not understand.

He was not afraid.

The splash of icy-sweet pleasure, when it reached him, won him completely. This was the half-remembered feeling he had come back for. This was the way it began.

Before the long-awaited rush of sensation swallowed him completely, he saw Lilith lie down alongside the ooloi, saw the second sensory arm loop around her neck. He tried to reach out to her across the body of the ooloi, to touch her, touch the warm Human flesh. It seemed to him that he reached and reached, yet she remained too far away to touch.

He thought he shouted as the sensation deepened, as it took him. It seemed that she was with him suddenly, her body against his own. He thought he said her name and repeated it, but he could not hear the sound of his own voice.

7

Akin took his first few steps toward Tino's outstretched hands. He learned to take food from Tino's plate, and he rode on Tino's back whenever the man would carry him. He did not forget Dichaan's warning not to be alone with Tino, but he did not take it seriously. He came to trust Tino very quickly. Eventually everyone came to trust Tino.

Thus, as it happened, Akin was alone with Tino when a party of raiders came looking for children to steal.

Tino had gone out to cut wood for the guest house. He was not yet able to perceive the borders of Lo. He had gotten into the habit of taking Akin along to spot for him after breaking an ax he had borrowed from Wray Ordway on a tree that was not a tree. The Lo entity shaped itself according to the desires of its occupants and the patterns of the surrounding vegetation. Yet it was the larval form of a space-going entity. Its hide and its organs were better protected than any living thing native to Earth. No ax or machete could mark it. Until it was older, no native vegetation would grow within its boundries. That was why Lilith and a few other people' had gardens far from the village. Lo would have provided good food from its own substance—the Oankali could stimulate food production and separate the food from Lo. But most Humans in the village did

53

spent days screaming at or not speaking at all to Nikanj,
screaming at or not speaking to Lilith, sitting alone and staring
at nothing. Once he left the village for three days, and Dichaan
followed him and led him back when he was ready to return.
He could have gone away until the effects of his mating with
Nikanj had passed from his body. He could have found another
village, a sterile Human-only mating. He had had several of
those, though. Akin had heard him speak of them during those
first few bad days. They were not what he wanted. But neither
was this. Now he was like Lilith. Very much attached to the
family and content with it most of the time, yet poisonously
resentful and bitter sometimes. But only Akin and the rest of
the younger children of the house worried that he might leave
permanently. The adults seemed certain he would stay.

Now he cut the tree he had felled into pieces and cut
lianas to bundle the wood. Then he came to collect Akin. He
stopped abruptly and whispered. "My god!"

Akin was tasting a large caterpillar. He had allowed it to
crawl onto his forearm. It was, in fact, almost as large as his
forearm. It was bright red and spotted with what appeared to
be tufts of long, stiff black fur. The tufts, Akin knew, were
deadly. The animal did not have to sting. It had only to be
touched on one of the tufts. The poison was strong enough to
kill a large Human. Apparently Tino knew this. His hand
moved toward the caterpillar, then stopped.

Akin split his attention, watching Tino to see that he made
no further moves and tasting the caterpillar gently, delicately,
with his skin and with a flick of his tongue to its pale, slightly
exposed underside. Its underside was safe. It did not poison
what it crawled on.

It ate other insects. It even ate small frogs and toads.
Some ooloi had given it the characteristics of another crawling
creature—a small, multilegged, wormlike peripatus. Now both
caterpillar and peripatus could project a kind of glue to snare
prey and hold it until it could be consumed.

The caterpillar itself was not good to eat. It was too
poisonous. The ooloi who had assembled it had not intended
that it be food for anything while it was alive, though it might
be killed by ants or wasps if it chose to hunt in one of the trees
protected by these. It was safe, though, in the tree it had

chosen. Its kind would give the tree a better chance to mature and produce food.

Akin held his arm against the trunk of the sapling and carefully maneuvered the caterpillar into crawling back to it. The moment it had left his arm, Tino snatched him up, shouting at him.

"*Never* do anything so crazy again! *Never!* That thing could kill you! It could kill me!"

Someone grabbed him from behind.

Someone else grabbed Akin from his arms.

Now, far too late, Akin saw, heard, and smelled the intruders. Strangers. Human males with no scent of the Oankali about them. Resisters. Raiders. Child thieves!

Akin screamed and twisted in the arms of his captor. But physically, he was still little more than a baby. He had let his attention be absorbed by Tino and the caterpillar, and now he was caught. The man who held him was large and strong. He held Akin without seeming to notice Akin's struggles.

Meanwhile, four men had surrounded Tino. There was blood on Tino's face where someone had hit him, cut him. One of the four had a piece of gleaming silver metal around one of his fingers. That must have been what had cut Tino.

"Hold it!" one of Tino's captors said. "This guy used to be Phoenix." He frowned at Tino. "Aren't you the Leal kid?"

"I'm Augustino Leal," Tino said, holding his body very straight. "I was Phoenix. I was Phoenix before you ever heard of it!" His voice did not tremble, but Akin could see that his body was trembling slightly. He looked toward his ax, which now lay on the ground several feet from him. He had leaned it against a tree when he came to get Akin. His machete, though, had still been at his belt. Now it was gone. Akin could not see where it had gone.

The raiders all had long wood-and-metal sticks, which they now pointed at Tino. The man holding Tino also had such a stick, strapped across his back. These were weapons, Akin realized. Clubs—or perhaps guns? And these men knew Tino. One of them knew Tino. And Tino did not like that one. Tino was afraid. Akin had never seen him more afraid.

The man who held Akin had put his neck within easy

reach of Akin's tongue. Akin could sting him, kill him. But then what would happen? There were four other men.

Akin did nothing. He watched Tino, hoping the man would know what was best.

"There were no guns in Phoenix when I left," Tino was saying. So the sticks were guns.

"No, and you didn't want there to be any, did you?" the same man asked. He made a point of jabbing Tino with his gun.

Tino began to be a little less afraid and more angry. "If you think you can use those to kill the Oankali, you're as stupid as I thought you were."

The man swung his gun up so that its end almost touched Tino's nose.

"Is it Humans you mean to kill?" Tino asked very softly. "Are there so many Humans left? Are our numbers increasing so fast?"

"You've joined the traitors!" the man said.

"To have a family," Tino said softly. "To have children." He looked at Akin. "To have at least part of myself continue."

The man holding Akin spoke up. "This kid is as human as any I've seen since the war. I can't find anything wrong with him."

"No tentacles?" one of the four asked.

"Not a one."

"What's he got between his legs?"

"Same thing you've got. Little smaller, maybe."

There was a moment of silence, and Akin saw that three of the men were amused and one was not.

Akin was afraid to speak, afraid to show the raiders his un-Human characteristics: his tongue, his ability to speak, his intelligence. Would these things make them let him alone or make them kill him? In spite of his months with Tino, he did not know. He kept quiet and began trying to hear or smell any Lo villager who might be passing nearby.

"So we take the kid," one of the men said. "What do we do with him?" He gestured sharply toward Tino.

Before anyone could answer, Tino said, "No! You can't take him. He still nurses. If you take him, he'll starve!"

The men looked at one another uncertainly. The man

holding Akin suddenly turned Akin toward him and squeezed the sides of Akin's face with his fingers. He was trying to get Akin's mouth open. Why?

It did not matter why. He would get Akin's mouth open, then be startled. He was Human and a stranger and dangerous. Who knew what irrational reaction he might have. He must be given something familiar to go with the unfamiliar. Akin began to twist in the man's arm and to whimper. He had not cried so far. That had been a mistake. Humans always marveled at how little construct babies cried. Clearly a Human baby would have cried more.

Akin opened his mouth and wailed.

"Shit!" muttered the man holding him. He looked around quickly as though fearing someone might be attracted by the noise. Akin, who had not thought of this, cried louder. Oankali had hearing more sensitive than most Humans realized.

"Shut up!" the man shouted, shaking him. "Good god, it's got the ugliest goddamn gray tongue you ever saw! Shut up, you!"

"He's just a baby," Tino said. "You can't get a baby to shut up by scaring him. Give him to me." He had begun to step toward Akin, holding his arms out to take him.

Akin reached toward him, thinking that the resisters would be less likely to hurt the two of them together. Perhaps he could shield Tino to some degree. In Tino's arms he would be quiet and cooperative. They would see that Tino was useful.

The man who had first recognized Tino now stepped behind him and smashed the wooden end of his gun into the back of Tino's head.

Tino dropped to the ground without a cry, and his attacker hit him again, driving the wood of the gun down into Tino's head like a man killing a poisonous snake.

Akin screamed in terror and anguish. He knew Human anatomy well enough to know that if Tino were not dead, he would die soon unless an Oankali helped him.

And there was no Oankali nearby.

The resisters left Tino where he lay and strode away into the forest, carrying Akin who still screamed and struggled.

PHOENIX

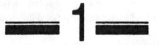

1

D ichaan slipped from the deep-
est part of the broad lake, shifted from breathing in water to
breathing in air, and began to wade to shore.

Humans called this an oxbow lake—one that had originally
been part of the river. Dichaan had kept the Lo entity from
engulfing it so far because the entity would have killed the
plant life in it and that would have eventually killed the animal
life. Even with help, Lo could not have been taught to provide
what the animals needed in a form they would accept before
they died of hunger. The only useful thing the entity could
have provided at once was oxygen.

But now the entity was changing, moving into its next
growth stage. Now it could learn to incorporate Earth vegetation, sustain it, and benefit from it. On its own, it would learn
slowly, killing a great deal, culling native vegetation for that
vegetation's ability to adapt to the changes it made.

But the entity in symbiotic relationship with its Oankali
inhabitants could change faster, adapting itself and accepting
adapted plant life that Dichaan and others had prepared.

Dichaan stepped on shore through a natural corridor
between great profusions of long, thick, upright prop roots that
would slowly be submerged when the rainy season began and
the water rose.

Dichaan had made his way out of the mud, his body still savoring the taste of the lake—rich in plant and animal life— when he heard a cry.

He stood utterly still, listening, his head and body tentacles slowly swinging around to focus on the direction of the sound. Then he knew where it was and who it was, and he began to run. He had been under water all morning. What had been happening in the air?

Leaping over fallen trees, dodging around dangling lianas, undergrowth, and living trees, he ran. He spread his body tentacles against his skin. This way the sensitive parts of the tentacles could be protected from the thin underbrush that lashed him as he ran through it. He could not avoid it all and still move quickly.

He splashed through a small stream, then scrambled up a steep bank.

He came to a bundle of small logs and saw where a tree had been cut. The scent of Akin and of strange Human males was there. Tino's scent was there—very strong.

And now Tino cried out weakly, making only a shadow of the sound Dichaan had heard at the lake. It hardly seemed a Human sound at all, yet to Dichaan, it was unmistakably Tino. His head tentacles swept around, seeking the man, finding him. He ran to him where he lay, concealed by the broad, wedge-shaped buttresses of a tree.

His hair was stuck together in solid masses of blood, dirt, and dead leaves. His body twitched, and he made small sounds.

Dichaan folded to the ground, first probed Tino's wounds with several head tentacles, then lay down beside him and penetrated his body wherever possible with filaments from head and body tentacles.

The man was dying—would die in a moment unless Dichaan could keep him alive. It had been good having a Human male in the family. It had been a balance found after painful years of imbalance, and no one had felt the imbalance more than Dichaan. He had been born to work with a Human male parallel—to help raise children with the aid of such a person, and yet he had had to limp along without this essential other. How were children to learn to understand the Human male side of themselves—a side they all possessed whatever their eventual sex?

Now, here was Tino, childless and unused to children, but quickly at ease with them, quickly accepted by them.

Now, here was Tino, nearly dead at the hands of his own kind.

Dichaan linked with his nervous system and kept his heart beating. The man was a beautiful, terrible physical contradiction, as all Humans were. He was a walking seduction, and he would never understand why. He could not be lost. He could not be another Joseph.

There was some brain damage. Dichaan could perceive it, but he could not heal it. Nikanj would have to do that. But Dichaan could keep the damage from growing worse. He stopped the blood loss, which was not as bad as it looked, and made certain the living brain cells had intact blood vessels to nourish them. He found damage to the skull and perceived that the damaged bone was exerting abnormal pressure on the brain. This, he did not tamper with. Nikanj would handle it. Nikanj could do it faster and more certainly than a male or female could.

Dichaan waited until Tino was as stable as he could be, then left him for a moment. He went to the edge of Lo to one of the larger buttresses of a pseudotree and struck it several times in the code of pressures he would have used to supplement exchanged sensory impressions. The pressures would normally be used very rapidly, soundlessly, against another person's flesh. It would take a moment for this drumming to be perceived as communication. But it would be noticed. Even if no Oankali or construct heard it, the Lo entity would pick up the familiar groups of vibrations. It would alert the community the next time someone opened a wall or raised a platform.

Dichaan pounded out the message twice, then went back to Tino and lay down to monitor him and wait.

Now there was time to think about what he had been too late to prevent.

Akin was gone—had been gone for some time. His abductors had been Human males—resisters. They had run toward the river. No doubt they had already headed up- or downriver toward their village—or perhaps they had crossed the river and traveled over land. Either way, their scent trail would probably vanish along the river. He had included in his message instructions to search for them, but he was not hopeful. All resister villages had to be searched. Akin would be found. Phoenix in particular would be checked, since it had once been Tino's home. But would men from Phoenix have hated Tino so much? He did not seem to be the kind of man people could know and still hate. The people of Phoenix who had watched him grow up as the village's only child must have felt as parents toward him. They would have been more likely to abduct him along with Akin.

Akin.

They would not hurt him—not intentionally. Not at first. He still nursed, but he did it more for comfort than for nutrition. He had an Oankali ability to digest whatever he was given and make the most of it. If they fed him what they ate, he would satisfy his body's needs.

Did they know how intelligent he was? Did they know he could talk? If not, how would they react when they found out? Humans reacted badly to surprise. He would be careful, of course, but what did he know of angry, frightened, frustrated Humans? He had never been near even one person who might hate him, who might even hurt him when they discovered that he was not as Human as he looked.

= 2 =

Upriver.

The Humans had a long, smooth, narrow canoe, light and easy to row. Two pairs of men took turns at the oars, and the boat cut quickly through the water. The current was not strong. Working in relay as they were, the men never slowed to rest.

Akin had screamed as loudly as he could as long as there had been any chance of his being heard. But no one had come. He was quiet now, exhausted and miserable. The man who had caught him still held him, had once dangled him by his feet and threatened to dunk him in the river if he did not be quiet. Only the intervention of the other men had stopped him from doing this. Akin was terrified of him. The man honestly did not seem to understand why murder and abduction should disturb Akin or stop him from following orders.

Akin stared at the man's broad, bearded, red face, breathed his sour breath. His was a bitter, angry face whose owner might hurt him for acting like a baby, yet might kill him for acting like anything else. The man held him as disgustedly as he had once seen another man hold a snake. Was he as alien as a snake to these people?

The bitter man looked down, caught Akin staring. "What the hell are you looking at?" he demanded.

Akin ceased to watch the man with his eyes, but kept him

in view with other light-sensitive parts of his body. The man stank of sweat and of something else. Something was wrong with his body—some illness. He needed an ooloi. And he would never go near one.

Akin lay very still in his arms and, somehow, eventually, fell asleep.

He awoke to find himself lying between two pairs of feet on a piece of soggy cloth at the bottom of the boat. Water sloshing on him had awakened him.

He sat up cautiously, knowing before he moved that the current was stronger here and that it was raining. Raining hard. The man who had been holding Akin began to bail water from the boat with a large gourd. If the rain continued or got worse, surely they would stop.

Akin looked around at the land and saw that the banks were high and badly eroded—cliffs with vegetation spilling over the edges. He had never seen such things. He was farther from home than he had ever been, and still traveling. Where would they take him? . . . into the hills? . . . into the mountains?

The men gave up their effort and rowed for the bank. The water was gray-brown and rough, and the rain was coming down harder. They did not quite make it to shore before the canoe sank. The men cursed and jumped out to pull the boat onto a broad mud flat, while Akin stayed where he was, all but swimming. They dumped the boat, tipping both him and the water over one side, laughing when he slid along the mud.

One of them grabbed him by a leg and tried to hand him to the man who had captured him.

His captor would not take him. "You babysit for a while," the man said. "Let him piss on you."

Akin was barely able to stop himself from speaking out in indignation. He had not urinated on anyone for months—not since his family had been able to make him understand that he should not, that he should warn them when he needed to urinate or move his bowels. He would not have urinated even on these men.

"No thanks," said the man holding Akin by the foot. "I just rowed the damn boat god knows how many miles while you sat there and watched the scenery. Now you can watch the kid." He put Akin down on the mud flat and turned to help carry the boat to a place where they might be able to make their way up the bank. The mud flat was exactly that—a sliver of soft, wet, bare silt collected only just above the water. It was neither safe nor comfortable in the downpour. And night was coming. Time to find a place to camp.

Akin's babysitter stared at Akin with cold dislike. He rubbed his stomach, and, for a moment, pain seemed to replace his general displeasure. Perhaps his stomach hurt him. How stupid to be sick and know where there was healing and decide to stay sick.

Abruptly, the man grabbed Akin, lifted him by one arm, thrust him under one of the man's own long, thick arms, and followed the others up the steep, muddy trail.

Akin shut his eyes during the climb. His captor was not surefooted. He kept falling but somehow never fell on Akin or dropped him. He did, however, hold him so tightly that Akin could hardly breathe, so tightly the man's fingers hurt and bruised him. He whimpered and sometimes cried out, but most of the time he tried to keep quiet. He feared this man as he had never before feared anyone. This man who had been eager to dunk him in water that might contain predators, who had gripped him and shaken him and threatened to punch him because he was crying, this man who was apparently willing to endure pain rather than go to someone who would heal him and ask nothing of him—this man might kill him before anyone could act to stop him.

At the top of the bluff, Akin's captor threw him down. "You can walk," the man muttered.

Akin sat still where he had landed, wondering whether Human babies had been thrown about this way—and if so, how they had survived? Then he followed the men as quickly as he could. If he were mature, he would run away. He would go back to the river and let it take him home. If he were mature he could breathe underwater and fend off predators with a simple chemical repellent—the equivalent of a bad smell.

But then, if he were mature, the resisters would not want him. They wanted a helpless infant—and they had very nearly gotten one. He could think, but his body was so small and weak that he could not act. He would not starve in the forest, but he might be poisoned by something that bit or stung him unexpectedly. Near the river, he might be eaten by an anaconda or a caiman.

Also, he had never been alone in the forest before.

As the men drew away from him, he grew more and more frightened. He fell several times but refused to cry again. Finally, exhausted, he stopped. If the men meant to leave him, he could not prevent them. Did they carry off construct children to abandon in the forest?

He urinated on the ground, then found a bush with edible, nutritious leaves. He was too small to reach the best possible food sources—sources the men could have reached but probably could not recognize. Tino had known a great deal, but he did not know much about the forest plants. He ate only obvious things—bananas, figs, nuts, palm fruit—wild versions of things his people grew in Phoenix. If a thing did not look or taste familiar to him, he would not eat it. Akin would eat anything that would not poison him and that would help to keep him alive. He was eating an especially nutritious gray fungus when he heard one of the men coming back for him.

He swallowed quickly, muddied one hand deliberately, and wiped it over his face. If he were simply dirty, the men would pay no attention. But if only his mouth were dirty, they might decide to try to make him throw up.

The man spotted him, cursed him, snatched him up, and carried him under one arm to where the others were building a shelter.

They had found a relatively dry place, well protected by the forest canopy, and they had swept it clean of leaf litter. They had stretched latex-sealed cloth from a pair of small trees to the ground. This cloth had apparently been in the boat, out of Akin's sight. Now they were cutting small branches and sapling trees for flooring. At least they did not plan to sleep in the mud.

They built no fire. They ate dry food—nuts, seeds, and dry fruit mixed together, and they drank something that was not water. They gave Akin a little of the drink and were amused to see that once he had tasted it, he would not take it again.

"It didn't seem to bother him, though," one of them said. "And that stuff is strong. Give him some food. Maybe he can handle it. He's got teeth, right?"

"Yeah."

He had been born with teeth. They gave him some of their food, and he ate slowly, one small fragment at a time.

"So that Phoenix we killed was lying," Akin's captor said. "I thought he might be."

"I wonder if it was really his kid."

"Probably. It looks like him."

"Jesus. I wonder what he had to do to get it. I mean, he didn't just fuck a woman."

"You know what he did. If you didn't know, you would have died of old age or disease by now."

Silence.

"So what do you think we can get for the kid?" a new voice asked.

"Whatever we want. A boy, almost perfect? Whatever they've got. He's so valuable I wonder if we shouldn't keep him."

"Metal tools, glass, good cloth, a woman or two... And this kid might not even live to grow up. Or he might grow up and grow tentacles all over. So what if he looks good now. Doesn't mean a thing."

"And I'll tell you something else," Akin's captor put in. "Our chances, any man's chances of seeing that kid grow up are rat shit. The worms are going to find him sooner or later, dead or alive. And the village they find him in is fucked."

Someone else agreed. "The only way is to get rid of him fast and get out of the area. Let someone else worry about how to hold him and how not to wind up dead or worse."

Akin went out of the shelter, found a place to relieve himself and another place—a clearing where one of the larger trees had recently fallen—where the rain fell heavily enough for him to wash himself and to catch enough water to satisfy his thirst.

The men did not stop him, but one of them watched him. When he reentered the shelter, wet and glistening, carrying broad, flat wild banana leaves to sleep on, the men all stared at him.

"Whatever it is," one of them said, "it isn't as Human as we thought. Who knows what it can do? I'll be glad to get rid of it."

"It's just what we knew it was," Akin's captor said. "A mongrel baby. I'll bet it can do a lot more that we haven't seen."

"I'll bet if we walked off and left it here it would survive and get home," the man who had killed Tino said. "And I'll bet if we poisoned it, it wouldn't die."

An argument broke out over this as the men passed around their alcoholic drink and listened to the rain, which stopped then began again.

Akin grew more afraid of them, but even his fear could not keep him awake after a while. He had been relieved to know that they would trade him away to some other people—to Phoenix, perhaps. He could find Tino's parents. Perhaps they would imagine that he looked like Tino, too. Perhaps they would let him live with them. He wanted to be among people who did not grab him painfully by a leg or an arm and carry him as though he had no more feeling than a piece of dead wood. He wanted to be among people who spoke to him and cared for him instead of people who either ignored him or drew away from him as though he were a poisonous insect or laughed at him. These men not only frightened him, they made him agonizingly lonely.

Sometime after dark, Akin awoke to find someone holding him and someone else trying to put something in his mouth.

He knew at once that the men had all had too much of their alcoholic drink. They stank of it. And their speech was thicker, harder to understand.

They had begun a small fire somehow, and in the light of it Akin could see two of them sprawled on the floor, asleep. The other three were busy with him, trying to feed him some beans they had mashed up.

He knew without his tongue touching the mashed beans that they were deadly. They were not to be eaten at all. Mashed as they were, they might incapacitate him before he could get rid of them. Then they would surely kill him.

He struggled and cried out as best he could without opening his mouth. His only hope, he thought, was to awaken the sleeping men and let them see how their trade goods were being destroyed.

But the sleeping men slept on. The men who were trying

to feed him the beans only laughed. One of them held his nose and pried his mouth open.

In desperation, Akin vomited over the intruding hand.

The man jumped back cursing. He fell over one of the sleeping men and was thrown off into the fire.

There was a terrifying confusion of shouting and cursing and the shelter stank of vomit and sweat and drink. Men struggled with one another, not knowing what they were doing. Akin escaped outside just before they brought the shelter down.

Frightened, confused, lonely almost to sickness, Akin fled into the forest. Better to try to get home. Better to chance hungry animals and poisonous insects than to stay with these men who might do anything, any irrational thing. Better to be completely alone than lonely among dangerous creatures that he did not understand.

But it was aloneness that really frightened him. The caimans and the anacondas could probably be avoided. Most stinging or biting insects were not deadly.

But to be alone in the forest . . .

He longed for Lilith, for her to hold him and give him her sweet milk.

= 3 =

The men realized quickly that he was gone.

Perhaps the pain of the fire and the wild blows, the collapse of the shelter, and the sudden wash of rain brought them to their senses. They scattered to search for him.

Akin was a small, frightened animal, unable to move quickly or coordinate his movements well. He could hear and occasionally see them, but he could not get away from them quickly enough. Nor could he be as quiet as he wished. Fortunately, the rain hid his clumsiness.

He moved inland—deeper into the forest, into the darkness where he could see and the Humans could not. They glowed with body heat that they could not see. Akin glowed with it as well and used it and the heat-light from the vegetation to guide him. For the first time in his life, he was glad Humans did not have this ability.

They found him without it.

He fled as quickly as he could. The rain ceased, and there were only insect and frog noises to conceal his mistakes. Apparently these were not enough. One of the men heard him. He saw the man jerk around to look. He froze, hoping he would not be seen, half-covered as he was by the leaves of several small plants.

"Here he is!" the man shouted. "I've found him!"

Akin scrambled away past a large tree, hoping the man would trip in the dangling lianas or run into a buttress. But beyond the tree was another man blundering toward the sound of the shout. He almost certainly did not see Akin. He did not seem even to see the tree. He tripped over Akin, fell against the tree, then twisted around, both arms extended, and swept them before him almost in swimming motions. Akin was not quick enough to escape the groping hands.

He was caught, felt roughly all over, then lifted and carried.

"I've got him," the man yelled. "He's all right. Just wet and cold."

Akin was not cold. His normal body temperature was slightly lower than the man's though, so his skin would always feel cool to Humans.

Akin rested against the man wearily. There was no escape. Not even at night when his ability to see gave him an advantage. He could not run away from grown men who were determined to keep him.

What could he do then? How could he save himself from their unpredictable violence? How could he live at least until they sold him?

He put his head against the man's shoulder and closed his eyes. Perhaps he could not save himself. Perhaps there was nothing for him to do but wait until they killed him.

The man who was carrying him rubbed his back with a free hand. "Poor kid. Shaking like hell. I hope those fools haven't made you sick. What do we know about taking care of a sick kid—or for that matter, a well one."

He was only muttering to himself, but he was at least not blaming Akin for what had happened. And he had not picked Akin up by an arm or a leg. That was a pleasant change. Akin wished he dared ask the man not to stroke him. Being stroked across the back was very much like being rubbed across eyes that could not protect themselves by closing.

Yet the man meant to be kind.

Akin looked at the man curiously. He had the shortest, brightest hair and beard of the group. Both were copper-colored and striking. He had not been the one to hit Tino. He had been asleep when his friends had tried to poison Akin. In the boat, he had been behind Akin, rowing, resting, or bailing. He had paid little attention to Akin beyond momentary curiosity. Now, though, he held Akin comfortably, supporting his body, and letting him hold on instead of clutching him and squeezing out his breath. He had stopped the rubbing now, and Akin was comfortable. He would stay close to this man if the man would let him. Perhaps with this man's help, he would survive to be sold.

4

Akin slept the rest of the night with the red-haired man. He simply waited until the man adjusted his sleeping mat under the newly built shelter and lay down. Then Akin crawled onto the mat and lay beside him. The man raised his head, frowned at Akin, then said, "Okay, kid, as long as you're housebroken."

The next morning while the red-haired man shared his sparse breakfast with Akin, his original captor vomited blood and collapsed.

Frightened, Akin watched from behind the red-haired man. This should *not* be happening. *It should not be happening!* Akin hugged himself, trembling, panting. The man was in pain, bleeding, sick, and all his friends could do was help him lie flat and turn his head to one side so that he did not reswallow the blood.

Why didn't they find an ooloi? How could they just let their friend bleed? He might bleed too much and die. Akin had heard of Humans doing that. They could not stop themselves from hemorrhaging without help. Akin could do this within his own body, but he did not know how to teach the skill to a Human. Perhaps it could not be taught. And he could not do it for anyone else the way the ooloi could.

One of the men went down to the river and got water.

Another sat with the sick man and wiped away the blood—
though the man continued to bleed.

"Jesus," the red-haired man said, "he's never been that
bad before." He looked down at Akin, frowned, then picked
Akin up and walked away toward the river. They met the man
who had gone for water coming back with a gourdful.

"Is he all right?" the man asked, stopping so quickly he
spilled some of his water.

"He's still throwing up blood. I thought I'd get the kid
away."

The other man hurried on, spilling more of his water.

The red-haired man sat on a fallen tree and put Akin down
beside him.

"Shit!" he muttered to himself. He put one foot on the
tree trunk, turning away from Akin.

Akin sat, torn, wanting to speak, yet not daring to, almost
sick himself about the bleeding man. It was *wrong* to allow
such suffering, *utterly wrong* to throw away a life so unfinished,
unbalanced, unshared.

The red-haired man picked him up and held him, peering
into his face worriedly. "You're not getting sick, too, are you?"
he asked. "Please, God, no."

"No," Akin whispered.

The man looked at him sharply. "So you can talk. Tilden
said you ought to know a few words. Being what you are, you
probably know more than a few, don't you?"

"Yes."

Akin did not realize until later that the man had not
expected an answer. Human beings talked to trees and rivers
and boats and insects the way they talked to babies. They
talked to be talking, but they believed they were talking to
uncomprehending things. It upset and frightened them when
something that should have been mute answered intelligently.
All this, Akin realized later. Now he could only think of the
man vomiting blood and perhaps dying *so* incomplete. And the
red-haired man had been kind. Perhaps he would listen.

"He'll die," Akin whispered, feeling as though he were
using shameful profanity.

The red-haired man put him down, stared at him with
disbelief.

"An ooloi would stop the bleeding and the pain," Akin said. "It wouldn't keep him or make him do anything. It would just heal him."

The man shook his head, let his mouth sag open. "What the hell are you?" There was no longer kindness or friendliness in his voice. Akin realized he had made a mistake. How to recoup? Silence? No, silence would be seen as stubbornness now, perhaps punished as stubbornness.

"Why should your friend die?" he asked with all the passionate conviction he felt.

"He's sixty-five," the man said, drawing away from Akin. "At least he's been awake for sixty-five years in all. That's a decent length of time for a Human being."

"But he's sick, in pain."

"It's just an ulcer. He had one before the war. The worms fixed it, but after a few years it came back."

"It could be fixed again."

"I think he'd cut his own throat before he'd let one of those things touch him again. I know I would."

Akin looked at the man, tried to understand his new expression of revulsion and hatred. Did he feel these things toward Akin as well as toward the Oankali? He was looking at Akin.

"What the hell are you?" he said.

Akin did not know what to say. The man knew what he was.

"How old are you really?"

"Seventeen months."

"Crap! Jesus, what are the worms doing to us? What kind of mother did you have?"

"I was born to a Human woman." That was what he really wanted to know. He did not want to hear that Akin had two female parents just as he had two male parents. He knew this, though he probably did not understand it. Tino had been intensely curious about it, had asked Akin questions he was too embarrassed to ask his new mates. This man was curious, too, but it was like the kind of curiosity that made some Humans turn over rotting logs—so that they could enjoy being disgusted by what lived there.

"Was that Phoenix your father?"

Akin began to cry in spite of himself. He had thought of Tino many times, but he had not had to speak of him. It hurt to speak of him. "How could you hate him so much and still want me? He was Human like you, and I'm not, but one of you killed him."

"He was a traitor to his own kind. He chose to be a traitor."

"He never hurt other Humans. He wasn't even trying to hurt anyone when you killed him. He was just afraid for me." Silence.

"How can what he did be wrong if I'm valuable?"

The man looked at him with deep disgust. "You may not be valuable."

Akin wiped his face and stared his own dislike back at this man who defended the killing of Tino, who had never harmed him. "I will be valuable to you," he said. "All I have to do is be quiet. Then you can be rid of me. And I can be rid of you."

The man got up and walked away.

Akin stayed where he was. The men would not leave him. They would come this way when they went down to the river. He was frightened and miserable and shaking with anger. He had never felt such a mix of intense emotions. And where had his last words come from? They made him think of Lilith when she was angry. Her anger had always frightened him, yet here it was inside him. What he had said was true enough, but he was not Lilith, tall and strong. It might have been better for him not to speak his feelings.

Yet there had been some fear in the red-haired man's expression before he went away.

"Human beings fear difference," Lilith had told him once. "Oankali crave difference. Humans persecute their different ones, yet they need them to give themselves definition and status. Oankali seek difference and collect it. They need it to keep themselves from stagnation and overspecialization. If you don't understand this, you will. You'll probably find both tendencies surfacing in your own behavior." And she had put her hand on his hair. "When you feel a conflict, try to go the Oankali way. Embrace difference."

Akin had not understood, but she had said, "It's all right. Just remember." And of course, he had remembered every word. It was one of the few times she had encouraged him to express Oankali characteristics. But now...

How could he embrace Humans who, in their difference, not only rejected him but made him wish he were strong enough to hurt them?

He climbed down from his log and found fungi and fallen fruit to eat. There were also fallen nuts, but he ignored them because he could not crack them. He could hear the men talking occasionally, though he could not hear what they said. He was afraid to try to run away again. When they caught him this time, they might beat him. If Red-Hair told them how well he could talk and understand, they might want to hurt him.

When he had eaten his fill he watched several ants, each the size of a man's forefinger. These were not deadly, but adult Humans found their sting agonizing and debilitating. Akin was gathering his courage to taste one, to explore the basic structure of it, when the men arrived, snatched him up, and stumbled and slipped down the path to the river. Three men carried the boat. One man carried Akin. There was no sign of the fifth man.

Akin was placed alone on the fifth seat in the center of the boat. No one spoke to him or paid any particular attention to him as they threw their gear into the boat, pushed the boat into deeper water, and jumped in.

The men rowed without speaking. Tears streamed down the face of one. Tears for a man who seemed to hate everyone, and who had apparently died because he would not ask an ooloi for help.

What had they done with his body? Had they buried it? They had left Akin alone for a long time—long enough, perhaps, even to escape if he had dared. They were getting a very late start in spite of their knowledge that they were being pursued. They had had time to bury a body.

Now they were dangerous. They were like smoldering wood that might either flare into flame or gradually cool and become less deadly. Akin made no sound, hardly moved. He must not trigger a flaring.

═ 5 ═

Dichaan helped Ahajas to a sitting position, then placed himself behind her so that she could rest against him if she wished. She never had before. But she needed him near her, needed contact with him during this one act—the birth of her child. She needed all her mates near her, touching her, needed to be able to link into them and feel the parts of her child that had come from them. She could survive without this contact, but that would not be good for her or for the child. Solitary births produced children with tendencies to become ooloi. It was too soon for construct ooloi. Such a child would have been sent to the ship to grow up among Lo relatives there.

Lilith had accepted this. She had shared all Ahajas's births as Ahajas had shared all of hers. She knelt now beside Dichaan, slightly behind Ahajas. She waited with false patience for the child to find its way out of Ahajas's body. First Tino had had to be transported to the ship for healing. He would probably not die. He would heal physically and emotionally during a short period in suspended animation. He might, however, lose some of his memory.

Then, when he was gone and Lilith was ready to join those already looking for Akin, Ahajas's child decided to be born. That was the way with children, Human or Oankali. When their bodies were ready, they insisted on being born. Eleven months for the Human-born instead of their original nine. Fifteen months for the Oankali-born instead of the original eighteen. Humans were so quick about everything. Quick and potentially deadly. Construct births on both sides had to be more carefully conventional than Human or Oankali births. Missing parents had to be simulated by the ooloi. The world had to be introduced very slowly after the child had gotten to know its parents. Lilith could not simply assist at the birth, then leave. Nikanj had all it could do simulating Joseph and being itself for the child. More would be uncertain—unsafe for the construct child.

Nikanj sat searching with its sensory arms for the place from which the child would eventually emerge. Lilith's Human way of giving birth was simpler. The child emerged from an existing orifice—the same one each time. Its birth hurt Lilith, but Nikanj always took away her pain. Ahajas had no birth orifice. Her child had to make its own way out of her body.

This did not hurt Ahajas, but it weakened her momentarily, made her want to sit down, made her focus her whole attention on following the child's progress, helping it if it seemed in distress. It was the duty of her mates to protect her from interference and reassure her that they were with her—were part of her child that was part of her. All interconnected, all united—a network of family into which each child should fall. This should be the best possible time for a family. But with Tino badly injured and Akin abducted, it was a time of confused feelings. The moments of union and anticipation were squeezed between moments of fear for Akin and worry that the Tino they got back might not know them or want them.

Surely the raiders would not hurt Akin. Surely. . .

But they did not belong to any resister village. That much had already been learned. They were nomads—traveling traders when they had trade goods, raiders when they had nothing. Would they try to keep Akin and raise him to be one of them, use his Oankali senses against the Oankali? Others had tried that before them, but they had never tried it with a child so young. They had never tried it with a Human-born male child, since there had been none before Akin. That worried Dichaan most. He was Akin's only living same-sex parent, and he felt uncertain, apprehensive, and painfully responsible. Where in the vast rain forest was the child? He probably could not escape and return home as so many others had before him. He simply did not have the speed or the strength. He must know that by now, and he must know he had to cooperate with the men, make them value him. *If* he were still alive, he *must* know.

The child would emerge from Ahajas's left side. She lay down on her right side. Dichaan and Lilith moved to maintain contact while Nikanj stroked the area of slowly rippling flesh. In tiny circular waves, the flesh withdrew itself from a central point, which grew slowly to show a darker gray—a temporary orifice within which the child's head tentacles could be seen moving slowly. These tentacles had released the substance that began the birth process. They were responsible now for the way Ahajas's flesh rippled aside.

Nikanj exposed one of its sensory hands, reached into the orifice, and lightly touched the child's head tentacles.

Instantly, the head tentacles grasped the sensory arm—the familiar thing amid so much strangeness. Ahajas, feeling the sudden movement and understanding it, rolled carefully onto her back. The child knew now that it was coming into an accepting, welcoming place. Without that small contact, its body would have prepared it to live in a harsher place—an environment less safe because it contained no ooloi parent. In truly dangerous environments, ooloi were likely to be killed trying to handle hostile new forms of life. That was why children who had no ooloi parents to welcome them at birth tended to become ooloi themselves when they matured. Their bodies assumed the worst. But in order for them to mature in the assumed hostile environment, they had to become unusually hardy and resilient early. This child, though, would not have to undergo such changes. Nikanj was with it. And someday it would probably be female to balance Akin—if Akin returned in time to influence it.

Nikanj caught the child as it slipped easily through its birth orifice. It was gray with a full complement of head tentacles, but only a few small body tentacles. It had a startlingly Human face—eyes, ears, nose, mouth—and it had a functioning sair orifice at its throat surrounded by pale, well-developed tentacles. The tentacles quivered slightly as the child breathed. That meant the small Human nose was probably only cosmetic.

It had a full set of teeth, as many construct newborns did, and unlike Human-born constructs, it would be using them at once. It would be given small portions of what everyone else ate. And once it had shown to Nikanj's satisfaction that it was not likely to poison itself, it would have the freedom to eat whatever it found edible—to graze, as the Humans said.

Akin might be doing that now to keep himself alive— grazing or browsing on whatever he could find. The resisters might or might not feed him. If they simply let him feed himself in the forest, it would be enough. Humans, though, were always frightened when they saw a young child putting something strange in its mouth. If the raiders were conscientious, normal Humans, they might kill him.

= 6 =

The river branched and branched, and the men never seemed in doubt about which branch to take. The journey seemed endless. Five days. Ten days. Twelve days. . . .

Akin said nothing as they traveled. He had made one mistake. He was afraid to make another. The red-haired man, whose name was Galt, nèver told anyone about his talking. It was as though the man did not quite believe he had heard Akin speak. He kept away from Akin as much as he could, never spoke to him, hardly spoke of him. The three others swung Akin around by his arms and legs or shoved him with their feet or carried him when necessary.

It took Akin days to realize that the men were not, in their own minds, treating him cruelly. There were no more drunken attempts to poison him, and no one hit him. They did hit each other occasionally. Twice, a pair of them rolled in the mud, punching and clutching at one another. Even when they did not fight, they cursed each other and cursed him.

They did not wash themselves often enough, and sometimes they stank. They talked at night about their dead comrade Tilden and about other men they had traveled with and raided with. Most of these, it seemed, were also dead. So many men, uselessly dead.

When the current grew too strong against them, they hid the boat and began to walk. The land was rising now. It was still rain forest, but it was climbing slowly into the hills. There, they hoped to trade Akin to a rich resister village called Hillmann where the people spoke German and Spanish. Tilden had been the group's German speaker. His mother, someone said, had been German. The men believed it was necessary to speak German because the majority of the people in the village were German, and they were likely to have the best trade goods. Yet only one other man, Damek, the man who had hit Tino, spoke any German at all. And he spoke only a little. Two people spoke Spanish—Iriarte and Kaliq. Iriarte had lived in a place called Chile before the war. The other, Kaliq, had spent years in Argentina. It was decided that bargaining would be done in Spanish. Many of the Germans spoke their neighbors' language. The traders would pretend not to know German, and Damek would listen to what he was not supposed to hear. Villagers who thought they could not be understood might talk too much among themselves.

Akin looked forward to seeing and hearing different kinds of Humans. He had heard and learned some Spanish from Tino. He had liked the sound of it when Tino had gotten Nikanj to speak it to him. He had never heard German at all. He wished that someone other than Damek spoke it. He avoided Damek as best he could, remembering Tino. But the thought of meeting an entirely new people was almost enticing enough to ease his grief and his disappointment at not being taken to Phoenix, where he believed he would have been welcomed by Tino's parents. He would not have pretended to them to be Tino's son, but if the color of his skin and the shape of his eyes reminded them of Tino, he would not have been sorry. Perhaps the Germans would not want him.

The four resisters and Akin approached Hillmann through fields of bananas, papaya trees, pineapple plants, and corn. The fields looked well kept and fruitful. They looked more impressive to Akin than Lilith's gardens because they were so much larger and so many more trees had been cut down. There was a great deal of cassava and rows of something that had not yet come up. Hillmann must have lost a great deal of top soil to the rain in all those long, neat rows. How long could they farm this way before the land was ruined and they had to move? How much land had they already ruined?

The village was two neat rows of thatched-roof wooden houses on stilts. Within the village, several large trees had been preserved. Akin liked the way the place looked. There was a calming symmetry to it.

But there were no people in it.

Akin could see no one. Worse, he could hear no one. Humans were noisy even when they tried not to be. These Humans, though, should be talking and working and going about their lives. Instead, there was absolutely no sound of them. They were not hiding. They were simply gone.

Akin stared at the village from the arms of Iriarte and wondered how long it would take the men to realize that something was wrong.

Iriarte seemed to notice first. He stopped, stood staring straight ahead. He glanced at Akin whose face was so close to his own, saw that Akin had turned in his arms and was also staring with his eyes.

"What is it?" he asked as though expecting Akin to answer. Akin almost did—almost forgot himself and spoke aloud. "Something is crazy here," Iriarte said to the others.

Immediately Kaliq took the opposite position. "It's a nice place. Still looks rich. There's nothing wrong."

"No one is here," Iriarte said.

"Why? Because they don't rush out to meet us? They're around somewhere, watching."

"No. Even the kid noticed something."

"Yes," Galt agreed. "He did. I was watching him. His kind are supposed to see and hear better than we are." He gave Akin a look of suspicion. "What we walk into, you walk into with us, kid."

"For godsake," Damek said, "he's a baby. He doesn't know anything. Let's go."

He had gone out several steps ahead before the others began to follow. He drew even farther ahead, showing his scorn for their caution, but he drew neither bullets nor arrows. There was no one to shoot him. Akin rested his chin on Iriarte's shoulder and savored the strange pale scents—all pale now. Humans had been gone from this place for several days. There was food spoiling in some of the houses. The scent of that grew stronger as they neared the village. Many men, a few women, spoiling food, and agoutis—the small rodents that some resisters ate.

And Oankali.

Many Oankali had been here several days ago. Did it have anything to do with Akin's abduction? No. How could it? The Oankali would not empty a village on his account. If someone in the village had harmed him, they would certainly find that person, but they would not bother anyone else. And this emptying may have occurred before he was abducted.

"There's nobody here," Damek said. He had stopped, finally, in the middle of the village, surrounded by empty houses.

"I told you that a long time ago," Iriarte muttered. "I think it's okay for us, though. The kid was nervous before, but he's relaxed now."

"Put him down," Galt said. "Let's see what he does."

"If he's not nervous, maybe we ought to be." Kaliq looked around warily, peered through the open doorway of a house. "Oankali did this. They must have."

"Put the kid down," Galt repeated. He had ignored Akin for most of Akin's captivity, had seemed to forget or deny Akin's precocity. Now he seemed to want something.

Iriarte put Akin down, though Akin would have been content to stay in the man's arms. But Galt seemed to expect something. Best to give him something and keep him quiet. Akin turned slowly, drawing breaths over his tongue. Something unusual but not likely to stimulate fear or anger.

Blood in one direction. Old human blood, dry on dead wood. No. It would do no good to show them that.

An agouti nearby. Most of these had gone—apparently either carried away by the villagers or released into the forest. This one was still in the village, eating the seedpods that had fallen from one of the few remaining trees. Best not to make the men notice it. They might shoot it. They craved meat. Within the last few days, they had caught, cooked, and eaten several fish, but they talked a great deal about real meat—steaks and chops and roasts and burgers...

A faint smell of the kind of vegetable dye Humans at Lo

used to write with. Writing. Books. Perhaps the people of Hillmann had left some record of the reason for their leaving.

Without speaking, the men followed Akin to the house that smelled strongest of the dye, the ink, Lilith called it. She used it so often that the smell of it made Akin see her in his mind and almost cry with wanting her.

"Just like a bloodhound," Damek said. "He doesn't waste a step."

"He eats mushrooms and flowers and leaves," Kaliq said inconsequentially. "It's a wonder he hasn't poisoned himself."

"What's that got to do with anything? What's he found?" Iriarte picked up a large book that Akin had been trying to reach. The paper, Akin could see, was heavy and smooth. The cover was of polished, dark-stained wood.

"Shit," Iriarte muttered. "It's in German." He passed the book to Damek.

Damek rested the book on the little table and turned pages slowly. *"Ananas . . . bohnen . . . bananen . . . mangos . . . .* This is just stuff about crops. I can't read most of it, but it's . . . records. Crop yelds, farming methods . . ." He turned several more pages to the end of the book. "Here's some Spanish, I think."

Iriarte came back to look. "Yeah. It says . . . shit. Ah, shit!"

Kaliq pushed forward to look. "I don't believe this," he said after a moment. "Someone was forced to write this!"

"Damek," Iriarte said, gesturing. "Look at this German shit up here. The Spanish says they gave it up. The Oankali invited them again to join the trade villages, and they voted to do it. To have Oankali mates and kids. They say, 'Part of what we are will continue. Part of what we are will go to the stars someday. That seems better than sitting here, rotting alive or dying and leaving nothing. How can it be a sin for the people to continue?'" Iriarte looked at Damek. "Does it say anything like that in German?"

Damek studied the book for so long that Akin sat down on the floor to wait. Finally Damek faced the others, frowning. "It says just about that," he told them. "But there are two writers. One says 'We're joining the Oankali. Our blood will continue.' But the other one says the Oankali should be killed—that to join with them is against God. I'm not sure, but I think one group went to join the Oankali and another went to kill the Oankali. God knows what happened."

"They just walked away," Galt said. "Left their homes, their crops..." He began looking through the house to see what else had been left. Trade goods.

The other men scattered through the village to carry on their own searches. Akin looked around to be certain he was unobserved, then went out to watch the agouti. He had not seen one close up before. Lilith claimed they looked like a cross between deer and rats. Nikanj said they were larger now than they had been before the war, and they were more inclined now to seek out insects. They had lived mainly on fruits and seeds before, though even then they took insects as well. This agouti was clearly more interested in the insect larvae that infested the seedpods than in the pods themselves. Its forelegs ended in tiny hands, and it sat back on its haunches and used the hands to pluck out the white larvae. Akin watched it, fascinated. It looked at him, tensed for a moment, then selected another seedpod. Akin was smaller than it was. Apparently it did not see him as a threat. He stooped near it and watched it. He inched closer, wanting to touch it, see how the furred body felt.

To his amazement, the animal let him touch it, let him stroke the short fur. He was surprised to find that the fur did not feel like hair. It was smooth and slightly stiff in one direction and rough in the other. The animal moved away when he rubbed its fur against the grain. It sniffed his hand and stared at him for a moment. It clutched a large, half-eaten larva in its hands.

An instant later the agouti flew sideways in a roar of Human-made thunder. It landed on its side some distance from Akin, and it made small, useless running motions with its feet. It could not get up.

Akin saw at once that it was Galt who had shot the animal. The man looked at Akin and smiled. Akin understood then that the man had shot the inoffensive animal not because he was hungry for its meat, but because he wanted to hurt and frighten Akin.

Akin went to the agouti, saw that it was still alive, still struggling to run. Its hind feet did not work, but its forefeet made small running steps through the air. There was a gaping hole in its side.

Akin bent to its neck and tasted it, then, for the first time, deliberately injected his poison. A few seconds later, the agouti stopped struggling and died.

Galt stepped up and nudged the animal with his foot.

"It was beginning to feel terrible pain," Akin said. "I helped it die." He swayed slightly, even though he was seated on the ground. He had tasted the agouti's life and its pain, but all he could give it was death. If he had not gone near it, Galt might never have noticed it. It might have lived.

He hugged himself, trembling, feeling sick.

Galt nudged him with a foot, and he fell over. He picked himself up and stared at the man, wanting desperately to be away from him.

"How come you only talk to me?" Galt asked.

"First because I wanted to help Tilden," Akin whispered quickly. The others were coming. "Now because I have to . . . have to help you. You shouldn't eat the agouti. The poison I gave it would kill you."

Akin managed to dodge the vicious kick Galt aimed at his head. Iriarte picked Akin up and held him protectively.

"You fool, you'll kill him!" Iriarte shouted.

"Good riddance," Galt yelled back. "Shit, there's plenty of trade goods here. We don't need that mongrel bastard!"

Kaliq had come up to stand beside Iriarte. "What have you found here that we could trade for a woman?" he demanded.

Silence.

"That boy is to us what gold used to be," Kaliq spoke softly now.

"In fact," Iriarte said, "he's more valuable to us than you are."

"He can talk!" Galt shouted.

Kaliq took a step closer to him. "Man, I don't care if he can fly! There are people who'll pay *anything* for him. He *looks* okay, that's what's important."

Iriarte looked at Akin. "Well, he always knew he could understand us better than any normal kid his age. What did he say?"

Galt drew his mouth into a thin smile. "After I shot the

agouti, he bit it on the neck, and it died. He told me not to eat it because he had poisoned it."

"Yeah?" Iriarte held Akin away from him and stared. "Say something, kid."

Akin was afraid the man would drop him if he spoke. He was also afraid he would lose Iriarte as a protector—as he had lost Galt. He tried to look as frightened as he felt, but he said nothing.

"Give him to me," Galt said. "I'll make him talk."

"He'll talk when he gets ready," Iriarte said. "Hell, I had seven kids before the war. They'd talk all the time until you wanted them to."

"Listen, I'm not talking about baby talk!"

"I know. I believe you. Why does it bother you so?"

"He can talk as well as you can!"

"So? It's better than being covered with tentacles or gray skin. It's better than being without eyes or ears or a nose. Kaliq is right. It's looks that are important. But you know as well as I do that he isn't Human, and it's *got* to come out somehow."

"He claims to be poison," Galt said.

"He may be. The Oankali are."

"So you go on holding him next to your neck. You do that."

To Akin's surprise, Iriarte did just that. Later, when he was alone with Akin, he said, "You don't have to talk if you don't want to." He ran a hand across Akin's hair. "I think I'd rather you didn't, really. You look so much like one of my kids, it hurts."

Akin accepted this silently.

"Don't kill anything else," he said. "Even if it's suffering, let it alone. Don't scare these guys. They get crazy."

7

At Siwatu village, the people looked much like Lilith. They spoke English, Swahili, and a scattering of other languages. They examined Akin and wished very much to buy him, but they would not send one of the village women away with foreign men. The women took Akin and fed him and bathed him as though he could do nothing for himself. Several of them believed that their breasts could be made to produce milk if they kept Akin with them.

The men were so fascinated with him that his captors became frightened. They took him and stole out of the village one moonless night. Akin did not want to go. He liked being with the women who knew how to lift him without hurting him and who gave him interesting food. He liked the way they smelled and the softness of their bosoms and their voices, high and empty of threat.

But Iriarte carried him away, and he believed that if he cried out, the man might be killed. Certainly some people would be killed. Perhaps it would only be Galt who kicked at him whenever he was nearby and Damek who had clubbed Tino down. But more likely, it would be all four of his abductors and several village men. He might die himself. He had seen that men could go mad when they were fighting. They could do things that afterward amazed and shamed them.

Akin let himself be carried to the raiders' canoes. They had two now—the one they had begun with and a light, new one found in Hillmann. Akin was put into the new one between two balanced mounds of trade goods. Behind one mound Iriarte rowed. In front of the other, Kaliq rowed. Akin was glad, at least, not to have to worry about Galt's feet or his oar. And he continued to avoid Damek when he could, though the man showed him friendliness. Damek acted as though Akin had not seen him club Tino down.

been afraid. Curious, suspicious, startled when an un-Human-looking child touched him, but not frightened. Not dangerous.

And the people of Phoenix were his people.

Phoenix was larger and more beautiful than Hillmann. The houses were large and colored white or blue or gray. They had the glass windows Tino had boasted of—windows that glittered with reflected light. There were broad fields and storage buildings and an ornate structure that must have been the church. Tino had described it to Akin and tried to make Akin understand what it was for. Akin still did not understand, but he could repeat Tino's explanation if he had to. He could even say his prayers. Tino had taught him, thinking it scandalous that he had not known them before.

Human men worked in the fields, planting something. Human men came out of their houses to look at the visitors. There was a faint scent of Oankali in the village. It was many days old—searchers who had come and searched and waited and finally left. None of the searchers had been members of his family.

Where were his parents looking?

And in this village, where were the Human women?

Inside. He could smell them in their houses—could smell their excitement.

"Don't say a word until I tell you to," Iriarte whispered.

Akin moved to show that he had heard, then he twisted in Iriarte's arms to face the large, well-built, low-stilted house they were walking toward and the tall, lean man who awaited them in the shade of its roof in what seemed to be a partially enclosed room. The walls were only as high as the man's waist, and the roof was held up by regularly spaced, rounded posts. The half-room reminded Akin of a drawing he had seen by a Human Lo woman, Cora: great buildings whose overhanging roofs were supported by huge, ornately decorated, round posts.

"So that's the kid," the tall man said. He smiled. He had a short, well-tended black beard and short hair, very black. He wore a white shirt and short pants, displaying startlingly hairy arms and legs.

A small blond woman came from the house to stand beside

"I wouldn't eat them," Galt said. "Anything that wasn't here before the war, I don't need."

Kaliq took two of the nuts in one hand and squeezed. Akin could hear the shells cracking. When he opened his hand, several small round nuts rolled around amid the shell fragments. Kaliq offered them to Akin, and Akin took most of them gratefully. He ate them with such obvious enjoyment that Kaliq laughed and ate one of them himself. He chewed slowly, tentatively.

"It tastes like . . . I don't know." He ate the rest. "It's very good. Better than anything I've had for a long time." He settled to breaking and eating the rest while Akin brought another leafful to Iriarte. There were not many good nuts on the ground. Most were insect-infested. He checked each one with his tongue to make sure they were all right. When Damek went out and gathered nuts of his own, almost every one was infested with insect larvae. This made him stare at Akin with suspicion and doubt. Akin watched him without facing him, watched him without eyes until he shrugged and threw the last of his nuts away in disgust. He looked at Akin once more and spat on the ground.

— 9 —

Phoenix.

The four resisters had been avoiding it, they said, because they knew it was Tino's home village. The Oankali would check it first, perhaps stay there the longest. But Phoenix was also the richest resister village they knew of. It sent people into the hills to salvage metal from prewar sites and had people who knew how to shape the metal. It had more women than any other village because it traded metal for them. It grew cotton and made soft, comfortable clothing. It raised and tapped not only rubber trees, but trees that produced a form of oil that could be burned in their lamps without refinement. And it had fine, large houses, a church, a store, vast farms...

It was, the raiders said, more like a prewar town—and less like a group of people who have given up, whose only hope was to kill a few Oankali before they died.

"I almost settled there once," Damek said when they had hidden the canoes and begun their single-file walk toward the hills and Phoenix. Phoenix was many days south of Hillmann on a different branch of the river, but it, too, was located closer to the mountains than most trader and resister villages. "I swear," Damek continued, "they've got everything there but kids."

Iriarte, who was carrying Akin, sighed quietly. "They'll

him. "My god," she said, "that's a beautiful child. Isn't there anything wrong with him?"

Iriarte walked up several steps and put Akin into the woman's arms. "He is beautiful," Iriarte told her quietly. "But he has a tongue you'll have to get used to—in more than one way. And he is very, very intelligent."

"And he is for sale," the tall man said, his eyes on Iriarte. "Come in, gentlemen. My name is Gabriel Rinaldi. This is my wife Tate."

The house was cool and dark and sweet-smelling inside. It smelled of herbs and flowers. The blond woman took Akin into another room with her and gave him a chunk of pineapple to eat while she poured some drinks for the guests.

"I hope you won't wet the floor," she said, glancing at him.

"I won't," he said impulsively. Something made him want to talk to this woman. He had wanted to speak to the women of Siwatu, but he had been afraid. He was never alone with one of them. He had feared their group reaction to his un-Human aspect.

The woman looked at him, eyes momentarily wide. Then she smiled with only the left side of her mouth. "So that's what the raider meant about that tongue of yours." She lifted him and put him on a counter so that she could talk to him without bending or stooping. "What's your name?"

"Akin." No one else had asked his name during his captivity. Not even Iriarte.

"Ah-keen," she pronounced. "Is that right?"

"Yes."

"How old are you?"

"Seventeen months." Akin thought for a moment. "No, eighteen now."

"Very, very intelligent," Tate said, echoing Iriarte. "Shall we buy you, Akin?"

"Yes, but..."

"But?"

"They want a woman."

Tate laughed. "Of course they do. We might even find them one. Men aren't the only ones who get itchy feet. But, Jesus, four men! She'd better have another itchy part or two."

"What?"

"Nothing, little one. Why do you want us to buy you?"

Akin hesitated, said finally, "Iriarte likes me and so does Kaliq. But Galt hates me because I look more Human than I am. And Damek killed Tino." He looked at her blond hair, knowing she was no relative of Tino's. But perhaps she had known him, liked him. It would be hard to know him and not like him. "Tino used to live here," he said. "His whole name is Augustino Leal. Did you know him?"

"Oh, yes." She had become very still, totally focused on Akin. If she had been Oankali, all her head tentacles would have been elongated toward him in a cone of living flesh. "His parents are here," she said. "He . . . couldn't have been your father. You look like him, though."

"My Human father is dead. Tino took his place. Damek called him a traitor and killed him."

She closed her eyes, turned her face away from Akin. "Are you sure he's dead?"

"He was alive when they took me away, but the bones of his head had been broken with the wooden part of Damek's gun. There was no one around to help him. He must have died."

She took Akin down from the counter and hugged him. "Did you like him, Akin?"

"Yes."

"We loved him here. He was the son most of us never had. I knew he was going, though. What was there for him in a place like this? I gave him a packet of food to take with him and aimed him toward Lo. Did he reach it?"

"Yes."

She smiled again with only half her mouth. "So you're from Lo. Who's your mother?"

"Lilith Iyapo." Akin did not think she would have liked hearing Lilith's long Oankali name.

"Son of a bitch!" Tate whispered. "Listen, Akin, don't say that name to anyone else. It may not matter anymore, but don't say it."

"Why?"

"Because there are people here who don't like your mother. There are people here who might hurt you because they can't get at her. Do you understand?"

Akin looked into her sun-browned face. She had very blue eyes—not like Wray Ordway's pale eyes, but a deep, intense color. "I don't understand," he said, "but I believe you."

"Good. If you do that, we'll buy you. I'll see to it."

"At Siwatu, the raiders took me away because they were afraid the men were going to try to steal me."

"Don't you worry. Once I drop this tray and you in the living room, I'll see to it that they don't go anywhere until our business with them is done."

She carried the tray of drinks and let Akin walk back to her husband and the resisters. Then she left them.

Akin climbed onto Iriarte's lap, knowing he was about to lose the man, missing him already.

"We'll have to have our doctor look at him," Gabriel Rinaldi was saying. He paused. "Let me see your tongue, kid."

Obligingly Akin opened his mouth. He did not stick his tongue out to its full extent, but he did nothing to conceal it.

The man got up and looked for a moment, then shook his head. "Ugly. And he's probably venomous. The constructs usually are."

"I saw him bite an agouti and kill it," Galt put in.

"But he's never made any effort to bite any of us," Iriarte said with obvious irritation. "He's done what he's been told to do. He's taken care of his own toilet needs. And he knows better than we do what's edible and what isn't. Don't worry about his picking up things and eating them. He's been doing that since we took him—seeds, nuts, flowers, leaves, fungi . . . and he's never been sick. He won't eat fish or meat. I wouldn't force him to if I were you. The Oankali don't eat it. Maybe it would make him sick."

"What I want to know," Rinaldi said, "is just how un-Human he is . . . mentally. Come here, kid."

Akin did not want to go. Showing his tongue was one thing. Deliberately putting himself in hands that might be unfriendly was another. He looked up at Iriarte, hoping the man would not let him go. Instead Iriarte put him down and gave him a shove toward Rinaldi. Reluctantly, he edged toward the man.

Rinaldi got up impatiently and lifted Akin into his arms.

He sat down, turned Akin about on his lap looking at him, then held Akin facing him. "Okay, they say you can talk. So talk."

Again Akin turned to look at Iriarte. He did not want to begin talking in a room full of men when talking had already made one of those men hate him.

Iriarte nodded. "Talk, niño. Do as he says."

"Tell us your name," Rinaldi said.

Akin caught himself smiling. Twice now, he had been asked his name. These people seemed to care who he was, not just what he was. "Akin," he said softly.

"Ah-keen?" Rinaldi frowned down at him. "Is that a Human name?"

"Yes."

"What language?"

"Yoruba."

"Yor—. . . what? What country?"

"Nigeria."

"Why should you have a Nigerian name? Is one of your parents Nigerian?"

"It means *hero*. If you put an *s* on it, it means *brave boy*. I'm the first boy born to a Human woman on Earth since the war."

"That's what the worms hunting for you said," Rinaldi agreed. He was frowning again. "Can you read?"

"Yes."

"How can you have had time to learn to read?"

Akin hesitated. "I don't forget things," he said softly.

The raiders looked startled. "Ever?" Damek demanded. "Anything?"

Rinaldi only nodded. "That's the way the Oankali are," he said. "They can bring out the ability in Humans when they want to—and when the Humans agree to be useful to them. I thought that was the boy's secret."

Akin, who had considered lying, was glad he had not. He had always found it easy to tell the truth and difficult to make himself lie. He could lie very convincingly, though, if lying would keep him alive and spare him pain among these men. It was easier, though, to divert questions—as he had diverted the question about his parents.

"Do you want to stay here, Akin?" Rinaldi asked.

"If you buy me, I'll stay," Akin said.

"Shall we buy you?"

"Yes."

"Why?"

Akin glanced at Iriarte. "They want to sell me. If I have to be sold, I'd like to stay here."

"Why?"

"You aren't afraid of me, and you don't hate me. I don't hate you, either."

Rinaldi laughed. Akin was pleased. He had hoped to make the man laugh. He had learned back in Lo that if he made Humans laugh, they were more comfortable with him—though, of course, in Lo, he had never been exposed to people who might injure him simply because he was not Human.

Rinaldi asked his age, the number of languages he spoke, and the purpose of his long, gray tongue. Akin withheld information only about the tongue.

"I smell and taste with it," he said. "I can smell with my nose, too, but my tongue tells me more." All true, but Akin had decided not to tell anyone what else his tongue could do. The idea of his tasting their cells, their genes, might disturb them too much.

A woman called a doctor came in, took Akin from Rinaldi, and began to examine, poke, and probe his body. She did not talk to him, though Rinaldi had told her he could talk.

"He's got some oddly textured spots on his back, arms, and abdomen," she said. "I suspect they're where he'll grow tentacles in a few years."

"Are they?" Rinaldi asked him.

"I don't know," Akin said. "People never know what they'll be like after metamorphosis."

The doctor stumbled back from him with a wordless sound.

"I told you he could talk, Yori."

She shook her head. "I thought you meant . . . baby talk."

"I meant like you and me. Ask him questions. He'll answer."

"What can you tell me about the spots?" she asked.

"Sensory spots. I can see and taste with most of them." And he could complete sensory connections with anyone else who had sensory tentacles or spots. But he would not talk to Humans about that.

"Does it bother you when we touch them?"

"Yes. I'm used to it, but it still bothers me."

Two women came into the room and called Rinaldi away.

A man and woman came in to look at Akin—just to stand and stare at him and listen as he answered the doctor's questions. He guessed who they were before they finally spoke to him.

"Did you really know our son?" the woman asked. She was very small. All the women he had seen so far were almost tiny. They would have looked like children alongside his mother and sisters. Still, they were gentle and knew how to lift him without hurting him. And they were neither afraid of him nor disgusted by him.

"Was Tino your son?" he asked the woman.

She nodded, mouth pulled tight. Small lines had gathered between her eyes. "Is it true?" she asked. "Have they killed him?"

Akin bit his lips, suddenly caught by the woman's emotion. "I think so. Nothing could save him unless an Oankali found him quickly—and no Oankali heard when I screamed for help."

The man stepped close to Akin, wearing an expression Akin had never seen before—yet he understood it. "Which one of them killed him?" the man demanded. His voice was very low, and only Akin and the two women heard. The doctor, slightly behind the man, shook her head. Her eyes were like his Human father Joseph's had been—more narrow than round. Akin had been waiting for a chance to ask her whether she was Chinese. Now, though, her eyes were big with fear. Akin knew fear when he saw it.

"One who died," Akin lied quietly. "His name was Tilden. He had a sickness that made him bleed and hurt and hate everyone. The other men called it an ulcer. One day, he threw up too much blood, and he died. I think the others buried him. One of them took me away so I wouldn't see."

"You know that he's dead? You're sure?"

"Yes. The others were angry and sad and dangerous for a long time after that. I had to be very careful."

The man stared at him for a long time, trying to see what any Oankali would have known at a touch, what this man would never know. He had loved Tino, this man. How could Akin, even without the doctor's warning, send him with his bare hands to face a man who had a gun, who had three friends with guns?

Tino's father turned from Akin and went to the other side of the room, where both Rinaldis, the two women who had come in, and the four raiders were talking, shouting, gesturing. They had, Akin realized, begun the business of trading for him. Tino's father was smaller than most of the men, but when he stalked into their midst, everyone stopped talking. Perhaps it was the look on the man's face that made Iriarte finger the rifle beside him.

"Is there one of you called Tilden?" Tino's father asked. His voice was calm and soft.

The raiders did not answer for a moment. Then, ironically, it was Damek who said, "He died, mister. That ulcer of his finally got him."

"Did you know him?" Iriarte asked.

"I would like to have met him," Tino's father said. And he walked out of the house. Tate Rinaldi looked over at Akin, but no one else seemed to pay attention to him. Attention shifted from Tino's father back to the subject of the trade. Tino's mother smoothed back Akin's hair and looked into his face for a moment.

"What was my son to you?" she asked.

"He took the place of my dead Human father."

She closed her eyes for a moment, and tears ran down her face. Finally she kissed his cheek and went away.

"Akin," the doctor said softly, "did you tell them the truth?"

Akin looked at her and decided not to answer. He wished he had not told Tate Rinaldi the truth. She had sent Tino's parents to him. It would have been better not to meet them at all until the raiders had gone away. He had to remember, had to keep reminding himself how dangerous Human beings were.

"Never tell them," Yori whispered. His silence had apparently told her enough. "There has been enough killing. We die and die and no one is born." She put her hands on either side of his face and looked at him, her expression shifting from pain to hatred to pain to something utterly unreadable. She hugged him suddenly, and he was afraid she would crush him or scratch him with her nails or thrust him away from her and hurt him. There was so much suppressed emotion in her, so much deadly tension in her body.

She left him. She spoke for a few moments with Rinaldi, then left the house.

= 10 =

Bargaining went on into the night. People ate and drank and told stories and tried to outtrade one another. Tate gave Akin what she called a decent vegetarian meal, and he did not tell her that it was not decent at all. It did not contain nearly enough protein to satisfy him. He ate it, then slipped out a door at the back of the house and supplemented his meal with peas and seed from her garden. He was eating these things when the shooting began inside.

The first shot startled him so much that he fell over. As he stood up, there were more shots. He took several steps toward the house, then stopped. If he went in, someone might shoot him or step on him or kick him. When the shooting stopped, he would go in. If Iriarte or Tate called him, he would go in.

There was the noise of furniture smashing—heavy bodies thrown about, people shouting, cursing. It was as though the people inside intended to destroy both the house and themselves.

Other people rushed into the house, and the sounds of fighting increased, then died.

When there had been several moments of silence, Akin went up the steps and into the house, moving slowly but not quietly. He made small noises deliberately, hoping he would be heard and seen and known not to be dangerous.

He saw first broken dishes. The clean, neat room where

Tate had given him pineapple and talked to him was now littered with broken dishes and broken furniture. He had to move very carefully to avoid cutting his feet. His body healed faster than the bodies of Humans, but he found injuring himself just as painful as they seemed to.

Blood.

He could smell it strongly enough to be frightened. Someone must be dead with so much blood spilled.

In the living room, there were people lying on the floor and others tending them. In one corner, Iriarte lay untended.

Akin ran toward the man. Someone caught him before he could reach Iriarte and picked him up in spite of his struggles and cries.

Rinaldi.

Akin yelled, twisted, and bit the man's thumb.

Rinaldi dropped him, shouting that he had been poisoned—which he had not—and Akin scrambled to Iriarte.

But Iriarte was dead.

Someone had struck him several times across the body with what must have been a machete. He had gaping, horrible wounds, some spilling entrails onto the floor.

Akin screamed in shock and frustration and grief. When he came to know a man, the man died. His Human father was dead without Akin ever knowing him except through Nikanj. Tino was dead. Now Iriarte was dead. His years had been cut off unfinished. His Human children had died in the war, and his construct children, created from material the ooloi had collected long ago, would never know him, never taste him and find themselves in him.

Why?

Akin looked around the room. Yori and a few others were doing what they could for the injured, but most of the people in the room were just staring at Akin or at Gabriel Rinaldi.

"He's not poisoned!" Akin said with disgust. "You're the ones who kill people, not me!"

"He's all right?" Tate said. She was standing with her husband, looking frightened.

"Yes." He looked at her for a moment, then looked again at Iriarte. He looked around, saw that Galt also appeared to be dead, hacked about the head and shoulders. Yori was working over Damek. What irony if Damek lived while Iriarte died for the murder Damek had committed.

Tino's murder *must* be the reason for all this.

On the floor near Damek lay Tino's father, wounded in his left thigh, his left arm, and his right shoulder. His wife was weeping over him, but he was not dead. A man was using something other than water to clean away blood from the shoulder wound. Another man was holding Tino's father down.

There were other wounded and dead around the room. Akin found Kaliq dead behind a long cushion-covered wooden bench. He had only one wound, bloody but small. It was a chest wound, probably involving his heart.

Akin sat beside him while others in the house helped the injured and carried out the dead. No one came for Kaliq while he sat there. Behind him, someone began to scream. Akin looked back and saw that it was Damek. Akin tried not to feel the anguish that came to him reflexively when he saw a Human suffering. One part of his mind screamed for an ooloi to save this irreplaceable Human, this man whom some ooloi somewhere had made prints of, but whom no Oankali or construct truly knew.

Another part of his mind hoped Damek would die. Let him suffer. Let him scream. Tino had not even had time to scream.

Tino's father did not scream. He grunted. Bits of metal were cut from his flesh while he held a piece of folded cloth between his teeth and grunted.

Akin came out of his corner to look at one of the bits of metal—a gray pellet covered with the blood of Tino's father.

Tate came over to him and picked him up. To his own surprise, he held on to her. He put his head on her shoulder and did not want to be put down.

"Don't you bite me," she said. "If you want to get down, you tell me. Bite me and I'll bounce you off a wall."

He sighed, feeling alone even in her arms. She was not the haven he had needed. "Put me down," he said.

She held him away from her and looked at him. "Really?"

Surprised, he looked back. "I thought you didn't want to hold me."

"If I didn't want to hold you, I wouldn't have picked you up. I just want us to understand each other. Okay?"

"Yes."

And she held him to her again and answered his questions, told him about bullets and how they were fired from guns, how Tino's father Mateo had come with his friends to take revenge on the raiders in spite of their guns. There were no guns in Phoenix before the raiders arrived.

"We voted not to have them," she said. "We have enough things to hurt each other with. Now... well, we've got our first four. I'll bury the damned things if I get the chance."

She had taken him in among the broken dishes and sat him on the counter. He watched while she lit a lamp. The lamp reminded him suddenly, painfully, of the guest house back in Lo.

"You want anything else to eat?" she asked.

"No."

"No, what?"

"No... what?"

"Shame on Lilith. 'No, thank you,' little one. Or 'Yes, please.' Understand?"

"I didn't know resisters said those things."

"In my house they do."

"Did you tell Mateo who killed Tino?"

"God, no. I was afraid you told him. I forgot to tell you to keep that to yourself."

"I told him the man who killed Tino was dead. One of the raiders really did die. He was sick. I thought if Mateo believed it was that one, he wouldn't hurt anyone else."

She nodded. "That should have worked. You're brighter than I thought. And Mateo is crazier than I thought." She sighed. "Hell, I don't know. I never had any kids. I don't know how I would have reacted if I had one and someone killed him."

"You shouldn't have told Tino's parents anything at all until the raiders were gone," Akin said quietly.

She looked at him, then looked away. "I know. All I said was that you had known Tino and that he had been killed. Of course they wanted to know more, but I told them to wait until we had settled you in—that you were just a baby, after all." She looked at him again, frowning, shaking her head. "I wonder what the hell you really are."

"A baby," he said. "A Human-Oankali construct. I wish I were something more because the Oankali part of me scares people, but it doesn't help me when they try to hurt me."

"I'm not going to hurt you."

Akin looked at her, then looked toward the room in which Iriarte lay dead.

Tate made herself very busy cleaning up the broken dishes and glass.

"Have you had all you wanted to eat out here?"

"Yes."

"You follow me, then. I've got this fruit to carry." She stooped and lifted the large basket of fruit to her head. When she was satisfied with its placement, she stood up and turned back toward the village.

"Tate?" he called.

"What?" She did not look at him.

"It went back to the ship, you know. It's still Dinso. It will have to come to Earth sometime. But it did not want to live here with any of the Humans it could have. I never knew why before."

"Nobody ever mentioned us?"

Us, Akin thought. Tate and Gabe. They had both known Kahguyaht. And Gabe was probably the reason Tate had not gone to Kahguyaht. "Kahguyaht would come back if Nikanj called it," he said.

"You really didn't know about us?" she insisted.

"No. But the walls in Lo aren't like the walls here. You can't hear through Lo walls. People seal themselves in and no one knows what they're saying."

She stopped, put one hand up to balance the basket, then stared down at him. "Good god!" she said.

It occurred to him then that he should not have let her know he could hear through Phoenix walls.

"What is Lo!" she demanded. "Is it just a village, or..."

Akin did not know what to say, did not know what she wanted.

"Do the walls really seal?" she asked.

"Yes, except at the guest house. You've never been there?"

"Never. Traders and raiders have told us about it, but never that it was... What is it, for godsake! A baby ship?"

Akin frowned. "It could be someday. There are so many on Earth, though. Maybe Lo will be one of the males inside one of those that become ships."

"But... but someday it will leave Earth?"

Akin knew the answer to this question, but he realized he must not give it. Yet he liked her and found it difficult to lie to her. He said nothing.

"I thought so," she said. "So someday the people of

Lo—or their descendants—will be in space again, looking for
some other people to infect or afflict or whatever you call it."

"Trade."

"Oh, yeah. The goddamn gene trade! And you want to
know why I can't go back to Kahguyaht."

She walked away, leaving him to make his own way back to
the village. He made no effort to keep up with her, knowing he
could not. The little she had guessed had upset her enough to
make her not care that he, valuable being that he was, was left
alone in the groves and gardens where he might be stolen.
How would she have reacted if he had told her all he knew—
that it was not only the descendants of Humans and Oankali
who would eventually travel through space in newly mature
ships. It was also much of the substance of Earth. And what
was left behind would be less than the corpse of a world. It
would be small, cold, and as lifeless as the moon. Maturing
Chkahichdahk left nothing useful behind. They had to be
worlds in themselves for as long as it took the constructs in
each one to mature as a species and find another partner
species to trade with.

The salvaged Earth would finally die. Yet in another way, it
would live on as single-celled animals lived on after dividing.
Would that comfort Tate? Akin was afraid to find out.

He was tired, but he had nearly reached the houses when
Tate returned for him. She had already put away her basket of
fruit. Now she picked him up without a word and carried him
back to her home. He fell asleep in her arms before they
reached it.

= 12 =

No one came for him.
No on would take him home or let him go.

He felt both unwanted and wanted too much. If his parents could not come because of his sibling's birth, then others should have come. His parents had done this kind of service for other families, other villages who had had their children stolen. People helped each other in searching for and recovering children.

And yet, his presence seemed to delight the people of Phoenix. Even those who were disturbed by the contrast between his tiny body and his apparent maturity grew to like having him around. Some always had a bit of food ready for him. Some asked question after question about his life before he was brought to them. Others liked to hold him or let him sit at their feet and tell him stories of their own prewar lives. He liked this best. He learned not to interrupt them with questions. He could learn afterward what kangaroos, lasers, tigers, acid rain, and Botswana were. And since he remembered every word of their stories, he could easily think back and insert explanations where they should go.

He liked it less when people told him stories that were clearly not true—stories peopled by beings called witches or elves or gods. Mythology, they said; fairy tales.

He told them stories from Oankali history—past partnerships that contributed to what the Oankali were or could become today. He had heard such stories from all three of his Oankali parents. All were absolutely true, yet the Humans believed almost none of them. They liked them anyway. They would gather around close so that they could hear him. Sometimes they let their work go and came to listen. Akin liked the attention, so he accepted their fairy tales and their disbelief in his stories. He also accepted the pairs of short pants that Pilar Leal made for him. He did not like them. They cut off some of his perception, and they were harder than skin to clean once they were soiled. Yet it never occurred to him to ask anyone else to wash them for him. When Tate saw him washing them, she gave him soap and showed him how to use it on them. Then she smiled almost gleefully and went away.

People let him watch them make shoes and clothing and paper. Tate persuaded Gabe to take him up to the mills—one where grain was ground and one where wooden furniture, tools, and other things were being made. The man and woman there were making a large canoe when Akin arrived.

"We could build a textile mill," Gabe told him. "But foot-powered spinning wheels, sewing machines, and looms are enough. We already make more than we need, and people need to do some things at their own pace with their own designs."

Akin thought about this and decided he understood it. He had often watched people spinning, weaving, sewing, making things they did not need in the hope of being able to trade with villages that had little or no machinery. But there was no urgency. They could stop in the middle of what they were doing and come to listen to his stories. Much of their work was done simply to keep them busy.

"What about metal?" he asked.

Gabe stared down at him. "You want to see the blacksmith's shop?"

"Yes."

Gabe picked him up and strode off with him. "I wonder how much you really understand," he muttered.

"I usually understand," Akin admitted. "What I don't understand, I remember. Eventually I understand."

"Jesus! I wonder what you'll be like when you grow up."

"Not as big as you," Akin said wistfully.

"Really? You know that?"

Akin nodded. "Strong, but not very big."

"Smart, though."

"It would be terrible to be small and foolish."

Gabe laughed. "It happens," he said. "But probably not to you."

Akin looked at him and smiled himself. He was still pleased when he could make Gabe laugh. It seemed that the man was beginning to accept him. It was Tate who had suggested that Gabe take him up the hill and show him the mills. She pushed them together when she could, and Akin understood that she wanted them to like each other.

But if they did what would happen when his people finally came for him? Would Gabe fight? Would he kill? Would he die?

Akin watched the blacksmith make a machete blade, heating, pounding, shaping the metal. There was a wooden crate of machete blades in one corner. There were also scythes, sickles, axes, hammers, saws, nails, hooks, chains, coiled wire, picks... And yet there was no clutter. Everything, work tools and products, had their places.

"I work here sometimes," Gabe said. "And I've helped salvage a lot of our raw materials." He glanced at Akin. "You might get to see the salvage site."

"In the mountains?"

"Yeah."

"When?"

"When things start to get warm around here."

It took Akin several seconds to realize that he was not talking about the weather. He would be hidden at the salvage site when his people came looking for him.

"We've found artifacts of glass, plastic, ceramic, and metal. We've found a lot of money. You know what money is?"

"Yes. I've never seen any, but people have told me about it."

Gabe reached into his pocket with his free hand. He brought out a bright, golden disk of metal and let Akin hold it. It was surprisingly heavy for its size. On one side was something that looked like a large letter *t* and the words, "He is risen. We shall rise." On the other side there was a picture of a bird flying up from fire. Akin studied the bird, noticing that it was a kind he had never seen pictured before.

"Phoenix money," Gabe said. "That's a phoenix rising from its own ashes. A phoenix was a mythical bird. You understand?"

"A lie," Akin said thoughtlessly.

Gabe took the disk from him, put it back into his pocket, and put Akin down.

"Wait!" Akin said. "I'm sorry. I call myths that in my mind. I didn't mean to say it out loud."

Gabe looked down at him. "If you're always going to be small, you ought to learn to be careful with that word," he said.

"But . . . I didn't say *you* were lying."

"No. You said my dream, the dream of everyone here, was a lie. You don't even know what you said."

"I'm sorry."

Gabe stared at him, sighed, and picked him up again. "I don't know," he said. "Maybe I ought to be relieved."

"At what?"

"That in some ways you really are just a kid."

= 13 =

Weeks later, traders arrived bringing two more stolen children. Both appeared to be young girls. The traders took away not a woman but as many metal tools and as much gold as they could carry, plus books that were more valuable than gold. Two couples in Phoenix worked together with occasional help from others to make paper and ink and print the books most likely to be desired by other villages. Bibles—using the memories of every village they could reach, Phoenix researchers had put together the most complete Bible available. There were also how-to books, medical books, memories of prewar Earth, listings of edible plants, animals, fish, and insects and their dangers and advantages, and propaganda against the Oankali.

"We can't have kids, so we make all this stuff," Tate told Akin as they watched the traders bargain for a new canoe to carry all their new merchandise in. "Those guys are now officially rich. For all the good it will do them."

"Can I see the girls?" Akin asked.

"Why not? Let's go over."

She walked slowly and let him follow her over to the Wilton house where the girls were staying. Macy and Kolina Wilton had been quick enough to seize both children for themselves. They were one half of Phoenix's publishers. They would probably be expected to give up one child to another couple, but for now they were a family of four.

The girls were eating roasted almonds and cassava bread with honey. Kolina Wilton was spooning a salad of mixed fruit into small bowls for them.

"Akin," she said when she saw him. "Good. These little girls don't speak English. Maybe you can talk to them."

They were brown girls with long, thick black hair and dark eyes. They wore what appeared to be men's shirts, belted with light rope and cut off to fit them. The bigger of the two girls had already managed to free her arms from the makeshift garment. She had a few body tentacles around her neck and shoulders, and confining them was probably blinding, itching torment. Now all her small tentacles focused on Akin, while the rest of her seemed to go on concentrating on the food. The smaller girl had a cluster of tentacles at her throat, where they probably protected a sair breathing orifice. That meant her small, normal-looking nose was probably ornamental. It might also mean the girl could breathe underwater. Oankali-born, then, in spite of her human appearance. That was unusual. If she was Oankali-born, then she was *she* only by courtesy. She could not know yet what her sex would be. But such children, if they had Human-appearing sex organs at all, tended to look female. The children were perhaps three and four years old.

"You'll have to go into their gardens and into the forest to find enough protein," Akin told them in Oankali. "They try, but they never seem to give us enough."

Both girls climbed down from their chairs, came to touch him and taste him and know him. He became so totally focused on them and on getting to know them that he could not perceive anything else for several minutes.

They were siblings—Human-born and Oankali-born. The smaller one was Oankali-born and the more androgenous-looking of the two. It would probably become male in response to its sibling's apparent femaleness. Its name, it had signaled, was Shkaht—Kaalshkaht eka Jaitahsokahldahktohj aj Dinso. It was a relative. They were both relatives through Nikanj, whose people were Kaal. Happily, Akin gave Shkaht the Human version of his own name, since the Oankali version did not give enough information about Nikanj. Akin Iyapo Shing Kaalnikanjlo.

= 14 =

The next day, all three children were arranged in backpacks and carried toward the mountains. They were not allowed to walk. Gabe carried Akin atop a bundle of supplies, and Tate walked behind, carrying even more supplies. Amma rode on Macy Wilton's back and surreptitiously tasted him with one of her small body tentacles. She had a normal Human tongue, but each of her tentacles would serve her as well as Akin's long, gray Oankali tongue. Shkaht's throat tentacles gave her a more sensitive sense of smell and taste than Akin, and she could use her hands for tasting. Also, she had slender, dark tentacles on her head, mixed with her hair. She could see with these. She could not see with her eyes. She had learned, though, to seem to look at people with her eyes—to turn and face them and to move her slender head tentacles as she moved her head so that Humans were not disturbed by her hair seeming to crawl about. She would have to be very careful because Humans, for some reason, liked to cut people's hair. They cut their own, and they had cut Akin's. Even back in Lo, men in particular either cut their own hair or got others to cut it. Akin did not want to think about what it might feel like to have sensory tentacles cut off. Nothing could hurt worse. Nothing would be more likely to cause an Oankali or a construct to sting reflexively, fatally.

The Humans walked all day, stopping for rest and food only once at noon. They did not talk about where they were going or why, but they walked quickly, as though they feared pursuit.

They were a party of twenty, armed, in spite of Tate's efforts, with the four guns of Akin's captors. Damek was still alive, but he could not walk. He was being cared for back at Phoenix. Akin suspected that he had no idea what was going on—that his gun was gone, that Akin was gone. What he did not know, he could not resent or tell.

That night the Humans erected tents and made beds of blankets and branches or bamboo—whatever they could find. Some stretched hammocks between trees and slept outside the tents since they saw no sign of rain. Akin asked to sleep outside with someone and a woman named Abira simply reached out of her hammock and lifted him in. She seemed glad to have him in spite of the heat and humidity. She was a short, very strong woman who carried a pack as heavy as those of men half again her size, yet she handled him with gentleness.

"I had three little boys before the war," she said in her strangely accented English. She had come from Israel. She gave his head a quick rub—her favorite caress—and went to sleep, leaving him to find his own most comfortable position.

Amma and Shkaht slept together on their own bed of blanket-covered bamboo. Humans valued them, fed them, sheltered them, but they did not like the girls' tentacles—would not deliberately allow themselves to be touched by the small sensory organs. Amma had only managed to taste Macy Wilton because she was riding on his back and her tentacles were able to burrow through the clothing he had put between himself and her.

No Human wanted to sleep with them. Even now Neci Roybal and her husband Stancio were whispering about the possibility of removing the tentacles while the girls were young.

Alarmed, Akin listened carefully.

"They'll learn to do without the ugly little things if we take them off while they're so young," Neci was saying.

"We have no proper anesthetics," the man protested. "It would be cruel." He was his wife's opposite, quiet, steady, kind. People tolerated Neci for his sake. Akin avoided him in order to avoid Neci. But Neci had a way of saying a thing and saying a thing over and over until other people began to say it—and believe it.

"They won't feel much now," she said. "They're so young... And those little worm things are so small. Now is the best time to do it."

Stancio said nothing.

"They'll learn to use their Human senses," Neci whispered. "They'll see the world as we do and be more like us."

"Do you want to cut them?" Stancio asked. "Little girls. Almost babies."

"Don't talk foolishness. It can be done. They'll heal. They'll forget they ever had tentacles."

"Maybe they'd grow back."

"Cut them off again!"

There was a long silence.

"How many times, Neci," the man said finally. "How many times would you torture children? Would you torture them if they had come from your body? Will you torture them now because they did not?"

Nothing more was said. Akin thought Neci cried a little. She made small, wordless sounds. Stancio made only regular breathing sounds. After a time, Akin realized he had fallen asleep.

═ 15 ═

They spent days walking through forest, climbing forested hills. But it was cooler now, and Akin and the girls had to fight off attempts to clothe them more warmly. There was still plenty to eat, and their bodies adjusted quickly and easily to the temperature change. Akin went on wearing the short pants Pilar Leal had made for him. There had been no time for clothing to be made for the girls, so they wore lengths of cloth wrapped around their waists and tied at the top. This was the only clothing they did not deliberately shed and lose.

Akin had begun sleeping with them on the second night of the journey. They needed to learn more English and learn it quickly. Neci was doing as Akin had expected—saying over and over to different people in quiet, intense conversation that the girls' tentacles should be removed now, while they were young, so that they would look more Human, so that they would learn to depend on their Human senses and perceive the world in a Human way. People laughed at her behind her back, but now and then, Akin heard them talking about the tentacles—how ugly they were, how much better the girls would look without them . . .

"Will they cut us?" Amma asked him when he told them. All her tentacles had flattened invisibly to her flesh.

Amma linked more deeply into both of them, giving them her frustration. She did not understand.

"He is being left here," Shkaht explained silently. She deliberately soothed her sibling with her own calm certainty. "They want him to know the Humans," she said. "They would not have sent him to them, but since he's here and not being hurt, they want him to learn so that later he can teach."

"What about us?"

"I don't know. They couldn't come for us without taking him. And they probably didn't know where we would be sold—or even whether we would be sold. I think we'll be left here until they decide to come for him—unless we're in danger."

"We're in danger now," Amma whispered aloud.

"No. Akin will talk to Tate. If Tate can't help us, we'll disappear some night soon."

"Run away?"

"Yes."

"The Humans would catch us!"

"No. We'd travel at night, hide during the day, take to the nearest river when it's safe."

"Can you breathe underwater?" Akin asked Amma.

"Not yet," she answered, "but I'm a good swimmer. I always went in whenever Shkaht did. If I get into trouble, Shkaht helps—links with me and breathes for me."

As Akin's sibling would have been able to help him. He withdrew from them, reminded by their unity of his own solitude. He could talk to them, communicate with them nonvocally, but he could never have the special closeness with them that they had with each other. Soon he would be too old for it—if he wasn't already. And what was happening to his sibling?

"I don't believe they're leaving me with the Humans deliberately," he said. "My parents wouldn't do that. My Human mother would come alone if no one would come with her."

Both girls were back in contact with him at once. "No!" Shkaht was saying. "When resisters find women alone, they keep them. We saw it happen at a village where our captors tried to trade us."

"What did you see?"

"Some men came to the village. They lived there, but they had been traveling. They had a woman with them, her arms tied with rope and a rope tied around her neck. They said they had found her and she was theirs. She screamed at them, but no one knew her language. They kept her."

"No one could do that to my mother," Akin said. "She wouldn't let them. She travels alone whenever she wants to."

"But how would she find you alone? Maybe every resister village she went to would try to tie her up and keep her. Maybe if they couldn't they would hurt her or kill her with guns."

Maybe they would. They seemed to do such things so easily. Maybe they already had.

Some communication he did not catch passed between Amma and Shkaht. "You have three Oankali parents," Shkaht whispered aloud. "They know more about resisters than we do. They wouldn't let her go alone, would they? If they couldn't stop her, they would go with her, wouldn't they?"

". . . yes," Akin answered, feeling no certainty at all. Amma and Shkaht did not know Lilith, did not know how she became so frightening sometimes that everyone stayed away from her. Then she vanished for a while. Who knew what might happen to her while she roamed the forests alone?

The girls had placed him between them. He did not realize until it was too late that they were calming him with their own deliberate calm, soothing him, putting themselves and him to sleep.

Akin awoke the next day still miserable, still frightened for his mother and lonely for his sibling. Yet he went to Tate and asked her to carry him for a while so that he could talk to her.

She picked him up at once and took him to the small, fast-running stream where the camp had gotten its water.

"Wash," she said, "and talk to me here. I don't want people watching the two of us whispering together."

He washed and told her about Neci's efforts to have Amma's and Shkaht's tentacles removed. "They would grow back," he said. "And until they did, Shkaht wouldn't be able to see at all or breathe properly. She would be very sick. She might die. Amma probably wouldn't die, but she would be crippled. She wouldn't be able to use any of her senses to their full advantage. She wouldn't be able to recognize smells and tastes that should be familiar to her—as though she could touch them, but not grasp them—until her tentacles grew back. They would always grow back. And it would hurt her to have them cut off—maybe the way it would hurt you to have your eyes cut out."

Tate sat on a fallen log, ignoring its fungi and its insects. "Neci has a way of convincing people," she said.

"I know," he said. "That's why I came to you."

"Gabe said something to me about a little surgery on the girls. Are you sure it was Neci's idea?"

"I heard her talking about it on the first night after we left Phoenix."

"God." Tate sighed. "And she won't quit. She never quits. If the girls were older, I'd like to give her a knife and tell her to go try it." She stared at Akin. "And since neither of those two is an ooloi, I assume that would be fatal to her. Wouldn't it, Akin?"

"... yes."

"What if the girls were unconscious?"

"It wouldn't matter. Even if they... Even if they were dead and hadn't been dead very long, their tentacles would still sting anyone who tried to cut them or pull them."

"Why didn't you tell me that instead of telling me how badly the girls would be hurt?"

"I didn't want to scare you. We don't want to scare anyone."

"No? Well, sometimes it's a good thing to scare people. Sometimes fear is all that will keep them from doing stupid things."

"You're going to tell them?"

"In a way. I'm going to tell them a story. Gabe and I once saw what happened to a man who injured an Oankali's body tentacles. That was back on the ship. There are other people in Phoenix who remember, but none of them are with us here. Your mother was with us then, Akin, though I don't intend to mention her."

Akin looked away from her, stared across the stream bed, and wondered if his mother were still alive.

"Hey," Tate said. "What's the matter?"

"You should have taken me home," he said bitterly. "You say you know my mother. You should have taken me back to her."

Silence.

"Shkaht says men in resister villages tie up women when they catch them, and they keep them. My mother probably knows that, but she would look for me anyway. She wouldn't let them keep her, but they might shoot her or cut her."

More silence.

"*You should have taken me home.*" He was crying openly now.

"I know," she whispered. "And I'm sorry. But I can't take you home. You mean too much to my people." She had crossed her arms in front of her, the fingers of each hand curved around an elbow. She had made a bar against him like the wooden bars she used to secure her doors. He went to her and put his hands on her arms.

"They won't let you keep me much longer," he said. "And even if they did . . . Even if I grew up in Phoenix and Amma and Shkaht grew up there, you would still need an ooloi. And there are no construct ooloi."

"You don't know what you'll need!"

This surprised him. How could she think he did not know? She might wish he did not know, but of course he did. "I've known since I touched my sibling," he said. "I couldn't have said it then, but I knew we were two-thirds of a reproductive unit. I know what that means. I don't know how it feels. I don't know how threes of adults feel when they come together to mate. But I know there must be three, and one of those three must be an ooloi. My body knows that."

She believed him. Her face said she believed him.

"Let's get back," she said.

"Will you help me get home?"

"No."

"But why?"

Silence.

"Why!" He pulled futilely at her locked arms.

"Because..." She waited until he remembered to turn his face up to meet her gaze. "Because these are my people. Lilith has made her choice, and I've made mine. That's something you'll probably never understand. You and the girls are hope to these people, and hope is something they haven't had for more years than I want to think about."

"But it's not real. We can't do what they want."

"Do yourself a favor. Don't tell them."

Now he did not have to remind himself to stare at her.

"Your people will come for you, Akin. I know that, and so do you. I like you, but I'm not good at self-delusion. Let my people hope while they can. Keep quiet." She drew a deep breath. "You'll do that, won't you?"

"You've taken my sibling from me," he said. "You've kept me from having what Amma and Shkaht have, and that's something you don't understand or even care about. My mother might die because you keep me here. You know her, but you don't care. And if you don't care about my people, why should I care about yours?"

She looked downward, then gazed into the running water. Her expression reminded him of Tino's mother's expression when she asked if her son were dead. "No reason," she said finally. "If I were you, I'd hate our guts." She unbarred her arms and picked him up, put him on her lap. "We're all you've got, though, kid. It shouldn't be that way, but it is."

She stood up with him, holding him tighter than necessary, and turned to see Gabe coming toward them.

"What's going on?" he asked. Akin thought later that he looked a little frightened. He looked uncertain, then relieved, yet slightly frightened—as though something bad still might happen.

"He had some things to tell me," Tate said. "And we have work to do."

"What work?" He took Akin from her as they walked back toward camp, and there was somehow more to the gesture than simply relieving her of a burden. Akin had seen this odd tension in Gabe before, but he did not understand it.

"We have to see to it that our little girls aren't forced to kill anyone," Tate said.

= 16 =

The salvage site that was their destination was a buried town. "Smashed and covered by the Oankali," Gabe told Akin. "They didn't want us living here and remembering what we used to be."

Akin looked at the vast pit the salvage crew had dug over the years, excavating the town. It had not been wantonly smashed as Gabe believed. It had been harvested. One of the shuttles had partially consumed it. The small ship-entities fed whenever they could. There was no faster way to destroy a town than to land a shuttle on it and let the shuttle eat its fill. Shuttles could digest almost anything, including the soil itself. What the people of Phoenix were digging through were leavings. Apparently these were enough to satisfy their needs.

"We don't even know what this place used to be called," Gabe said bitterly.

Piles of metal, stone, and other materials lay scattered about. Salvagers were tying some things together with jute rope so that they could be carried. They all stopped their work, though, when they saw the party of newcomers. They gathered around first, shouting and greeting people by name, then falling silent as they noticed the three children.

Men and women, covered with sweat and dirt, clustered around to touch Akin and make baby-talk noises at him. He did

139

not surprise them by speaking to them, although both girls
were trying out their new English on their audience.

Gabe knelt down, slipped out of his pack, then lifted Akin
free. "Don't goo-goo at him," he said to a dusty woman
salvager who was already reaching for him. "He can talk as well
as you can—and understand everything you say."

"He's beautiful!" the woman said. "Is he ours? Is he—"

"We got him in trade. He's more Human-looking than the
girls, but that probably doesn't mean anything. He's construct.
He's not a bad kid, though."

Akin looked up at him, recognizing the compliment—the
first he had ever received from Gabe, but Gabe had turned
away to speak to someone else.

The salvager picked Akin up and held him so that she
could see his face. "Come on," she said. "I'll show you a damn
big hole in the ground. Why don't you talk like your friends?
You shy?"

"I don't think so," Akin answered.

The woman looked startled, then grinned. "Okay. Let's go
take a look at something that probably used to be a truck."

The salvagers had hacked away thick, wild vegetation to
dig their hole and to plant their crops along two sides of it, but
the wild vegetation was growing back. People with hoes,
shovels, and machetes had been clearing it away. Now they
were talking with newly arrived Humans or getting acquainted
with Amma and Shkaht. Three Humans trailed after the woman who carried Akin, talking to each other about him and
occasionally talking to him.

"No tentacles," one of them said, stroking his face. "So
Human. So beautiful..."

Akin did not believe he was beautiful. These people liked
him simply because he looked like them. He was comfortable
with them, though. He talked to them easily and ate the bits of
food they kept giving him and accepted their caresses, though
he did not enjoy them any more than he ever had. Humans
needed to touch people, but they could not do so in ways that
were pleasurable or useful. Only when he felt lonely or frightened was he glad of their hands, their protection.

They passed near a broad trench, its sides covered with
grass. At its center flowed a clear stream. No doubt there were

wet seasons when the entire riverbed was filled, perhaps to overflowing. The wet and dry seasons here would be more pronounced than in the forest around Lo. There, it rained often no matter what the season was supposed to be. Akin knew about such things because he had heard adults talk about them. It was not strange to see this shrunken river. But when he looked up as he was carried toward the far end of the pit, he saw for the first time between the green hills to the distant, snow-covered peaks of the mountains.

"Wait!" Akin shouted as the salvager—Sabina, her name was—would have carried him on toward the houses on the far side of the hole. "Wait, let me look."

She seemed pleased to do this. "Those are volcanic," she said. "Do you know what that means?"

"A broken place in the Earth where hot liquid rock comes up," Akin said.

"Good," she said. "Those mountains were pushed up and built by volcanic activity. One of them went off last year. Not close enough to us to matter, but it was exciting. It still steams now and then, even though it's covered with snow. Do you like it?"

"Dangerous," he said. "Did the ground shake?"

"Yes. Not much here, but it must have been pretty bad there. I don't think there are any people living near there."

"Good. I like to look at it, though. I'd like to go there some day to understand it."

"Safer to look from here." She took him on to the short row of houses where salvagers apparently lived. There was a flattened rectangular metal frame—Sabina's "truck" apparently. It looked useless. Akin had no idea what Humans had once done with it, but now it could only be cut up into metal scrap and eventually forged into other things. It was huge and would probably yield a great deal of metal. Akin wondered how the feeding shuttle had missed it.

"I'd like to know how the Oankali smashed it flat this way," another woman said. "It's as though a big foot stepped on it."

Akin said nothing. He had learned that people did not really want him to give them information unless they asked him directly—or unless they were so desperate they didn't care where their information came from. And information about the

Oankali tended to frighten or anger them no matter how they
received it.

Sabina put him down, and he looked more closely at the
metal. He would have tasted it if he had been alone. Instead,
he followed the salvagers into one of the houses. It was a
solidly built house, but it was plain, unpainted, roofed with
sheets of metal. The guest house at Lo was a more interesting
building.

But inside there was a museum.

There were stacks of dishes, bits of jewelry, glass, metal.
There were boxes with glass windows. Behind the windows was
only a blank, solid grayness. There were massive metal boxes
with large, numbered wheels on their doors. There were metal
shelves, tables, drawers, bottles. There were crosses like the
one on Gabe's coin—crosses of metal, each with a metal man
hanging from them. Christ on the cross, Akin remembered.
There were also pictures of Christ rapping with his knuckles on
a wooden door and others of him pulling open his clothing to
reveal a red shape that contained a torch. There was a picture
of Christ sitting at a table with a lot of other men. Some of the
pictures seemed to move as Akin viewed them from different
angles.

Tate, who had reached the house before him, took one of
the moving pictures—a small one of Christ standing on a hill
and talking to people—and handed it to Akin. He moved it
slightly in his hand, watching the apparent movement of Christ,
whose mouth opened and closed and whose arm moved up and
down. The picture, though scratched, was hard and flat—made
of a material Akin did not understand. He tasted it—then
threw it hard away from him, disgusted, nauseated.

"Hey!" one of the salvagers yelled. "Those things are
valuable!" The man retrieved the picture, glared at Akin, then
glared at Tate. "What the hell would you give a thing like that
to a baby for anyway?"

But both Tate and Sabina had stepped quickly to see what
was wrong with Akin.

Akin went to the door and spat outside several times, spat
away pure pain as his body fought to deal with what he had
carelessly taken in. By the time he was able to talk and tell

what was wrong, he had everyone's attention. He did not want
it, but he had it.

"I'm sorry," he said. "Did the picture break?"

"What's the matter with you?" Tate said with unmistakable
concern.

"Nothing now. I got rid of it. If I were older, I could have
handled it better—made it harmless."

"The picture—the plastic—was harmful to you?"

"The stuff it was made of. Plastic?"

"Yes."

"It's so sealed and covered with dirt that I didn't feel the
poison before I tasted it. Tell the girls not to taste it."

"We won't," Amma and Shkaht said in unison, and Akin
jumped. He did not know when they had come in.

"I'll show you later," he said in Oankali.

They nodded.

"It was . . . more poison packed tight together in one place
than I've ever known. Did Humans make it that way on
purpose?"

"It just worked out that way," Gabe said. "Hell, maybe
that's why the stuff is still here. Maybe it's so poisonous—or so
useless—that not even the microbes would eat it. Nonbiode-
gradable, I think the prewar word was."

Akin looked at him sharply. The shuttle had not eaten the
plastic. And the shuttle could eat anything. Perhaps the plastic,
like the truck, had simply been overlooked. Or perhaps the
shuttle had found it useless as Gabe had said.

"Plastics used to kill people back before the war," a woman
said. "They were used in furniture, clothing, containers, appliances,
just about everything. Sometimes the poisons leached into food
or water and caused cancer, and sometimes there was a fire and
plastics burned and gassed people to death. My prewar husband was a fireman. He used to tell me."

"I don't remember that," someone said.

"I remember it," someone else contradicted. "I remember
a house fire in my neighborhood where everybody died trying
to get out because of poison gas from burning plastics."

"My god," Sabina said, "should we be trading this stuff?"

"We can trade it," Tate said. "The only place that has
enough of it to be a real danger is right here. Other people

need things like this—pictures and statues from another time, something to remind them what we were. What we are."

"Why did people use it so much if it killed them?" Akin asked.

"Most of them didn't know how dangerous it was," Gabe said. "And some of the ones who did know were making too damn much money selling the stuff to worry about fire and contamination that might or might not happen." He made a wordless sound—almost a laugh, although Akin could detect no humor in it. "That's what Humans are, too, don't forget. People who poison each other, then disclaim all responsibility. In a way, that's how the war happened."

"Then . . ." Akin hesitated. "Then why don't you paint new pictures and make statues from wood or metal?"

"It wouldn't be the same for them," Shkaht said in Oankali. "They really do need the old things. Our Human father got one of the little crosses from a traveling resister. He always wore it on a cord around his neck."

"Was it plastic?" Akin asked.

"Metal. But prewar. Very old. Maybe it even came from here."

"Independent resisters take our stuff to your villages?" Tate asked when Akin translated.

"Some of them trade with us," Akin said. "Some stay for a while and have children. And some only come to steal children."

Silence. The Humans went back to their trade goods, broke into groups, and began exchanging news.

Tate showed Akin the house where he was to sleep—a house filled with mats and hammocks, cluttered with small objects the salvagers had dug up, and distinguished by a large, cast-iron wood stove. It made the one in Tate's kitchen seem child-sized.

"Stay away from that," Tate said. "Even when it's cold. Make a habit of staying away from it, you hear?"

"All right. I wouldn't touch anything hot by accident, though. And I'm finally too old to poison, so—"

"You just poisoned yourself!"

"No. I was careless, and it hurt, but I wouldn't have gotten very sick or died. It was like when you hit your toe and stumbled on the trail. It didn't mean you don't know how to walk. You were just careless."

"Yeah. That may or may not be a good analogy. You stay away from the stove anyway. You want something to eat or has everyone already stuffed you with food?"

"I'll have to get rid of some of what I've already eaten so that I can eat some more protein."

"Want to eat with us or would you rather go out and eat leaves?"

"I'd rather go out and eat leaves."

She frowned at him for a second, then began to laugh "Go," she said. "And be careful."

= 17 =

Neci Roybal wanted one of the girls. And she had not given up the idea of having both girls' tentacles removed. She had begun again to campaign for that among the salvagers. The tentacles looked more like slugs than worms most of the time, she said. It was criminal to allow little girls to be afflicted with such things. Girl children who might someday be the mothers of a new Human race ought to look Human—ought to see Human features when they looked in the mirror...

"They're not Oankali," Akin heard her tell Abira one night. "What happened to the man Tate and Gabe knew—that might only happen with Oankali."

"Neci," Abira told her, "if you go near those kids with a knife, and they don't finish you, I will."

Others were more receptive. A pair of salvagers named Senn converted quickly to Neci's point of view. Akin spent much of his third night at the salvage camp lying in Abira's hammock, listening as in the next house Neci and Gilbert and Anne Senn strove to convert Yori Shinizu and Sabina Dobrowski. Yori, the doctor, was obviously the person they hoped would remove the girls' tentacles.

"It's not just the way the tentacles look," Gil said in his soft voice. Everyone called him Gil. He had a soft, ooloilike

146

voice. "Yes, they are ugly, but it's what they represent that's important. They're alien. Un-Human. How can little girls grow up to be Human women when their own sense organs betray them?"

"What about the boy?" Yori asked. "He has the same alien senses, but they're located in his tongue. We couldn't remove that."

"No," Anne said, soft-voiced like her husband. She looked and sounded enough like him to be his sister, but Humans did not marry their siblings, and these two had been married before the war. They had come from a place called Switzerland and had been visiting a place called Kenya when the war happened. They had gone to look at huge, fabulous animals, now extinct. In her spare time, Anne painted pictures of the animals on cloth or paper or wood. Giraffes, she called them, lions, elephants, cheetahs . . . She had already shown Akin some of her work. She seemed to like him.

"No," she repeated. "But the boy must be taught as any child should be taught. It's wrong to let him always put things into his mouth. It's wrong to let him eat grass and leaves like a cow. It's wrong to let him lick people. Tate says he calls it tasting them. It's disgusting."

"She lets him give in to any alien impulse," Neci said. "She had no children before. I heard there was some sickness in her family so that she didn't dare have children. She doesn't know how to care for them."

"The boy loves her," Yori said.

"Because she spoils him," Neci said. "But he's young. He can learn to love other people."

"You?" Gil asked.

"Why not me! I had two children before the war. I know how to bring them up."

"We also had two," Anne said. "Two little girls." She gave a low laugh. "Shkaht and Amma look nothing like them, but I would give anything to make one of those girls my daughter."

"With or without tentacles?" Sabina said.

"If Yori would do it, I would want them removed."

"I don't know whether I'd do it," Yori said. "I don't believe Tate was lying about what she saw."

"But what she saw was between a Human and an adult

Oankali," Anne said. "These are children. Almost babies. And they're almost Human."

"They *look* almost Human," Sabina put in. "We don't know what they really are."

"Children," Anne said. "They're children."

Silence.

"It should be done," Neci said. "Everyone knows it should be done. We don't know how to do it yet, but, Yori, you should be finding out how. You should study them. You came along to guard their health. Doesn't that mean you should spend time with them, get to know more about them?"

"That won't help," Yori said. "I already know they're venomous. Perhaps I could protect myself, and perhaps I couldn't. But... this is cosmetic surgery, Neci. Unnecessary. And I'm no surgeon anyway. Why should we risk the girls' health and my life just because they have what amounts to ugly birthmarks? Tate says the tentacles grow back, anyway." She drew a deep breath. "No, I won't do it. I wasn't sure before, but I am now. I won't do it."

Silence. Sounds of moving about, someone walking—Yori's short, light steps. Sound of a door being opened.

"Good night," Yori said.

No one wished her a good night.

"It's not that complicated," Neci said moments later. "Especially not with Amma. She has so few tentacles—eight or ten—and they're so small. Anyone could do it—with gloves for protection."

"I couldn't do it," Anne said. "I couldn't use a knife on anyone."

"I could," Gil said. "But... if only they weren't such little girls."

"Is there any liquor here?" Neci asked. "Even that foul cassava stuff the wanderers drink would do."

"We make the corn whiskey here, too," Gil said. "There's always plenty. Too much."

"So we give it to the girls and then do it."

"I don't know," Sabina said. "They're so young. And if they get sick..."

"Yori will care for them if they get sick. She'll care for

them, even if she doesn't like what we've done. And it will be done, as it should be."

"But—"

"It *must* be done! We must raise Human children, not aliens who don't even understand how we see things."

Silence.

"Tomorrow, Gil? Can it be done tomorrow?"

"I ... don't know. ...."

"We can collect the kids when they're out eating plants. No one will notice for a while that they're gone. Sabina, you'll get the liquor, won't you?"

"I—"

"Are there very sharp knives here? It should be done quickly and cleanly. And we'll need clean cloths for bandages, gloves for all of us, just in case, and that antiseptic Yori has. I'll get that. There probably won't be any infection, but we won't take chances." She stopped abruptly, then spoke one word harshly. "Tomorrow!"

Silence.

Akin got up, managed to struggle out of the hammock. Abira awoke, but only mumbled something and went back to sleep. Akin headed toward the next room where Amma and Shkaht shared a hammock. They met him coming out. All three linked instantly and spoke without sound.

"We have to go," Shkaht said sadly.

"You don't," Akin argued. "They're only a few, and not that strong. We have Tate and Gabe, Yori, Abira, Macy and Kolina. They would help us!"

"They would help us tomorrow. Neci would wait and recruit and try again later."

"Tate could talk to the salvagers the way she talked to the camp on the way up here. People believe her when she talks."

"Neci didn't."

"Yes she did. She just wants to have everything her way—even if her way is wrong. And she's not very smart. She's seen me taste metal and flesh and wood, but she thinks gloves will protect her hands from being tasted or stung when she cuts you."

"Plastic gloves?"

Surprised, Akin thought for a moment. "They might have

gloves made of some kind of plastic. I haven't seen plastic that soft, but it could exist. But once you understand the plastic it can't hurt you."

"Neci probably doesn't realize that. You said she wasn't smart. That makes her more dangerous. Maybe if other people stop her from cutting us tomorrow, she'll get angrier. She'll want to hurt us just to prove she can."

After a time, Akin agreed. "She would."

"We have to go."

"I want to go with you!"

Silence.

Frightened, Akin linked more deeply with them. "Don't leave me here alone!"

More silence. Very gently, they held him between them and put him to sleep. He understood what they were doing and resisted them angrily at first, but they were right. They had a chance without him. They were stronger, larger, and could travel faster and farther without rest. Communication between them was quicker and more precise. They could act almost as though they shared a single nervous system. Only paired siblings and adult mates came to know each other that well. Akin would hamper them, probably get them recaptured. He knew this, and they could feel his contradictory feelings. They knew he knew. Thus, there was no need to argue. He must simply accept the reality.

He accepted it finally and allowed them to send him into a deep sleep.

Tate frowned. "Were they going to give them the moonshine—the whiskey?"

"Yes. But it wouldn't make them drunk. I've seen drunk Humans. I don't think anything we could drink would make us like that. Our bodies would reject the drink."

"What would it have done to them?"

"Make them vomit or urinate a lot. It isn't strong or deadly. Probably they would just pass it through almost unchanged. They would urinate a lot."

"That stuff's damn strong."

"I mean . . . I mean it's not a deadly poison. Humans can drink it without dying. We can drink it without vomiting it up fast, without wrapping it in part of our flesh to keep it from injuring us on the way up."

"So it wouldn't hurt them—just in case Neci caught them."

"It wouldn't hurt them. They wouldn't like it, though. And Neci hasn't caught them."

"How lo you know?"

"I've heard her. She's been asking people where the girls are. No one's seen them. She's getting worried."

Tate stared at nothing, believing, absorbing. "We wouldn't have let her do it. All you had to do was tell me."

"You would have stopped her this time," he agreed. "She would have kept trying. People believe her after a while. They do what she wants them to."

She shook her head. "Not this time. Too many of us were against her on this. Little girls, for godsake! Akin, we could waste days searching for them, but you could track them faster with your Oankali hearing and sight."

"No."

"Yes. Oh, yes! How far do you think those girls will get before something happens to them? They're not much bigger than you are. They'll die out there!"

"I wouldn't. Why should they?"

Silence. She frowned down at him. "You mean you could get home from here?"

"I could if no Humans stopped me."

"And you think no Humans will stop the girls?"

"I think . . . I think they're afraid. I think they're frightened enough to sting."

= 18 =

He slept naked on the floor until Tate found him the next morning. She awoke him by lifting him and was startled when he grabbed her around the neck and would not let go. He did not cry or speak. He tasted her but did not study her. Later he realized he had actually tried to become her, to join with her as he might with his closest sibling. It was not possible. He was reaching for a union the Humans had denied him. It seemed to him that what he needed was just beyond his grasp, just beyond that final crossing he could not make, as with his mother. As with everyone. He could know so much and no more, feel so much and no more, join so close and no closer.

Desperately, he took what he could get. She could not comfort him or even know how deeply he perceived her. But she could, simply by permitting the attachment, divert his attention from himself, from his own misery.

Aside from her original jerk of surprise, Tate did not try to detach him. He did not know what she did. All his senses were focused on the worlds within the cells of her body. He did not know how long he was frozen to her, not thinking, not knowing or caring what she did as long as she did not disturb him.

When he finally drew away fom her, he found that she was sitting on a mat on the floor, leaning against a wall. She had

151

gone on holding him on her arm and resting her arm on her knees. Now as he straightened and reoriented himself, she took his chin between her fingers and turned his face toward hers

"Are you all right?" she asked.

"Yes."

"What was it?"

He said nothing for a moment, looked around the room.

"Everyone's at breakfast," she said. "I've had my regularly scheduled lecture about how I spoil you and a little extra to boot. Now, why don't you tell me exactly what happened."

She put him down beside her and stared down at him, waiting. Clearly she did not know the girls were gone. Perhaps no one had noticed yet, thanks to the morning grazing habits of all three children. He could not tell. Amma and Shkaht should have as much of a start as possible.

"It's too late for me to bond with my sibling," he said truthfully. "I was thinking about that last night. I was feeling... Lonely wouldn't really be the right word. This was more like... something died." Every word was true. His answer was simply incomplete. Amma and Shkaht had started his feelings—their union, their leaving...

"Where are the girls?" Tate asked.

"I don't know."

"Have they gone, Akin?"

He looked away. Why was she always so hard to hide things from? Why did he hesitate so to lie to her?

"Good god," she said, and started to get up.

"Wait!" Akin said. "They were going to cut them this morning. Neci and her friends were going to grab them while they were eating and hide them and cut off their sensory tentacles."

"The hell they were!"

"They were! We heard them last night! Yori wouldn't help them, but they were going to do it anyway. They were going to give them corn whiskey and—"

"Moonshine?"

"What?"

"They were going to make the girls drunk?"

"They couldn't."

"Oh, god."

"What if someone were going to cut your eyes out, and you had a gun?"

"I thought the new species was supposed to be above that kind of thing."

"They're afraid. They only want to go home. They don't want to be cut."

"No." She sighed. "Get dressed. Let's go to breakfast. The riot should be starting any time now."

"I don't think they'll find the girls."

"If what you say is true, I hope they don't. Akin?"

He waited, knowing what she would ask.

"Why didn't they take you with them?"

"I'm too small." He walked away from her, found his pants in the next room, and put them on. "I couldn't work with them the way they could work with each other. I would have gotten them caught."

"You wanted to go?"

Silence. If she did not know he had wanted to go, wanted desperately to go, she was stupid. And she was not stupid.

"I wonder why the hell your people don't come for you," she said. "They must know better than I do what they're putting you through."

"What *they're* putting me through?" he asked, amazed.

She sighed. "We, then. Whatever good that admission does you. Oankali drove us to become what we are. If they hadn't tampered with us, we'd have children of our own. We could live in our own ways, and they could live in theirs."

"Some of you would attack them," Akin said softly. "I think some Humans would have to attack them."

"Why?"

"Why did Humans attack one another?"

Suddenly there was shouting outside.

"Okay," Tate said. "They've realized the girls are gone. They'll be here in a moment."

Almost before she had finished speaking, Macy Wilton and Neci Roybal were at the door, looking around the room.

"Have you seen the girls?" Macy demanded.

Tate shook her head. "No, we haven't been out."

"Did you see them at all this morning?"

"No."

"Akin?"

"No." If Tate thought it was best to lie, then he would lie—although neither of them had begun lying yet.

"I heard you were sick, Akin," Neci said.

"I'm all right now."

"What made you sick?"

He stared at her with quiet dislike, wondering what it might be safe to say.

Tate spoke up with uncharacteristic softness. "He had a dream that upset him. A dream about his mother."

Neci raised an eyebrow skeptically. "I didn't know they dreamed."

Tate shook her head, smiled slightly. "Neci, why not? He's at least as Human as you are."

The woman drew back. "You should be out helping to search for the girls!" she said. "Who knows what's happened to them!"

"Maybe someone decided to follow your advice, grab them, and cut off their sensory tentacles."

"What!" demanded Macy. He had gone into the room where he and the girls and his wife had slept. Now he came out, staring at Tate.

"She has an obscene sense of humor," Neci said.

Tate made a wordless sound. "These days, I have no sense of humor at all where you're concerned." She looked at Macy. "She was still pushing to have the girls' tentacles amputated. She's been talking to the salvagers about it." Now she looked directly at Neci. "Deny it."

"Why should I? They would be better off without them—more Human!"

"Just as much better off as you would be without your eyes! Let's go look for them, Macy. I hope to god they never heard the things Neci's been saying."

Amazed, Akin followed her out. She had put the blame for the girls' flight exactly where it belonged without involving him at all. She left him with a salvager who had injured his knee and joined the search as though she had every expectation of finding the girls quickly.

village or town. They got sick of one pointless, endless existence and chose another."

"Pointless because resisters can't have children?"

"That's it. It means a lot more than I could ever explain to you. We don't get old. We don't have kids, and nothing we do means shit."

"What would it mean . . . if you had a kid like me?"

"We have got a kid like you. You."

"You know what I mean."

"Go to sleep, Akin."

"Why are you afraid of guns?"

"They make killing too easy. Too impersonal. You know what that means?"

"Yes. I'll ask if you say something I don't understand."

"So we'll kill more of each other than we already do. We'll learn to make better and better guns. Someday, we'll take on the Oankali, and that will be the end of us."

"It would. What do you want to happen instead?"

Silence.

"Do you know?"

"Not extinction," she whispered. "Not extinction in any form. As long as we're alive, we have some chance."

Akin frowned, trying to understand. "If you had kids in the old way, your prewar way, with Gabe, would that mean you and Gabe were becoming extinct?"

"It would mean we weren't. Our kids would be Human like us."

"I'm Human like you—and Oankali like Ahajas and Dichaan."

"You don't understand."

"I'm trying to."

"Are you?" She touched his face. "Why?"

"I need to. It's part of me, too. It concerns me, too."

"Not really."

Abruptly he was angry. He hated her soft condescension. "Then why am I here! Why are you here! You and Gabe would be down in Phoenix if it didn't concern me. I would be back in Lo. Oankali and Human have done what Human male and female used to do. And they made me and Amma and Shkaht, and they're no more extinct than you would be if you had kids with Gabe!"

She turned slightly—turned her back to him as much as she could in a hammock. "Go to sleep, Akin."

But he did not sleep. It was his turn to lie awake thinking. He understood more than she thought. He recalled his argument with Amma and Shkaht that Humans should be permitted their own Akjai division—their own hedge against disaster and true extinction. Why should it be so difficult? There were, according to Lilith, bodies of land surrounded by vast amounts of water. Humans could be isolated and their ability to reproduce in their own way restored to them. But then what would happen when the constructs scattered to the stars, leaving the Earth a stripped ruin. Tate's hopes were in vain.

Or were they?

Who among the Oankali was speaking for the interests of resister Humans? Who had seriously considered that it might not be enough to let Humans choose either union with the Oankali or sterile lives free of the Oankali? Trade-village Humans said it, but they were so flawed, so genetically contradictory that they were often not listened to.

He did not have their flaw. He had been assembled within the body of an ooloi. He was Oankali enough to be listened to by other Oankali and Human enough to know that resister Humans were being treated with cruelty and condescension.

Yet he had not even been able to make Amma and Shkaht understand. He did not know enough yet. These resisters had to help him learn more.

═ 20 ═

Akin was with the people of Phoenix for over a year. He spent most of this time in the hills, watching the salvaging and taking part when the salvagers would let him. One of the men set him to cleaning small, decorative items—jewelry, figurines, small bottles, jars, eating utensils. He knew he was given the job mainly to keep him from underfoot, but the work pleased him. He tasted everything before he cleaned it and afterward. Often he found Human leavings protected within containers. There were bits of hair, skin, nail. From some of these he salvaged lost Human genetic patterns that ooloi could recreate if they needed the Human genetic diversity. Only an ooloi could tell him what was useful. He memorized everything to give to Nikanj someday.

Once Sabina caught him tasting the inside of a small bottle. She tried to snatch the bottle away. Fortunately, he managed to dodge her hands and withdraw the thin, searching filaments of his tongue before she broke them. She should have gone back to Phoenix when her group left. She had done her share of what she called grubbing in the dirt, but she had stayed. Akin believed she had stayed because of him. He had not forgotten that she had been willing to take part in cutting off Amma's and Shkaht's tentacles. But she seemed brighter than Neci, more able, more willing to learn.

160

"What was this called?" he asked her once there was no chance of her injuring him.

"It was a perfume bottle. You keep it out of your mouth."

"Where were you going?" he asked.

"What?"

"If you have time, I'll tell you why I put things in my mouth."

"All kids put things in their mouths—and sometimes they poison themselves."

"I *must* put things in my mouth to understand them. And I must try to understand them. Not to try would be like having hands and eyes and yet always being tied and blindfolded. It would make me . . . not sane."

"Oh, but—"

"And I'm too old now to poison myself. I could drink the fluid that used to be in this bottle and nothing would happen. It would pass through me quickly, almost unchanged, because it isn't very dangerous. If it were very dangerous, my body would either change its structure and neutralize it or . . . contain it in a kind of sealed flesh bottle and expel it. Do you see?"

"I . . . understand what you're saying, but I'm not sure I believe you."

"It's important that you understand. Especially you."

"Why?"

"Because just now, you almost hurt me a lot. You could have injured me more than any poison could. And you could have made me sting you. If I did that, you would die. That's why."

She had drawn back from him. Her face had changed slightly. "You always look so normal . . . sometimes I forget."

"Don't forget. But don't hate me either. I've never stung anyone, and I don't ever want to."

Some of the wariness left her eyes.

"Help me learn," he said. "I want to know the Human part of myself better."

"What can I teach you?"

He smiled. "Tell me why Human kids put things in their mouths. I've never known."

═ 22 ═

Gabe took him away from his tasting and cleaning for a while—took him higher into the hills where the great mountains in the distance could be seen clearly. One of them smoked and steamed into the blue sky and was somehow very beautiful—a pathway deep into the Earth. A breathing place. A kind of joint where great segments of the Earth's crust came together. Akin could look at the huge volcano and understand a little better how the Earth worked— how it would work until it was broken and divided between departing Dinso groups.

Akin chose the edible plants he thought would taste best to Gabe and introduced the man to them. In return, Gabe told him about a place called New York and what it had been like to grow up there. Gabe talked more than he ever had—talked about acting, which Akin did not understand at all at first.

Gabe had been an actor. People gave him money and goods so that he would pretend to be someone else—so that he would take part in acting out a story someone had made up.

"Didn't your mother ever tell you any stories?" he asked Akin.

"Yes," Akin said. "But they were true."

"She never told you about the three bears?"

"What's a bear?"

164

Gabe looked first angry, then resigned. "I still forget sometimes," he said. "A bear is just one more large, extinct animal. Forget it."

That night in a small, half-ruined stone shelter before a campfire, Gabe became another person for Akin. He became an old man. Akin had never seen an old man. Most of the old Humans who had survived the war had been kept aboard the ship. The oldest were dead by now. The Oankali had not been able to extend their lives for more than a few years, but they kept them healthy and free of pain for as long as possible.

Gabe became an old man. His voice became heavier, thicker. His body seemed heavier, too, and painfully weary, bent, yet hard to bend. He was a man whose daughters had betrayed him. He was sane, and then not sane. He was terrifying. He was another person altogether. Akin wanted to get up and run out into the darkness.

Yet he sat still, spellbound. He could not understand much of what Gabe said, though it seemed to be English. Somehow, though, he felt what Gabe seemed to want him to feel. Surprise, anger, betrayal, utter bewilderment, despair, madness. . . .

The performance ended, and Gabe was Gabe again. He turned his face upward and laughed aloud. "Jesus," he said. "*Lear* for a three-year-old. Damn. It felt good, anyway. It's been so long. I didn't know I remembered all that stuff."

"Don't you do that for the people in Phoenix?" Akin asked timidly.

"No. I never have. Don't ask me why. I don't know. I farm now or I work metal. I dig up junk from the past and turn it into stuff people can use today. That's what I do."

"I liked the acting. It scared me at first, and I couldn't understand a lot of it, but . . . It's like what we do—constructs and Oankali. It's like when we touch each other and talk with feelings and pressures. Sometimes you have to remember a feeling you haven't had for a long time and bring it back so you can transmit it to someone else or use a feeling you have about one thing to help someone understand something else."

"You do that?"

"Yes. We can't do it very well with Humans. The ooloi can, but males and females can't."

"Yeah." He sighed and lay down on his back. They had cleared some of the plant growth and rubble from the stone floor of the shelter and could wrap themselves in their blankets and lie on it in comfort.

"What was this place?" Akin asked, looking up at the stars through the roofless building. Only the overhang of the hill provided any shelter at all if it happened to rain that night.

"Don't know," Gabe said. "It could have been some peasant's house. I suspect it goes back further, though. I think it's an old Indian dwelling. Maybe even Inca or some related people."

"Who were they?"

"Short brown people. Probably looked something like Tino's parents. Something like you, maybe. They were here for thousands of years before people who look like me or Tate got here."

"You and Tate don't look alike."

"No. But we're both descended from Europeans. Indians were descended from Asians. The Incas are the ones everyone thinks of for this part of the world, but there were a lot of different groups. To tell the truth, I don't think we're far enough into the mountains to be seeing Inca ruins. This is a damn old place, though." He pulled his mouth into a smile. "Old and Human."

They walked for many days, exploring, finding other ruined dwellings, describing a great circle back to the salvage camp. Akin never asked why Gabe took him on the long trip. Gabe never volunteered an explanation. He seemed pleased that Akin insisted on walking most of the time and usually managed to keep up. He willingly tried eating plants Akin recommended and liked some of them well enough to take them back as small plants, seeds, stalks, or tubers. Akin guided him in this, too.

"What can I take back that will grow?" Gabe would say. He could not know how much his pleased Akin. What he and Gabe were doing was what the Oankali always did—collect life, travel and collect and integrate new life into their ships, their already vast collection of living things, and themselves.

He studied each plant very carefully, telling Gabe exactly what he must do to keep the plant alive. Automatically, he kept within himself a memory of genetic patterns or a few dormant cells from each sample. From these, an ooloi could recreate copies of the living organism. Ooloi liked cells from or memories of several individuals within a species. For the Humans, Akin saw that Gabe took seed when there was seed. Seed could be carried in a leaf or a bit of cloth tied with a twist of grass. And it would grow. Akin would see to that. Even without an ooloi to help, he could taste a plant and read its needs. With its needs met, it would thrive.

"This is about the happiest I've ever seen you," Gabe remarked as they neared the salvage camp.

Akin grinned at him but said nothing. Gabe would not want to know that Akin was collecting information for Nikanj. It was enough for him to know that he had pleased Akin very much.

Gabe did not smile back, but only because he made an obvious effort not to.

When they reached camp a few days later, Gabe met Tate with none of the odd anxiety he often showed when she had been out of his sight for a while.

stroked his hair and finally held him away from her. "Three years old," she said. "So big. I kept worrying that you wouldn't remember me—but I knew you would. I knew you would."

He laughed at the impossible notion of his forgetting her and looked to see whether she was crying. She was not. She was examining him—his hands and arms, his legs...

A shout made them both look up. Tate and the other Human stood facing one another. The sound had been Tate shouting Tino's name.

Tino was smiling at her uncertainly. He did not speak until she took him by the arms and said, "Tino, don't you recognize me? Tino?"

Akin looked at Tino's expression, and he knew he did not recognize her. He was alive, but something was the matter with him.

"I'm sorry," Tino said. "I've had a head injury. I remember a lot of my past, but... some things are still coming back to me."

Tate looked at Lilith. Lilith looked back with no sign of friendliness. "They tried to kill him when they took Akin," she said. "They clubbed him down, fractured his skull so badly he nearly did die."

"Akin said he was dead."

"He had good reason to think so." She paused. "Was it worth his life for you to have my son?"

"She didn't do it," Akin said quickly. "She was my friend. The men who took me tried to sell me in a lot of places before... before Phoenix wanted to buy me."

"Most of the men who took him are dead," Tate said. "The survivor is paralyzed. There was a fight." She glanced at Tino. "Believe me, you and Tino are avenged."

The Oankali began communicating silently among themselves as they heard this. Akin could see his Oankali parents among them, and he wanted to go to them, but he also wanted to go to Tino, wanted to make the man remember him, wanted to make him sound like Tino again.

"Tate... ?" Tino said staring at her. "Is it... ? Are you... ?"

"It's me," she said quickly. "Tate Rinaldi. You did half of your growing up in my house. Tate and Gabe. Remember?"

"Kind of." He thought for a moment. "You helped me. I

was going to leave Phoenix and you said . . . you told me how to get to Lo."

Lilith looked surprised. "You did?" she asked Tate.

"I thought he would be safe in Lo."

"He should have been." Lilith drew a deep breath. "That was our first raid in years. We'd gotten careless."

Ahajas, Dichaan, and Nikanj detached themselves from the other Oankali and came over to the Human group. Akin could not wait any longer. He reached toward Dichaan, and Dichaan took him and held him for several minutes of relief and reacquaintance and joy. He did not know what the Humans said while he and Dichaan were locked together by as many of Dichaan's sensory tentacles as could reach him and by Akin's own tongue. Akin learned how Dichaan had found Tino and struggled to keep him alive and got home only to discover that Ahajas's child was soon to be born. The family could not search. But others had searched. At first.

"Was I left among them for so long so that I could study them?" Akin asked silently.

Dichaan rustled his free tentacles in discomfort. "There was a consensus," he said. "Everyone came to believe it was the right thing to do except us. We've never been alone that way before. Others were surprised that we didn't accept the general will, but they were wrong. They were wrong to even want to risk you!"

"My sibling?"

Silence. Sadness. "It remembers you as something there then not there. Nikanj kept you in its thoughts for a while, and the rest of us searched. As soon as we could leave it, we began searching. No one would help us until now."

"Why now?" Akin asked.

"The people believed you had learned enough. They knew they had deprived you of your sibling."

"It's . . . too late for bonding." He knew it was.

"Yes."

"There was a pair of construct siblings here."

"We know. They're all right."

"I saw what they had, how it was for them." He paused for a moment remembering, longing. "I'll never have that." Without out realizing it, he had begun to cry.

"Eka, you'll have something very like it when you mate. Until then, you have us." Dichaan did not have to be told how little this was. It would be long years before Akin was old enough to mate. And bonding with parents was not the same as bonding with a close sibling. Nothing he had touched was as sweet as that bonding.

Dichaan gave him to Nikanj, and Nikanj coaxed from him all the information he had discovered about plant and animal life, about the salvage pit. This could be given with great speed to an ooloi. It was the work of ooloi to absorb and assimilate information others had gathered. They compared familiar forms of life with what had been or should be. They detected changes and found new forms of life that could be understood, assembled, and used as they were needed. Males and females went to the ooloi with caches of biological information. The ooloi took the information and gave in exchange intense pleasure. The taking and the giving were one act.

Akin had experienced mild versions of this exchange with Nikanj all his life, but this experience taught him he had known nothing about what an ooloi could take and give until now. Locked to Nikanj, he forgot for a time the pain of being denied bonding with his sibling.

When he was able to think again, he understood why people treasured the ooloi. Males and females did not collect information only to please the ooloi or get pleasure from them. They collected it because the collecting felt necessary to them and pleased them.

But, still, they did know that at some point an ooloi must take the information and coordinate it so that the people could use it. At some point, an ooloi must give them the sensation that only an ooloi could give. Even Humans were vulnerable to this enticement. They could not deliberately gather the kind of specific biological information the ooloi wanted, but they could share with an ooloi all that they had recently eaten, breathed, or absorbed through their skins. They could share any changes in their bodies since their last contact with the ooloi. They did not understand what they gave the ooloi. But they knew what the ooloi gave them. Akin understood exactly what he was giving to Nikanj. And for the first time, he began to understand what an ooloi could give him. It did not take the place of ar ongoing closeness like Amma's and Shkaht's. Nothing could do that. But this was better than anything he had ever known. It was an easing of pain for now and a foreshadowing of healing for the distant, adult future.

Sometime later, Akin became aware again of the three Humans. They were sitting on the ground talking to one another. On the hill behind them, the hill that concealed them from the salvage camp, Gabe stood. Apparently, none of the Humans had seen him yet. All the Oankali must be aware of him. He was watching Tate, no doubt focusing on her yellow hair.

"Don't say anything," Nikanj told him silently. "Let them talk."

"He's her mate," Akin whispered aloud. "He's afraid she'll come with us and leave him."

"Yes."

"Let me go and get him."

"No, Eka."

"He's a friend. He took me all around the hills. It was because of him that I had so much information to give you."

"He's a resister. I won't give him the chance to use you as a hostage. You don't realize how valuable you are."

"He wouldn't do it."

"What if he simply picked you up and stepped over the hill and called his friends. There are guns in that camp, aren't there?"

Silence. Gabe might do such a thing if he thought he was losing both Akin and Tate. He might. Just as Tino's father had gathered his friends and killed so many even though he believed nothing he could do would bring Tino back or even properly avenge him.

"Come with us!" Lilith was saying. "You like kids? Have some of your own. Teach them everything you know about what Earth used to be."

"That's not what you used to say," Tate said softly.

Lilith nodded. "I used to think you resisters would find an answer. I hoped you would. But, Jesus, your only answer has been to steal kids from us. The same kids you're too good to have yourselves. What's the point?"

"Don't follow him. He isn't doing any harm."

"I'm his only same-sex parent. I should understand him better. I don't because his Human inheritance makes him do things that I don't expect."

"What would a twenty-year-old Oankali be doing?"

"Developing an affinity for one of the sexes. Beginning to know what it would become."

"He knows that. He doesn't know how he'll look, but he knows he'll become male."

"Yes."

"Well, a twenty-year-old Human male in a place like this would be exploring and hunting and chasing girls and showing off. He'd be trying to see to it that everyone knew he was a man and not a kid any more. That's what I was doing."

"Akin is still a kid, as you say."

"He doesn't look like one, in spite of his small size. And he probably doesn't feel like one. And whether he's fertile or not, he's damned interested in girls. And they don't seem to mind."

"Nikanj said he would go through a phase of quasi-Human sexuality."

Tino laughed. "This must be it, then."

"Later he'll want an ooloi."

"Yeah. I can understand that, too."

Dichaan hesitated. He had come to the question he most wanted to ask, and he knew Tino would not appreciate his asking. "Does he go to the resisters, Tino? Are they the reason for his wandering?"

Tino looked startled, then angry. "If you knew, why did you ask?"

"I didn't know. I guessed. He must stop!"

"No."

"They could kill him, Tino! They kill each other so easily!"

"They know him. They look after him. And he doesn't go far."

"You mean they know him as a construct man?"

"Yes. He's picked up some of their languages. But he hasn't hidden his identity from them. His size disarms them. Nobody that small could be dangerous, they think. On the other hand, that means he's had to fight a few times. Some guys think if he's small, he's weak, and if he's weak, he's fair game."

"Tino, he is too valuable for this. He's teaching us what a Human-born male can be. There are still so few like him because we're too unsure to form a consensus—"

"Then learn from him! Let him alone and learn!"

"Learn what? That he enjoys the company of resisters? That he enjoys fighting?"

"He doesn't enjoy fighting. He had to learn to do it in self-defense, that's all. And as for the resisters, he says he has to know them, has to understand them. He says they're part of him."

"What is there still for him to learn?"

Tino straightened his back and stared at Dichaan. "Does he know everything about the Oankali?"

"...no." Dichaan let his head and body tentacles hang limp. "I'm sorry. The resisters don't seem very complex—except biologically."

"Yet they resist. They would rather die than come here and live easy, pain-free lives with you."

Dichaan put his food aside and focused a cone of head tentacles on Tino. "Is your life pain-free?"

"Sometimes—biologically."

He did not like Dichaan to touch him. It had taken Dichaan a while to realize that this was not because Dichaan was Oankali, but because he was male. He touched hands with or threw an arm around other Human males, but Dichaan's maleness disturbed him. He had finally gone to Lilith for help in understanding this.

"You're one of his mates," she had told him solemnly. "Believe me, 'Chaan, he never expected to have a male mate. Nikanj was difficult enough for him to get used to."

Dichaan didn't see that Tino had found it difficult to get used to Nikanj. People got used to Nikanj very quickly. And in the long, unforgettable group matings, Tino had not seemed to have any difficulty with anyone. Though afterward, he did tend to avoid Dichaan. Yet Lilith did not avoid Ahajas.

Dichaan got up from his platform, left his salad, and went to Tino. The man started to draw back, but Dichaan took his arms.

"Let me try to understand you, Chkah. How many children have we had together? Be still."

Tino sat still and allowed Dichaan to touch him with a few long, slender head tentacles. They had had six children together. Three boys from Ahajas and three girls from Lilith. The old pattern.

"You chose to come here," Dichaan said. "And you've chosen to stay. I've been very glad to have you here—a Human father for the children and a Human male to balance group mating. A partner in every sense. Why does it hurt you to stay here?"

"How could it not hurt?" Tino asked softly. "And how could you not know? I'm a traitor to my people. Everything I do here is an act of betrayal. Someday, my people won't exist at all, and I will have helped their destroyers. I've betrayed my parents ... everyone." His voice had all but vanished even before he finished speaking. His stomach hurt him, and he was developing a pain in his head. He got very bad pains in his head sometimes. And he would not tell Nikanj. He would go away by himself and suffer. If someone found him, he might curse them. He would not struggle against help, though.

Dichaan moved closer to the platform on which Tino sat. He penetrated the flesh of the platform—of the Lo entity—and asked it to send Nikanj. It liked doing such things. Nikanj always pleasured it when it passed along such a message.

"Chkah, does Lilith feel the way you do?" he asked Tino.

"Do you really not know the answer to that?"

"I know she did at first. But she knows that resisters' genes are just as available to us as any other Human genes. She knows there are no resisters, living or dead, who are not already parents to construct children. The difference between them and her—and you—is that you have decided to act as parents."

"Does Lilith really believe that?"

"Yes. Don't you?"

Tino looked away, head throbbing. "I guess I believe it. But it doesn't matter. The resisters haven't betrayed themselves or their Humanity. They haven't helped you do what you're doing. They may not be able to stop you, but they haven't helped you."

"If all Humans were like them, our construct children would be much less Human, no matter how they looked. They would know only what we could teach them of Humans. Would that be better?"

"I tell myself it wouldn't," Tino said. "I tell myself there's some justification for what I'm doing. Most of the time, I think I'm lying. I wanted kids. I wanted . . . the way Nikanj makes me feel. And to get what I wanted, I've betrayed everything I once was."

Dichaan moved Tino's food off his platform and told him to lie down. Tino only looked at him. Dichaan rustled his body tentacles uncomfortably. "Nikanj says you prefer to endure your pain. It says you need to make yourself suffer so that you can feel that your people are avenged and you've paid your debt to them."

"That's shit!"

Nikanj came through a wall from the outside. It looked at the two of them and shot them a bad smell.

"He insists on hurting himself," Dichaan said. "I wonder if he hasn't convinced Akin to hurt himself, too."

"Akin does as he pleases!" Tino said. "He understands what I feel better than either of you could, but it's not what he feels. He has his own ideas."

"You aren't part of his body," Nikanj said, pushing him backward so that he would lie down. He did lie down this time. "But you're part of his thoughts. You've done more than Lilith would have to make him feel that the resisters have been wronged and betrayed."

"Resisters *have* been wronged and betrayed," Tino said. "I never told Akin that, though. I never had to. He saw it for himself."

"You're working on another ulcer," Nikanj said.

"So what?"

"You want to die. And yet you want to live. You love your children and your parents and that is a terrible conflict. You even love us—but you don't think you should." It climbed onto the platform and lay down alongside Tino. Dichaan touched the platform with his head tentacles, encouraging it to grow, to broaden and make room for him. He was not needed, but he wanted to know firsthand what happened to Tino.

"I remember Akin telling me about a Human who bled to death from ulcers," he said to Nikanj. "One of his captors."

"Yes. He gave the man's identity. I found the ooloi who had conditioned the man and learned that he had had ulcers since adolescence. The ooloi tried to keep him for his own sake, but the man wouldn't stay."

"What was his name?" Tino demanded.

"Joseph Tilden. I'm going to put you to sleep, Tino."

"I don't care," Tino muttered. After a time, he drifted off to sleep.

"What did you say to him?" Nikanj asked Dichaan.

"I asked him about Akin's disappearances."

"Ah. You should have asked Lilith."

"I thought Tino would know."

"He does. And it disturbs him very much. He thinks Akin is more loyal to Humanity than Tino himself. He doesn't understand why Akin is so focused on the resisters."

"I didn't realize how focused he was," Dichaan admitted. "I should have."

"The people deprived Akin of closeness with his sibling and handed him a compensating obsession. He knows this."

"What will he do?"

"Chkah, he's your child, too. What do you think he'll do?"

"Try to save them—what's left of them—from their empty, unnecessary deaths. But how?"

Nikanj did not answer.

"It's impossible. There's nothing he can do."

"Maybe not, but the problem will occupy him until his metamorphosis. Then I hope the other sexes will occupy him."

"But there must be more to it than that!"

Nikanj smoothed its body tentacles in amusement. "Anything to do with Humans always seems to involve contradictions." It paused. "Examine Tino. Inside him, so many very different things are working together to keep him alive. Inside his cells, mitochondria, a previously independent form of life, have found a haven and trade their ability to synthesize proteins and metabolize fats for room to live and reproduce. We're in his cells too now, and the cells have accepted us. One Oankali organism within each cell, dividing with each cell, extending life, and resisting disease. Even before we arrived, they had bacteria living in their intestines and protecting them from other bacteria that would hurt or kill them. They could not exist without symbiotic relationships with other creatures. Yet such relationships frighten them."

"Nika..." Dichaan deliberately tangled his head tentacles with those of Nikanj. "Nika, we aren't like mitochondria or helpful bacteria, and they know it."

Silence.

"You shouldn't lie to them. It would be better to say nothing."

"No, it wouldn't. When we keep quiet, they suppose it's because the truth is terrible. I think we're as much symbionts as their mitochondria were originally. They could not have evolved into what they are without mitochondria. Their earth might still be inhabited only by bacteria and algae. Not very interesting."

"Is Tino going to be all right?"

"No. But I'll take care of him."

"Can't you do something to stop him from hurting himself?"

"I could make him forget some of his past again."

"No!"

"You know I wouldn't. Even if I hadn't seen the pleasant, empty man he was before his memories came back after his injury, I wouldn't do it. I don't like to tamper with them that way. They lose too much of what I value in them."

"What will you do, then? You just go on repairing him until finally he leaves us and maybe kills himself?"

"He won't leave us."

It meant it would not let him go, *could* not. Ooloi could be that way when they found a Human they were strongly attracted to. Nikanj certainly could not let Lilith go, no matter how much it let her wander.

"Will Akin be all right?"

"I don't know."

Dichaan detached himself from Nikanj and sat up, folding his legs under him. "I'm going to separate him from the resisters."

"Why?"

"Sooner or later, one of them will kill him. We've collected their guns twice since they took him. They always make more, and the new ones are always more effective. Greater range, greater accuracy, greater safety for the Humans using them ... Humans are too dangerous. And they're only one part of him. Let him learn what else he is."

Nikanj drew its body tentacles in, upset, but it said nothing. If it had favorites among its children, Akin was one of them. It had no same-sex children, and that was a real deprivation. Akin was unique, and when he was at home, he spent much of his time with Nikanj. But Dichaan was still his same-sex parent.

"Not for long, Chkah," Dichaan said softly. "I won't keep him from you long. And he'll bring you all the changes he finds in Chkahichdahk."

"He always brings me things," Nikanj whispered. It seemed to relax, accepting Dichaan's decision. "He goes out of his way to find unusual things to taste and bring back. There's so little time until he metamorphoses and begins giving all his acquisitions to his mates."

"A year," Dichaan said. "I'll bring him back in only a year." He lay down again to comfort Nikanj and was not surprised to find that the ooloi needed comfort. It had been upset by the way Tino continually took his frustration and confusion out on his own body. Now it was even more upset. It was to lose a year of Akin's childhood. In its home with its large family all around, it felt alone and tired.

Dichaan linked himself into the nervous system of the ooloi. He could feel his own deep family bond stimulating Nikanj's. These bonds expanded and changed over the years, but they did not weaken. And they never failed to capture Nikanj's most intense interest.

Later Dichaan would tell Lo to signal the ship and have it send a shuttle. Later he would tell Akin it was time for him to learn more about the Oankali side of his heritage.

2

Sometimes it seemed to Akin that his world was made up of tight units of people who treated him kindly or coldly as they chose, but who could not let him in, no matter how much they might want to.

He could remember a time when blending into others seemed not only possible but inevitable—when Tiikuchahk was still unborn and he could reach out and taste it and know it as his closest sibling. Now, though, because he had not been able to bond with it, it was perhaps his least interesting sibling. He had spent as little time as possible with it.

Now it wanted to go to Chkahichdahk with him.

"Let it go and let me stay here," he had told Dichaan.

"It is alone, too," Dichaan had answered. "You and it both need to learn more about what you are."

"I know what I am."

"Yes. You are my same-sex child, near his metamorphosis."

Akin had not been able to answer this. It was time for him to listen to Dichaan, learn from him, prepare to be a mature male. He felt strongly inclined to obey.

Yet he had lost himself in the forest for days, resisting the inclination and deeply resenting it each time it returned to nag him.

No one came after him. And no one seemed surprised

185

when he came home. The shuttle had eaten a new clearing waiting for him.

He stood staring at it. It was a great green-shelled thing—a male itself to the degree that the ship-entities could be of one sex or the other. Each one had the capacity to become female. But as long as it received a controlling substance from the body of Chkahichdahk, it would remain small and male. It would extend the reach of Chkahichdahk by investigating planets and moons of solar systems, bringing back information, supplies of minerals, life. It would carry passengers and work wifh them in exploration. And it would ferry people to the ship and back.

Akin had never been inside one. He would not be allowed to link into one's nervous system until he was an adult. So much had to wait until he was an adult.

When he was an adult, he could speak for the resisters. Now, his voice could be ignored, would not even be heard without the amplification provided by one of the adult members of his family. He remembered Nikanj's stories of its own childhood—of being right, knowing it was right, and yet being ignored because it was not adult. Lilith had occasionally been hurt during those years because people did not listen to Nikanj, who knew her better than they did.

Akin would not make Nikanj's mistake. He had decided that long ago. But now... Why had Dichaan decided to send him to Chkahichdahk? Was it only to keep him out of danger or was there some other reason?

He moved closer to the shuttle, waiting to go inside but wanting first to walk around the thing, look at it, appreciate it with the senses he and the Humans shared.

It looked from every angle like a perfectly symmetrical high hill. Once it was airborne, it would be spherical. Its shell plates would slide around and lock—three layers of them—and nothing would get in or out.

"Akin."

He looked around without moving his body and saw Ahajas coming from the direction of Lo. Everyone else made some noise when they walked, but Ahajas, larger, taller than almost everyone else, seemed to flow along, sixteen-toed feet hardly seeming to touch the ground. If she did not want to be heard, no one heard her. Females had to be able to hide if possible and to fight if hiding was impossible or useless. Nikanj had said that.

He would not see Nikanj for a year. Perhaps longer.

She came towering over him, then folded herself into a sitting position opposite him the way some Humans used to stoop or kneel to talk to him when he was younger. Now his head and hers were at the same level.

"I wanted to see you before you left. You might not still be a child when you come back."

"I will be." He put his hand in among her head tentacles and felt them grasp and penetrate. "I'm still years away from changing."

"Your body can change faster than you think. The stress of having to adjust to a new environment could make things go more quickly. You should see everyone now."

"I don't want to."

"I know. You don't want to leave so you don't want to say goodbye. You didn't even go to your resister friends."

She didn't smell them on him. He had been particularly embarrassed to realize that she and others knew by scent when he had been with a woman. He washed, of course, but still they knew.

"You should have gone to them. You might change a great deal during your metamorphosis. Humans don't accept that easily."

"Lilith?"

"You know better. In spite of the things she says, I've never seen her reject one of her children. But would you want to leave without seeing her?"

Silence.

"Come on, Eka." She released his hand and stood up.

He followed her back to the village, feeling resentful and manipulated.

= 3 =

An outdoor feast was arranged for him. The people stopped their activities and came together in the center of the village for him and for Tiikuchahk. Tiikuchahk seemed to enjoy the party, but Akin simply endured it. Margit, who was known to be on the verge of her metamorphosis, came to sit beside him. She was still his favorite sibling, although she spent more time with her own paired sibling. She held out a gray hand to him, and he almost took it between his own before he noticed what she was showing him. She had always had too many fingers for a Human-born child—seven on each hand. But the hand she held out to him now had only five long, slender, gray fingers.

He stared at her, then carefully took the offered hand and examined it. There was no wound, no scars.

"How...?" he asked.

"I woke up this morning, and they were gone. Nothing left but the nail and some shriveled, dead skin."

"Did your hand hurt?"

"It felt fine. It still does. I'm sleepy, but that's all so far." She hesitated. "You're the first person I've told."

He hugged her and was barely able to stop himself from crying. "I won't even know you when I come back. You'll be someone else, probably mated and pregnant."

"I may be mated and pregnant, but you'll know me. I'll see to that!"

He only looked at her. Everyone changed, but, irrationally, he did not want her to change.

"What is it?" Tiikuchahk asked.

Akin did not understand why he did it, but after looking to see that it was all right with Margit, he took her hand and showed it to Tiikuchahk.

Tiikuchahk, who looked a great deal more Human than Margit did in spite of being Oankali-born, began to cry. It kissed her hand and let it go sadly. "Things are going to change too much while we're gone," it said, silent tears sliding down its gray face. "We'll be strangers when we come back." Its few small sensory tentacles tightened into lumps against its body, making it look the way Akin felt.

Now others wanted to know what was wrong, and Lilith came to them, looking as though she already knew.

"Margit?" she said softly.

Margit held up her hands and smiled. "I thought so," Lilith said. "Now this is your party, too. Come on." She led Margit away to show others.

Akin and Tiikuchahk got up together without speaking. They did sometimes act in unison in the way of paired siblings, but the phenomenon always startled them and somehow never gave the comfort it seemed to give to sibling pairs who had bonded properly in infancy. Now, though, they moved together toward Ayre, their oldest sister. She was a construct adult—the oldest construct adult in Lo—and she had been watching them, training several head tentacles on them as she sat talking to one of Leah's Oankali-born sons. She had been born in Chkahichdahk. She had passed her metamorphosis on Earth, mated, and borne several children. The things that they still faced, she had already survived.

"Sit with me," Ayre said as they came up to her. "Sit here." She positioned them on either side of her. She immediately tangled her long head tentacles with Tiikuchahk's. Akin had come to find having only one true sensory tentacle, and that one in his mouth, very inconvenient. Resisters liked it because they did not have to look at it, but it inhibited communication with Oankali and constructs. He had quickly grown too large to be held in someone's arms.

But Ayre, being Ayre, simply took him under one arm and pulled him against her so that it was easy for him to link with her as she used her body tentacles to link with him.

"We don't know what will happen to us," both he and Tiikuchahk said in silent unison. It was a cry of fear from both of them and, for Akin, also a cry of frustration. Time was being stolen from him. He knew the people and languages of a Chinese resister village, an Igbo village, three Spanish-speaking villages made up of people from many countries, a Hindu village, and two villages of Swahili-speaking people from different countries. So many resisters. Yet there were so many more. He had been driven out of, of all things, a village of English-speaking people because he was browner than the villagers were. He did not understand this, and he had not dared to ask anyone in Lo. But still, there were resisters he had never seen, resisters whose ideas he had not heard, resisters who believed their only hope was to steal construct children or to die as a species. There were stories now of a village whose people had gathered in their village square and drunk poison. No one Akin had talked to knew the name of this village, but everyone had heard about it.

Would there be any Humans left to save when he was finally old enough to have his opinions respected?

And would he still look Human enough to persuade them?

Or was all that foolishness? Would he truly be able to help them at all, no matter what happened? The Oankali would not stop him from doing anything they did not consider harmful. But if there were no consensus, they would not help him. And he could not help the Humans alone.

He did not intend to give them a ship entity. As long as they remained Human enough to satisfy their beliefs, they could not communicate with a ship. Some of them insisted on believing the ships were not alive—that they were metal things that anyone could learn to control. They had not understood at all when Akin tried to explain that ships controlled themselves. You either joined with them, shared their experiences, and let them share yours, or there was no trade. And without trade, the ships ignored your existence.

"You know you must help each other," Ayre said.

Akin and Tiikuchahk drew back reflexively.

"You can't be what you should have been, but you can help each other." Akin could not miss the certainty Ayre felt. "You're both alone. You'll both be strangers. And you're like one pea cut in half. Let yourselves depend on each other a little."

Neither Akin nor Tiikuchahk responded.

"Is a pea cut in half one wounded thing or two?" she asked softly.

"We can't heal each other," Tiikuchahk said.

"Metamorphosis will heal you, and it may be closer than you think."

And they were afraid again. Afraid of changing, afraid of returning to a changed, unrecognizable home. Afraid of going to a place even less their own than the one they were leaving. Ayre sought to divert them. "Ti, why do you want to go to Chkahichdahk?" she asked.

Tiikuchahk did not want to answer the question. Both Akin and Ayre received only a strong negative feeling from it.

"There are no resisters there," Ayre said. "That's it, isn't it?"

Tiikuchahk said nothing.

"Has Ahajas said you would be female?" Ayre asked.

"Not yet."

"Do you want to be?"

"I don't know."

"You think you might want to be male?"

"Maybe."

"If you want to be male, you should stay here. Let Akin go. Spend your time with Dichaan and Tino and with your sisters. Male parents, female siblings. Your body will know how to respond."

"I want to see Chkahichdahk."

"You could wait. See it after you change."

"I want to go with Akin." There was the strong negative again. It had said what it had not wanted to say.

"Then you will probably be female."

Sadness. "I know."

"Ti, maybe you want to go with Akin because you're still trying to heal the old wound. As I said, there are no resisters

left the village on one of her solitary treks, he had followed her, found her sitting on a log waiting for him when he finally caught her. They traveled together for several days, and she told him her story—why her name was an epithet among English-speaking resisters, how they blamed her for what the Oankali had done to them because she was the person the Oankali had chosen to work through. She had had to awaken groups of Humans from suspended animation and help them understand their new situation. Only she could speak Oankali then. Only she could open and close walls and use her Oankali-enhanced strength to protect herself and others. That was enough to make her a collaborator, a traitor in the minds of her own people. It had been safe to blame her, she said. The Oankali were powerful and dangerous, and she was not.

Now she faced him. "You couldn't possibly reach all the resisters," she said. "If you want to help them, you already have the information you need from them. Now you need to learn more about the Oankali. Do you see?"

He nodded slowly, his skin itching where there were sensory spots but no tentacles to coil tight and express the tension he felt.

"If there is anything you can do, now is the time to find out what it is and how to do it. Learn all you can."

"I will." He compared her long, brown hand to his own and wondered how there could be so little visible difference. Perhaps the first sign of his metamorphosis would be new fingers growing or old ones losing their flat Human nails. "I hadn't really thought of the trip being useful."

"Make it useful!"

"Yes." He hesitated. "Do you really believe I can help?"

"Do you?"

"I have ideas."

"Save them. You've been right to keep quiet about them so far."

It was good to hear her confirming what he had believed. "Will you come to the ship with me?"

"Of course."

"Now."

She looked out at the party, at the village. People had clustered at the guest house where someone was telling a story, and another group had gotten out flutes, drums, guitars, and a small harp. Their music would soon either drive the storytellers into one of the houses or, more likely, bring them into the singing and dancing.

Oankali did not like music. They began to withdraw into the houses—to save their hearing, they said. Most constructs enjoyed music as much as Humans did. Several Oankali-born construct males had become wandering musicians, more than welcome at any trade village.

"I'm not in a mood for singing or dancing or stories," he said. "Walk with me. I'll sleep at the ship tonight. I've said my goodbyes."

She stood up, towering over him in a way that made him feel oddly secure. No one spoke to them or joined them as they left the village.

Chkahichdahk. Dichaan went up with Akin and Tiikuchahk. The shuttle could simply have been sent home. It had eaten its fill and been introduced to several people who had reached adulthood recently. It was content and needed no guiding. But Dichaan went with them anyway. Akin was glad of this. He needed his same-sex parent more than he would have admitted.

Tiikuchahk seemed to need Dichaan, too. It stayed close to him in the soft light of the shuttle. The shuttle had made them a plain gray sphere within itself and left them to decide whether they wanted to raise platforms or bulkheads. The air would be kept fresh, the shuttle efficiently supplying them with the oxygen it produced and taking away the carbon dioxide they exhaled for its own use. It could also use any waste they produced, and it could feed them anything they could describe, just as Lo could. Even a child with only one functional sensory tentacle could describe foods he had eaten and ask for duplicate foods. The shuttle would synthesize them as Lo would have.

But only Dichaan could truly link with the shuttle and, through its senses, share its experience of flying through space. He could not share what he experienced until he had detached himself from the shuttle. Then he held Akin immobile as though holding an infant and showed him open space.

Akin seemed to drift, utterly naked, spinning on his own axis, leaving the wet, rocky, sweet-tasting little planet that he had always enjoyed and going back to the life source that was wife, mother, sister, haven. He had news for her of one of their children—of Lo.

But he was in empty space—surrounded by blackness, feeding from the impossibly bright light of the sun, falling away from the great blue curve of the Earth, aware over all the body of the great number of distant stars. They were gentle touches, and the sun was a great, confining hand, gentle but inescapable. No shuttle could travel this close to a star, then escape its gravitational embrace. Only Chkahichdahk could do that, powered by its own internal sun—its digestion utterly efficient, wasting nothing.

Everything was sharp, starkly clear, intense beyond enduring. Everything pounded the senses. Impressions came as blows. He was attacked, beaten, tormented...

And it ended.

Akin could not have ended it. He lay now, weak with shock, no longer annoyed at Dichaan's holding him, needing the support.

"That was only a second," Dichaan was saying. "Less than a second. And I cushioned it for you."

Gradually, Akin became able to move and think again. "Why is it like that?" he demanded.

"Why does the shuttle feel what it feels? Why do we experience its feelings so intensely? Eka, why do *you* feel what you feel? How would a coati or an agouti receive your feelings?"

"But—"

"It feels as it feels. Its feelings would hurt you, perhaps injure or kill you if you took them directly. Your reactions would confuse it and throw it off course."

"And when I'm an adult, I'll be able to perceive through it as you do?"

"Oh, yes. We never trade away our abilities to work with the ships. They're more than partners to us."

"But... what do we do for them, really? They allow us to travel through space, but they could travel without us."

He could not imagine such a life. It was not Human or
Oankali. How would he be able to help the resisters if he were
so solitary?

Nikanj knew a great deal, but it did not know everything.
Its children were always healthy and intelligent. But they did
not always do what it wanted or expected them to. It had
better luck sometimes predicting what Humans would do
under a given set of circumstances. Surely it did not know as
much as it thought it did about what Akin would do as an adult.

"This is a bad way to bring Humans in," Dichaan was
saying as they walked. "Most of them are disturbed at being so
closed in. If you ever have to bring any in, have the shuttle
take you as close as possible to one of the true corridors
and get them into that corridor as quickly as possible. They
don't like the flesh movement either. Try to keep them from
seeing it."

"They see it at home," Tiikuchahk said.

"Not this massive kind of movement. Lilith says it makes
her think of being swallowed alive by some huge animal. At
least she can stand it. Some Humans go completely out of
control and hurt themselves—or try to hurt us." He paused.
"Here's a true corridor. Now we ride."

Dichaan led them to a tilio feeding station and chose one
of the large, flat animals. The three of them climbed onto it,
and Dichaan touched several head tentacles to it. The animal
was curious and sent up pseudotentacles to investigate them.

"This one's never carried an Earth-born construct before,"
Dichaan said. "Taste it. Let it taste you. It's harmless."

It reminded Akin of an agouti or an otter, although it was
brighter than either of those animals. It carried them through
other riders and through pedestrians—Oankali, construct, and
Human. Dichaan had told it where he wanted to go, and it
found its way without trouble. And it enjoyed meeting strange-
tasting visitors.

"Will we have these animals on Earth eventually?" Tiikuchahk
asked.

"We'll have them when we need them," Dichaan said. "All
our ooloi know how to assemble them."

Assemble was the right word, Akin thought. The tilio had
been fashioned from the combined genes of several animals.

Humans put animals in cages or tied them to keep them from straying. Oankali simply bred animals who did not want to stray and who enjoyed doing what they were intended to do. They were also pleased to be rewarded with new sensations or pleasurable familiar sensations. This one seemed particularly interested in Akin, and he spent the journey telling it about Earth and about himself—giving it simple sensory impressions. Its delight with these gave him as much pleasure as he gave the tilio. When they reached the end of their journey, Akin hated to leave the animal. Dichaan and Tiikuchahk waited patiently while he detached himself from it and gave it a final touch of farewell.

"I liked it," he said unnecessarily as he followed Dichaan through a wall and up a slope toward another level.

Without turning, Dichaan focused a cone of head tentacles on him. "It paid a great deal of attention to you. More than to either of us. Earth animals pay attention to you, too, don't they?"

"They let me touch them sometimes, even let me taste them. But if someone else is with me, they run away."

"You can train here to look after animals—to understand their bodies and keep them healthy."

"Ooloi work?"

"You can be trained to do it. Everything except controlling their breeding. And ooloi must mix their young."

Of course. You controlled both animals and people by controlling their reproduction—controlling it absolutely. But perhaps Akin could learn something that would be of use to the resisters. And he liked animals.

"Would I be able to work with shuttles or with Chkahich-dahk?" he asked.

"If you choose to, after you change. There will be a need for people to do that kind of work during your generation."

"You told me once that people who work with the ship had to look different—really different."

"That change won't be needed on Earth for several generations."

"Working with animals won't affect the way I look at all?"

"Not at all."

"I want to do it then." After a few steps, he looked back at Tiikuchahk. "What will you do?"

"Find us an ooloi subadult," it said.

He would have walked faster if he had known the way. He wanted to get away from Tiikuchahk. The thought of it finding an ooloi—even an immature one—to unite the two of them, even briefly, was disturbing, almost disgusting.

"I meant what work will you do?"

"Gather knowledge. Collect information on Toaht and Akjai changes that have taken place since Dinso settled on Earth. I don't think I would be allowed to do much more. You know what your sex will be. It's as though you were never really eka. But I am."

"You won't be prevented from learning work," Dichaan said. "You won't be taken seriously, but no one will stop you from doing what you choose. And if you want help, people will help you."

"I'll gather knowledge," Tiikuchahk insisted. "Maybe while I'm doing that, I'll see some work that I want to do."

"This is Lo aj Toaht," Dichaan said, leading them into one of the vast living areas. Here grew great treelike structures bigger than any tree Akin had ever seen on Earth. Lilith had said they were as big as high-rise office buildings, but that had meant nothing to Akin. They were living quarters, storage space, internal support structures, and providers of food, clothing, and other desired substances such as paper, waterproof covering, and construction materials. They were not trees but parts of the ship. Their flesh was the same as the rest of the ship's flesh.

When Dichaan touched his head tentacles to what appeared to be the bark of one of them, it opened as walls opened at home, and inside was a familiar room, empty of resister-style furniture but containing several platforms grown for sitting or for holding containers of food. The walls and platforms were all a pale yellow-brown.

As the three of them entered, the wall on the opposite side of the room opened, and three Oankali Akin had never seen before came in.

Akin drew air over his tongue and his sense of smell told him that the male and female newcomers were Lo—close relatives, in fact. The ooloi must be their mate. There was no scent of family familiarity to it at all as there would have been if it had been ooan Dichaan. These were not parents, then. But they were relatives. Dichaan's brother and sister and their ooloi mate, perhaps.

The adults came together silently, head and body tentacles tangling together, locking together in intense feeling. After a time, probably after feelings and communications had slowed, cooled to something a child could tolerate, they drew Tiikuchahk in, handling and examining it with great curiosity. It examined them as well and made their acquaintance. Akin envied it its head tentacles. When the adults released it and took him into their midst, he could taste only one of them at a time, and there was no time to savor them all as he wished. Children and resisters were easier to cope with.

Yet these people welcomed him. They could see themselves in him and see his alien Humanity. The latter fascinated them, and they chose to take the time to perceive themselves through his senses.

The ooloi was particularly fascinated by him. Taishokaht its name was—Jahtaishokahtlo lel Surohahwahj aj Toaht. He had never touched a Jah ooloi before. It was shorter and stockier than ooloi from the Kaal or Lo. In fact, it was built rather like Akin himself, although it was taller than Akin. Everyone was taller than Akin. There was a feeling of intensity and confidence to the ooloi and a feeling almost of humor—as though he amused it very much, but it liked him.

"You don't know what an intricate mix you are," it told him silently. "If you're the prototype for Human-born males, there are going to be a great many of us who settle for daughters only from our Human mates. And that would be a loss."

"There are several others now," Dichaan told it aloud. "Study him. Maybe you'll mix the first for Lo Toaht."

"I don't know whether I'd want to."

Akin, still in contact with it, broke the contact and drew back to look at it. It wanted to. It wanted to badly. "Study me all you want," he said. "But share what you learn with me as much as you can."

"Trade, Eka," it said with amusement. "I'll be interested to see how much you can perceive."

Akin was not sure he liked the ooloi. It had a soft, paper-dry voice and an attitude that irritated Akin. The ooloi did not care that Akin was clearly going to be male and was close to metamorphosis. To it, he was eka: sexless child. Child trying to make adult bargains. Amusing. But that was what Dichaan had promised Tiikuchahk. They would be helped and taught with a certain lack of seriousness. In a sense, they would be humored. Children who lived in the safety of the ship did not have to grow up as quickly as those on Earth. Except for young ooloi who underwent two metamorphoses with their subadult years between, everyone was allowed a long, easy childhood. Even the ooloi were not seriously challenged until they proved they were to be ooloi—until they reached the subadult stage. No one abducted them in infancy or carried them around by their arms and legs. No one threatened them. They did not have to keep themselves alive among well-meaning but ignorant resisters.

Akin looked at Dichaan. "How can it be good for me to be treated as though I were younger than I am?" he asked. "What lesson is condescension supposed to teach me about this group of my people?"

He would not have spoken so bluntly if Lilith had been with him. She insisted on more respect for adults. Dichaan, though, simply answered his questions as he had expected. "Teach them who you are. Now they only know what you are. Both of you." He focused for a moment on Tiikuchahk. "You're here to teach as well as to learn." Which was just about what Taishokaht had said, but Taishokaht had said it as though to a much younger child.

At that moment, for no reason he could understand, Tiikuchahk touched him, and they fell into their grating, dissonant near-synchronization.

"This is what we are, too," he said to Taishokaht—only to hear the same words coming from Tiikuchahk. "This is what we need help with!"

The three Oankali tasted them, then drew back. The female, Suroh, drew her body tentacles tight against her and seemed to speak for all of them.

"We heard about that trouble. It's worse than I thought."

"It was wrong to separate them," Dichaan said softly.

Silence. What was there to say? The thing had been done by consensus years before. Adults of Earth and Chkahichdahk had made the decision.

"I know a Tiej family with an ooloi child," Suroh said. There could be no boy children, no girl children among the Oankali, but a subadult ooloi was often referred to as an ooloi child. Akin had heard the words all his life. Now adults would find an ooloi child for him and for Tiikuchahk. The thought made him shudder.

"My closest siblings have an ooloi child," Taishokaht said. "It's young, though. Just through its first metamorphosis."

"Too young," Dichaan said. "We need one who understands itself. Shall I stay and help choose?"

"We'll choose," the male said, smoothing his body tentacles flat against his skin. "There's more than one problem to be solved here. You've brought us something very interesting."

"I've brought you my children," Dichaan said quietly.

At once the three of them touched him, reassured him directly, drawing Akin and Tiikuchahk in to let them know that they had a home here, that they would be cared for.

Akin wanted desperately to go back to his true home. When food was served, he did not eat. Food did not interest him. When Dichaan left, it was all Akin could do to keep himself from following and demanding to be taken home to Earth. Dichaan would not have taken him. And no one present would have understood why he was making the gesture. Nikanj would understand, but Nikanj was back on Earth. Akin looked at the Toaht ooloi and saw that it was paying no attention to him.

Alone, and more lonely than he had been since the raiders abducted him, he lay down on his platform and went to sleep.

6

"Are you afraid?" Taishokaht asked. "Humans are always afraid of them."

"I'm not afraid," Akin said. They were in a large, dark, open area. The walls glowed softly with the body heat of Chkahichdahk. There was only body heat to see by here, deep inside the ship. Living quarters and travel corridors were above—or Akin thought of their direction as above. He had passed through areas where gravity was less, even where it was absent. Words like *up* and *down* were meaningless, but Akin could not keep himself from thinking them.

He could see Taishokaht by its body heat—less than his own and greater than that of Chkahichdahk. And he could see the other person in the room.

"I'm not afraid," he repeated. "Can this one hear?"

"No. Let it touch you. Then taste the limb it offers."

Akin stepped toward what his sense of smell told him was an ooloi. His sight told him it was large and caterpillarlike, covered with smooth plates that made a pattern of bright and dark as body heat escaped between the plates rather than through them. From what Akin had heard, this ooloi could seal itself within its shell and lose little or no air or body heat. It could slow its body processes and induce suspended animation

208

so that it could survive even drifting in space. Others like it had been the first to explore the war-ruined Earth.

It had mouth parts vaguely like those of some terrestrial insects. Even if it had possessed ears and vocal cords, it could not have formed anything close to Human or Oankali speech.

Yet it was as Oankali as Dichaan or Nikanj. It was as Oankali as any intelligent being constructed by an ooloi to incorporate the Oankali organelle within its cells. As Oankali as Akin himself.

It was what the Oankali had been, one trade before they found Earth, one trade before they used their long memories and their vast store of genetic material to construct speaking, hearing, bipedal children. Children they hoped would seem more acceptable to Human tastes. The spoken language, an ancient revival, had been built in genetically. The first Human captives awakened had been used to stimulate the first bipedal children to talk—to "remember" how to talk.

Now, most of the caterpillarlike Oankali were Akjai like the ooloi that stood before Akin. It or its children would leave the vicinity of Earth physically unchanged, carrying nothing of Earth or Humanity with it except knowledge and memory.

The Akjai extended one slender forelimb. Akin took the limb between his hands as though it were a sensory arm—and it seemed to be just that, although Akin learned in the first instant of contact that this ooloi had six sensory limbs instead of only two.

Its language of touch was the one Akin had first felt before his birth. The familiarity of this comforted him, and he tasted the Akjai, eager to understand the mixture of alienness and familiarity.

There was a long period of getting to know the ooloi and understanding that it was as interested in him as he was in it. At some point—Akin was not certain when—Taishokaht joined them. Akin had to use sight to find out for certain whether Taishokaht had touched him or touched the Akjai. There was an utter blending of the two ooloi—greater than any blending Akin had perceived between paired siblings. This, he thought, must be what adults achieved when they reached for a consensus on some controversial subject. But if it was, how did they continue to think at all as individuals? Taishokaht and Kohj, the

"Keeping you separated was a mistake," the Akjai agreed. "I can see now why it was done, but it was a mistake."

Only Akin's family had ever said that before. They had said it because he was one of them, and it hurt them to see him hurt. It hurt them to see the family unbalanced by paired siblings who had failed to pair. People who had never had close siblings or whose closest siblings had died did not damage the balance as much as close siblings who had failed to bond.

"You should go back to your relatives," the Akjai said. "Make them find a young ooloi for you and your sibling. You should not go through metamorphosis with so much pain cutting you off from your sibling."

"Ti was talking about finding a young ooloi before I left to study with you. I don't think I could stand to share an ooloi with it."

"You will," the Akjai said. "You must. Go back now, Eka. I can feel what you're feeling, but it doesn't matter. Some things hurt. Go back and reconcile with your sibling. Then come to me and I'll find new teachers for you—people who know the processes of changing a cold, dry, lifeless world into something Humans might survive on."

The Akjai straightened its body and broke contact with him. When Akin stood still, looking at it, not wanting to leave it, it turned and left him, opening the floor beneath itself and surging into the hole it had made. Akin let the hole seal itself, knowing that once it was sealed he would not find the Akjai again until it wished to be found.

= 8 =

The ooloi subadult was a relative of Taishokaht. Jahdehkiaht, its personal name was at this stage of its life. Dehkiaht. It had been living with Taishokaht's family and Tiikuchahk, waiting for him to return from the Akjai.

The young ooloi looked sexless but did not smell sexless. It would not develop sensory arms until its second metamorphosis. That made its scent all the more startling and disturbing.

Akin had never been aroused by the scent of an ooloi before. He liked them, but only resister and construct women had interested him sexually. What could an immature ooloi do for anyone sexually, anyway?

Akin took a step back the moment he caught the ooloi scent. He looked at Tiikuchahk who was with the ooloi, who had introduced it eagerly.

There was no one else in the room. Akin and Dehkiaht stared at each other.

"You aren't what I thought," it whispered. "Ti told me, showed me . . . and I still didn't understand."

"What didn't you understand?" Akin asked, taking another step backward. He did not want to feel so drawn to anyone who was clearly already on good terms with Tiikuchahk.

217

"That you are a kind of subadult yourself," Dehkiaht said. "Your growth stage now is more like mine than like Ti's."

That was something no one had said before. It almost distracted him from the ooloi's scent. "I'm not fertile yet, Nikanj says."

"Neither am I. But it's so obvious with ooloi that no one could make a mistake."

To Akin's amazement, he laughed. Just as abruptly, he sobered. "I don't know how this works."

Silence.

"I didn't want it to work before. I do now." He did not look at Tiikuchahk. He could not avoid looking at the ooloi, although he feared it would see that his motives for wanting success had little to do with it or Tiikuchahk. He had never felt as naked as he did before this immature ooloi. He did not know what to do or say.

It occurred to him that he was reacting exactly as he had the first time he realized a resister woman was trying to seduce him.

He took a deep breath, smiled, and shook his head. He sat down on a platform. "I'm reacting very Humanly to an un-Human thing," he said. "To your scent. If you can do anything to suppress it, I wish you would. It's confusing the hell out of me."

The ooloi smoothed its body tentacles and folded itself onto a platform. "I didn't know constructs talked about hell."

"We say what we've grown up hearing. Ti, what does its scent do to you?"

"I like it," Tiikuchahk said. "It makes me not mind that you're in the room."

Akin tried to consider this through the distracting scent. "It makes me hardly notice that you're in the room."

"See?"

"But . . . It . . . I don't want to feel like this all the time if I can't do anything about it."

"You're the only one here who *could* do anything about it," Dehkiaht said.

Akin longed to be back with his Akjai teacher, an adult ooloi who had never made him feel this way. No adult ooloi had made him feel this way.

Dehkiaht touched him.

He had not noticed the ooloi coming closer. Now he jumped. He felt himself more eager than ever for a satisfaction the ooloi could not give. Knowing this, he almost pushed Dehkiaht away in frustration. But Dehkiaht was ooloi. It did have that incredible scent. He could not push it or hit it. Instead, he twisted away from it. It had touched him only with its hand, but even that was too much. He had moved across the room to an outside wall before he could stop. The ooloi, clearly surprised, only watched him.

"You don't have any idea what you're doing, do you?" he said to it. He was panting a little.

"I think I don't," it admitted. "And I can't control my scent yet. Maybe I can't help you."

"No!" Tiikuchahk said sharply. "The adults said you could help—and you do help me."

"But I hurt Akin. I don't know how to stop hurting him."

"Touch him. Understand him the way you've understood me. Then you'll know how."

Tiikuchahk's voice stopped Akin from urging the ooloi to go. Tiikuchahk sounded . . . not just frightened but desperate. It was his sibling, as tormented by the situation as he was. And it was a child. Even more a child than he was—younger and truly eka.

"All right," he said unhappily. "Touch me, Dehkiaht. I'll hold still."

It held still itself, watching him silently. He had almost injured it. If he had fled from it only a little less quickly, he would have caused it a great deal of pain. And it probably would have stung him reflexively and caused him a great deal of pain. It needed more than Akin's words to assure it that he would not do such a thing again.

He made himself walk over to it. Its scent made him want to run to it and grab it. Its immaturity and its connection with Tiikuchahk made him want to run the other way. Somehow, he crossed the room to it.

"Lie down," it told him. "I'll help you sleep. When I'm finished, I'll know whether I can help you in any other way."

Akin lay down on the platform, eager for the relief of sleep. The light touches of the ooloi's head tentacles were an almost unendurable stimulant, and sleep was not as quick in coming as it should have been. He realized, finally, that his state of arousal was making sleep impossible.

The ooloi seemed to realize this at the same time. It did something Akin was not quick enough to catch, and Akin was abruptly no longer aroused. Then he was no longer awake.

9

Akin awoke alone.

He got up feeling slightly drowsy but unchanged and wandered through the Lo Toaht dwelling, looking for Tiikuchahk, for Dehkiaht, for anyone. He found no one until he went outside. There, people went about their business as usual, their surroundings looking like a gentle, incredibly well-maintained forest. True trees did not grow as large as the ship's treelike projections, but the illusion of rolling, forested land was inescapable. It was, Akin thought, too tame, too planned. No grazing here for exploring children. The ship gave food when asked. Once it was taught how to synthesize a food, it never forgot. There were no bananas or papayas or pineapples to pick, no cassava to pull, no sweet potatoes to dig, no growing, living things except appendages of the ship. Perfect "sweet potatoes" could be made to grow on the pseudotrees if an Oankali or a construct adult asked it of Chkahichdahk.

He looked up at the limbs above him and saw that nothing other than the usual hairlike, green, oxygen-producing tentacles hung from .he huge pseudotrees.

Why was he thinking about such things? Homesickness? Where were Dehkiaht and Tiikuchahk? Why had they left him?

He put his face to the pseudotree he had emerged from

221

He climbed onto the platform and looked at Tiikuchahk. "Will you take part?" he asked it.

"Yes," it said solemnly. "This will be the first time since before I was born that I'll be able to take impressions from you without things going wrong."

Akin lay down next to the ooloi. He drew close to it, his mouth against the flesh of its neck, its many head and body tentacles linked with him and with Tiikuchahk. Then, carefully, in the manner of a storyteller, he gave it the experience of his abduction, captivity, and conversion. All that he had felt, he made it feel. He did what he had not known he could do. He overwhelmed it so that for a time it was, itself, both captive and convert. He did to it what the abandonment of the Oankali had done to him in his infancy. He made the ooloi understand on an utterly personal level what he had suffered and what he had come to believe. Until he had finished, neither it nor Tiikuchahk could escape.

But when he had finished, when he had let them go, they both left him. They said nothing. They simply got up and left him.

10

The Akjai spoke to the people for Akin. Akin had not realized it would do this—an Akjai ooloi telling other Oankali that there must be Akjai Humans. It spoke through the ship and had the ship signal the trade villages on Earth. It asked for a consensus and then showed the Oankali and construct people of Chkahichdahk what Akin had shown Dehkiaht and Tiikuchahk.

As soon as the experience ended, people began objecting to its intensity, objecting to being so overwhelmed, objecting to the idea that this could have been the experience of such a young child...

No one objected to the idea of a Human Akjai. For some time, no one mentioned it at all.

Akin perceived what he could through the Akjai, drawing back whenever the transmission was too fast or too intense. Drawing back felt like coming up for air. He found himself gasping, almost exhausted each time. But each time he went back, needing to feel what the Akjai felt, needing to follow the responses of the people. It was rare for children to take part in a consensus for more than a few seconds. No child who was not deeply concerned would want to take part for longer.

Akin could feel the people avoiding the subject of Akjai Humans. He did not understand their reactions to it: a turning

=11=

Tiikuchahk and Dehkiaht were with him when he awoke. The Akjai was there, too, but he realized it had not been with him continually. He had a memory of it going away and coming back with Tiikuchahk and Dehkiaht. As Akin took in his surroundings, he saw the Akjai draw Dehkiaht into an alarming embrace, lifting the ooloi child and clasping it in over a dozen limbs.

"They wanted to learn about one another," Tiikuchahk said. These were the first words it had spoken to him since he caused it to experience his memories.

He sat up and focused on it questioningly.

"You shouldn't have been able to grab us and hold us that way," it said. "Dehkiaht and its parents say no child should be able to do that."

"I didn't know I could do it."

"Dehkiaht's parents say it's a teaching thing—the way adults teach subadult ooloi sometimes when the ooloi have to learn something they aren't really ready for. They've never heard of a subadult male."

"But Dehkiaht says that's what I am."

"It is what you are. Human-born construct females could be called subadults too, I guess. But you're a first. Again."

230

"I'm sorry you didn't like what I did. I'll try not to do it again."

"Don't. Not to me. The Akjai says you learned it here."

"I must have—without realizing it." He paused, watching Tiikuchahk. It was sitting next to him in apparent comfort. "Is it all right between us?"

"Seems to be."

"Will you help me?"

"I don't know." It focused narrowly on him. "I don't know what I am yet. I don't even know what I want to be."

"Do you want Dehkiaht?"

"I like it. It helped us, and I feel better when it's around. If I were like you, I would probably want to keep it."

"I do."

"It wants you, too. It says you're the most interesting person it's known. I think it will help you."

"If you become female, you could join us—mate with it."

"And you?"

He looked away from it. "I can't imagine how I would feel to have it and not you. What I've felt of it was . . . partly you."

"I don't know. No one knows yet what I'll be. I can't feel what you feel yet."

He managed to stop himself from arguing. Tiikuchahk was right. He still occasionally thought of it as female, but its body was neuter. It could not feel as he did. He was amazed at his own feelings, although they were natural. Now that Tiikuchahk was no longer a source of irritation and confusion, he could begin to feel about it the way people tended to feel about their closest siblings. He did not know whether he truly wanted to have it as one of his mates—or whether a wandering male of the kind he was supposed to be could be said to have mates. But the idea of mating with it felt right, now. It, Dehkiaht, and himself. That was the way it should be.

"Do you know what the people have decided?" he asked.

Tiikuchahk shook its head Humanly. "No."

After a time, Dehkiaht and the Akjai separated, and Dehkiaht climbed to the Akjai's long, broad back.

"Come join us," Dehkiaht called.

Akin got up and started toward it. Behind him, though, Tiikuchahk did not move.

Akin stopped, turned to face it. "Are you afraid?" he asked.

"Yes."

"You know the Akjai won't hurt you."

"It will hurt me if it thinks hurting me is necessary."

That was true. The Akjai had hurt Akin in order to teach him—and had taught Akin much more than he realized.

"Come anyway," Akin said. He wanted to touch Tiikuchahk now, draw it to him, comfort it. He had never before wanted to do such a thing. And in spite of the impulse, he found he was not willing to touch it now. It would not want him to. Dehkiaht would not want him to.

He went back to it and sat next to it. "I'll wait for you," he said.

It focused on him, head tentacles knotting miserably. "Join them," it said.

He said nothing. He sat with it, comfortably patient, wondering whether it feared the joining because it might find itself making decisions it did not feel ready to make.

Dehkiaht simply lay down on the Akjai's back, and the Akjai squatted, resting on its belly, waiting. Humans said no one knew how to wait better than the Oankali. Humans, perhaps remembering their earlier short life spans, tended to hurry without reason.

He did not know how much time had passed when Tiikuchahk stood up and he roused and stood up beside it. He focused on it, and when it moved, he followed it to the Akjai and Dehkiaht.

The Akjai drew its body into the familiar curve and welcomed Tiikuchahk and Akin to sit or lie against it. The Akjai gave each a sensory arm and gave Dehkiaht one too when it slid down one of the plates to settle beside them.

Now Akin learned for the first time what the people had decided. He felt now what he had not been able to feel before.

That the people saw him as something they had helped to make.

He was intended to decide the fate of the resisters. He was intended to make the decision the Dinso and the Toaht could not make. He was intended to see what must be done and convince others.

He had been abandoned to the resisters when they took him so that he could learn them as no adult could, as no Oankali-born construct could, as no construct who did not look quite Human could. Everyone knew the resisters' bodies, but no one knew their thinking as Akin did. No one except other Humans. And they could not be allowed to convince Oankali to do the profoundly immoral, antilife thing that Akin had decided must be done. The people had suspected what he would decide—had feared it. They would not have accepted it if he had not been able to stir confusion and some agreement among constructs, both Oankali-born and Human-born.

They had deliberately rested the fate of the resisters—the fate of the Human species—on him.

Why? Why not on one of the Human-born females? Some of them were adults before he was born.

The Akjai supplied him with the answer before he was aware of having asked the question. "You're more Oankali than you think, Akin—and far more Oankali than you look. Yet you're very Human. You skirt as close to the Contradiction as anyone has dared to go. You're as much of them as you can be and as much of us as your ooan dared make you. That leaves you with your own contradiction. It also made you the most likely person to choose for the resisters—quick death or long, slow death."

"Or life," Akin protested.

"No."

"A chance for life."

"Only for a while."

"You're certain of that . . . and yet you spoke for me?"

"I'm Akjai. How can I deny another people the security of an Akjai group? Even though for this people it's a cruelty. Understand that, Akin; it is a cruelty. You and those who help you will give them the tools to create a civilization that will

IV
HOME

For a time, Earth seemed wild
and strange to Akin—a profusion of life almost frightening in its
complexity. On Chkahichdahk, there was only a potential profusion stored in people's memories and in seed, cell, and
gene-print banks. Earth was still a huge biological bank itself,
balancing its own ecology with little Oankali help.

Akin could do nothing on the fourth planet—Mars, the
Humans called it—until after his metamorphosis. His training
too had gone as far as it could until his metamorphosis. His
teachers had sent him home. Tiikuchahk, now at peace with
him and with itself, seemed glad to come home. And Dehkiaht
had simply attached itself to Akin. When Dichaan came for
Akin and Tiikuchahk, even he did not suggest leaving Dehkiaht
behind.

Once they reached Earth, however, Akin had to get away
from Dehkiaht, away from everyone for a while. He wanted to
see some of his resister friends before his metamorphosis—
before he changed beyond recognition. He had to let them
know what had happened, what he had to offer them. Also, he
needed respected Human allies. He first thought of people he
had visited during his wanderings—men and women who knew
him as a small, nearly Human man. But he did not want to see
them. Not yet. He felt drawn toward another place—a place

239

where the people would hardly know him. He had not been there since his own third year. He would go to Phoenix—to Gabe and Tate Rinaldi, where his obsession with the resisters had begun.

He settled Dehkiaht with his parents and noticed that Tiikuchahk seemed to be spending more and more time with Dichaan. He watched this sadly, knowing that he was losing his closest sibling for the second time, the final time. If it chose later to help with the changing of Mars, it would not do so as a mate or a potential mate. It was becoming male.

He went to see Margit, who was brown now and mated and pregnant and content.

He asked his parents to find a female mate for Dehkiaht.

Then he left for Phoenix. He especially wanted to see Tate again while he still looked Human. He wanted to tell her he had kept his promise.

= 2 =

Phoenix was still more a town than a village, but it was a shabbier town. Akin could not help comparing Phoenix as he remembered it to Phoenix now.

There was trash in the street. Dead weeds, food waste, scrap wood, cloth, and paper. Some of the houses were obviously vacant. A couple of them had been partially torn down. Others seemed ready to fall down.

Akin walked into town openly as he had always walked into resister settlements. He had been shot doing this only once. That once had been nothing more than a painful nuisance. A Human would have died. Akin had simply run away and healed himself. Lilith had warned him that he must not let resisters see how his body healed—that the sight of wounds healing before their eyes could frighten them. And Humans were most dangerous, most unpredictable when they were afraid.

There were rifles pointed at him as he walked down the street of Phoenix. So Phoenix was armed now. He could see guns and people through the windows, although it seemed the people were trying not to be seen. A few people working or loitering in the street stared at him. At least two were too drunk to notice him.

241

Hidden guns and open drunkenness.

Phoenix was dying. One of the drunken men was Macy Wilton, who had acted as father to Amma and Shkaht. The other was Stancio Roybal, husband of Neci, the woman who had wanted to amputate Amma's and Shkaht's sensory tentacles. And where were Kolina Wilton and Neci? How could they let their mates—their husbands—lie in the mud half-conscious or unconscious?

And where was Gabe?

He reached the house that he had shared with Tate and Gabe, and for a moment he was afraid to climb the stairs to the porch and rap his knuckles against the door Human-fashion. The house was shut and looked well-kept, but . . . who might live there now?

A man with a gun came out onto the porch and looked down. Gabe.

"You speak English?" he demanded, pointing his rifle at Akin.

"I always have, Gabe." He paused, giving the man time to look at him. "I'm Akin."

The man stood staring at him, peering first from one angle, then moving slightly to peer from another. Akin had changed after all, had grown up. Gabe looked the same.

"I worried that you would be in the hills or out at another village," Akin said. "I never thought to worry that you might not recognize me. I've come back to keep a promise I made to Tate."

Gabe said nothing.

Akin sighed and settled to wait. It was not likely that anyone would shoot him as long as he stood still, hands in sight, unthreatening.

Men gathered around Akin, waiting for some sign from Gabe.

"Check him," Gabe said to one of them.

The man rubbed rough hands over Akin's body. He was Gilbert Senn. He and his wife Anne had once stood with Neci, feeling that sensory tentacles should be removed. Akin did not speak to him. Instead, he waited, eyes on Gabe. Humans needed the steady, visible gaze of eyes. Males respected it. Females found it sexually interesting.

"He ways he's that kid we bought almost twenty years ago," Gabe said to the men. "He says he's Akin."

The men stared at Akin with hostility and suspicion. Akin gave no indication that he saw this.

"No worms," one man said. "Shouldn't he have them by now?"

No one answered. Akin did not answer because he did not want to be told to be quiet. He wore only a pair of short pants as he had when these people knew him. Insects no longer bit him. He had learned to make his body unpalatable to them. He was a dark, even brown, small, but clearly not weak. And clearly not afraid.

"Are you an adult?" Gabe asked him.

"No," he said softly.

"Why not?"

"I'm not old enough."

"Why did you come here?"

"To see you and Tate. You were my parents for a while."

The rifle wavered slightly. "Come closer."

Akin obeyed.

"Show me your tongue."

Akin smiled, then showed his tongue. It did not look any more Human now than it had when Gabe had first seen it.

Gabe drew back, then took a deep breath. He let the rifle point toward the ground. "So it is you."

Almost shyly, Akin extended a hand. Human beings often shook one another's hands. Several had refused to shake his.

Gabe took the hand and shook it, then seized Akin by both shoulders and hugged him. "I don't believe it," he kept saying. "I don't fucking believe it.

"It's okay," he told the other men. "It's really him!"

The men watched for a moment longer, then began to drift away. Watching them without turning, Akin got the impression that they were disappointed—that they would have preferred to beat him, perhaps kill him.

Gabe took Akin into the house, where everything looked the same—cool and dark and clean.

Tate lay on a long bench against a wall. She turned her head to look at him, and he read pain in her face. Of course, she did not recognize him.

"She took a fall," Gabe said. There was deep pain in his voice. "Yori's been taking care of her. You remember Yori?"

"I remember," Akin said. "Yori once said she'd leave Phoenix if the people here made guns."

Gabe gave him an odd look. "Guns are necessary. Raids taught everyone that."

"Who . . . ?" Tate asked. And then, amazingly, "Akin?"

He went to her, knelt beside her, and took her hand. He did not like the slightly sour smell of her or the lines around her eyes. How much harm had been done to her?

How much help would she and Gabe tolerate?

"Akin," he echoed. "How did you fall? What happened?"

"You're the same," she said, touching his face. "I mean, you're not grown up yet."

"No. But I have kept my promise to you. I've found . . . I've found what may be the answer for your people. But tell me how you got hurt."

He had forgotten nothing about her. Her quick mind, her tendency to treat him like a small adult, the feeling she projected of being not quite trustworthy—just unpredictable enough to make him uneasy. Yet he had accepted her, liked her from his first moments with her. It troubled him more than he could express that she seemed so changed now. She had lost weight, and her coloring, like her scent, had gone wrong. She was too pale. Almost gray. Her hair, too, seemed to be graying. It was much less yellow than it had been. And she was far too thin.

"I fell," she said. Her eyes were the same. They examined his face, his body. She took one of his hands and looked at it. "My god," she whispered.

"We were exploring," Gabe said. "She lost her footing, fell down a hill. I carried her back to Salvage." He paused. "The old camp's a town itself now. People live there permanently. But they don't have their own doctor. Some of them helped me bring her down to Yori. That was... That was bad. But she's getting better now." She was not. He knew she was not.

She had closed her eyes. She knew it as well as he did. She was dying.

Akin touched her face so that she would open her eyes. Humans seemed almost not to be there when they closed their eyes. They could close off all visual awareness and shut themselves too completely within their own flesh. "When did it happen?" he asked.

"God. Two, almost three months ago."

She had suffered that long. Gabe had not found an ooloi to help her. Any ooloi would have done it at no cost to the Humans. Even some males and females could help. He believed he could. It was clear that she would die if nothing was done.

What was the etiquette of asking to save someone's life in an unacceptable way? If Akin asked in the wrong way, Tate would die.

Best not to ask at all. Not yet. Perhaps not at all. "I came back to tell you I'd kept my promise to you," he said. "I don't know if you and the others can accept what I have to offer, but it would mean restored fertility and... a place of your own."

Now her eyes were wide and intent on him. "What place?" she whispered. Gabe had come to stand near them and stare down.

"Where!" he demanded.

"It can't be here," Akin said. "You would have to build whole new towns in a new environment, learn new ways to live. It would be hard. But I've found people—other constructs— to help me make it possible."

"Akin, where?" she whispered.

"Mars," he said simply. They stared at him, wordless. He did not know what they might know about Mars, so he began to reassure them. "We can enable the planet to support Human life. We'll start as soon as I'm mature. The work has been given to me. No one else felt the need to do it as strongly as I did."

"Mars?" Gabe said. "Leave Earth to the Oankali? All of Earth?"

"Yes." Akin turned his face toward Gabe again. The man must understand as quickly as possible that Akin was serious.

He needed to have reason to trust Akin with Tate. And Tate needed a reason to continue to live. It had occurred to Akin that she might be weary of her long, pointless life. That, he realized, was something that would not occur to the Oankali. They would not understand even if they were told. Some would accept without understanding. Most would not.

Akin turned his face to Tate again. "They left me with you for so long so that you could teach me whether what they had done with you was right. They couldn't judge.· They were so . . . disturbed by your genetic structure that they couldn't do, couldn't even consider doing what I will do."

"Mars?" she said. "Mars?"

"I can give it to you. Others will help me. But . . . you and Gabe have to help me convince resisters."

She looked up at Gabe. "Mars," she whispered, and managed to shake her head.

"I've studied it," Akin told them. "With protection, you could live there now, but you would have to live underground or inside some structure. There's too much ultraviolet light, an atmosphere of carbon dioxide, and no liquid water. And it's cold. It will always be colder than it is here, but we can make it warmer than it is now."

"How?" Gabe asked.

"With modified plants and, later, modified animals. The Oankali have used them all before to make lifeless planets livable."

"Oankali plants?" Gabe demanded. "Not Earth plants?"

Akin sighed. "If something the Oankali have modified belongs to them, then you and all your people belong to them now."

Silence.

"The modified plants and animals work much faster than anything that could be found on Earth naturally. We need them to prepare the way for you relatively quickly. The Oankali won't allow your fertility to be restored here on Earth. You're older now than most Humans used to get. You can still live a long time, but I want you to leave as soon as possible so that you can still raise children there the way my mother has here and teach them what they are."

Tate's eyes had closed again. She put one hand over them,

and Akin restrained an impulse to move it away. Was she crying?

"We've lost almost everything already," Gabe said. "Now we lose our world and everything on it."

"Not everything. You'll be able to take whatever you want. And plant life from Earth will be added as the new environment becomes able to support it." He hesitated. "The plants that grow here . . . Not many of them will grow there outdoors. But a lot of the mountain plants will eventually grow there."

Gabe shook his head. "All that in our lifetimes?"

"If you keep yourselves safe, you'll live about twice as long as you already have. You'll live to see plants from Earth growing unprotected on Mars."

Tate took her hand away from her face and looked at him. "Akin, I probably won't live another month," she said. "Before now, I didn't want to. But now . . . Can you get help for me?"

"No!" Gabe protested. "You don't need help. You'll be okay!"

"I'll be dead!" She managed to glare at him. "Do you believe Akin?" she asked.

He looked from her to Akin, stared at Akin as he answered. "I don't know."

"What, you think he's lying?"

"I don't know. He's just a kid. Kids lie."

"Yes. And men lie. But don't you think you can lie to me after all these years. If there's something to live for, I want to live! Are you saying I should die?"

"No. Of course not."

"Then let me get the only help available. Yori has given up on me."

Gabe looked as though he still wanted to protest, but he only looked at her. After a time, he spoke to Akin. "Get someone to help her," he said. Akin could recall hearing him curse in that same tone of voice. Only Humans could do that: say, "Get someone to help her," with their mouths, and "Damn her to hell!" with their voices and bodies.

"I can help her," Akin said.

And both Humans were suddenly looking at him with a suspicion he didn't understand at all.

"I asked for training," he said. "Why are you looking at me that way?"

"If you aren't ooloi," Gabe said, "how can you heal anyone?"

"I told you, I asked to be taught. My teacher was ooloi. I can't do everything it could do, but I can help your flesh and your bones heal. I can encourage your organs to repair themselves even if they wouldn't normally."

"I've never heard that males could do that," Gabe said.

"An ooloi could do it better. You would enjoy what it did. The safest thing for me to do is make you sleep."

"That's what you'd do if you were an ooloi child, isn't it?" Tate asked.

"Yes. But it's what I'll always do, even as an adult. Ooloi change and become physically able to do more."

"I don't want more done," Tate said. "I want to be healed—healed of everything. And that's all."

"I can't do anything else."

Gabe made a short, wordless sound. "You can still sting, can't you?"

Akin suppressed an urge to stand up, to face Gabe. His body was almost tiny compared to Gabe's. Even if he had been larger, physical confrontation would have been pointless. He simply stared at the man.

After a time, Gabe came closer and bent to face Tate. "You really want to let him do this?"

She sighed, closed her eyes for a moment. "I'm dying. Of course I'm going to let him do it."

And he sighed, stroked her hair lightly. "Yeah." He turned to glare at Akin. "All right, do whatever it is you do."

Akin did not speak or move. He continued to watch Gabe, resenting the man's attitude, knowing that it did not come only from fear for Tate.

"Well?" Gabe said, standing straight and looking down. Tall men did this. They meant to intimidate. Some of them wanted to fight. Gabe simply intended to make a point he was in no position to make.

Akin waited.

Tate said, "Get out of here, Gabe. Leave us alone for a while."

"Leave you with him!"

"Yes. Now. I'm sick of feeling like shit that's been stepped in. Go."

He went. It was better for him to go because she wanted it than for him to give in to Akin. Akin would have preferred to let him go silently, but he did not dare.

"Gabe," he said as the man was going outside.

Gabe stopped but did not turn.

"Guard the door. An interruption could kill her."

Gabe closed the door behind him without speaking. Immediately, Tate let her breath out in a kind of moan. She looked at the door, then at Akin. "Do I have to do anything?"

"No. Just put up with having me on that bench with you."

This did not seem to disturb her. "You're small enough," she said. "Come on."

He was no smaller than she was.

Carefully, he settled himself between her and the wall. "I still have only my tongue to work with," he said. "That means this will look like I'm biting you on the neck."

"You used to do that whenever I'd let you."

"I know. Apparently, though, it looks more threatening or more suspicious now."

She tried to laugh.

"You don't think he'll come in, do you? It really could kill you if someone tried to pull us apart."

"He won't. He learned a long time ago not to do things like that."

"Okay. You won't sleep as quickly as you would with an ooloi because I can't sting you unconscious. I have to convince your body to do all the work. Keep still now."

He put one arm around her to keep her in position when she lost consciousness, then put his mouth to the side of her neck. From then on, he was aware only of her body—its injured organs and poorly healed fractures... and its activation of her old illness, her Huntington's disease. Did she know? Had the disease caused her to fall? It could have. Or she could have fallen deliberately in the hope of escaping the disease.

She had strained and bruised the ligaments in her back. She had dislocated one of the disks of cartilage between the vertebrae of her neck. She had broken her left kneecap badly.

Her kidneys were damaged. Both kidneys. How had she managed to do that? How far had she fallen?

Her left wrist had been broken but had been set and had almost healed. There were also two rib fractures, nearly healed.

Akin lost himself in the work—the pleasure—of finding injuries and stimulating her body's own healing ability. He stimulated her body to produce an enzyme that turned off the Huntington's gene. The gene would eventually become active again. She *must* have an ooloi take care of the disease permanently before she left Earth. He could not replace the deadly gene or trick her body into using genes she had not used since before her birth. He could not help her create new ova clean of the Huntington's gene. What he had already done to suppress the gene was as much as he dared to do.

= 3 =

Gabe's interruption of Akin's healing produced the only serious disruption in his memory Akin ever experienced. All he recalled of it later was abrupt agony.

In spite of his warning to Gabe, in spite of Tate's reassurance, Gabe came into the room before the healing was complete. Akin learned later that Gabe returned because hours had passed without a sound from Akin or Tate. He was afraid for Tate, afraid something had gone wrong, and suspicious of Akin.

He found Akin apparently unconscious, his mouth still against Tate's neck. Akin did not even seem to breathe. Nor did Tate. Her flesh was cool—almost cold—and that frightened Gabe. He believed she was dying, feared she might already be dead. He panicked.

First he tried to pull Tate free, alerting Akin on some level that something was wrong. But Akin's attention was too much on Tate. He had only begun to disengage when Gabe hit him.

Gabe was afraid of Akin's sting. He would not grasp Akin and try to pull him away from Tate. Instead, he tried to knock Akin away with quick, hard punches.

The first blow all but tore Akin loose. It hurt him more than he had ever been hurt, and he could not help passing some of his pain on to Tate.

Yet he managed not to poison her. He did not know when she began to scream. He continued automatically to hold her. That and the fact that he was stronger than the larger Gabe enabled him to withdraw from Tate's nervous system and then from her body without being badly injured—and without killing. Later he was amazed that he had done this. His teacher had warned him that males did not have the control to do such things. Oankali males and females avoided healing not only because they were not needed as healers but because they were more likely than ooloi to kill by accident. They could be driven to kill unintentionally by interruptions and even by their subjects if things went wrong. Even Gabe should have been in danger. Akin should have struck at him blindly, reflexively.

Yet he did not.

His body coiled into a painfully tight fetal knot and lay vulnerable and more completely unconscious than it had ever been.

= 4 =

When Akin became able to perceive the world around him again he discovered that he could not move or speak. He lay frozen, aware that sometimes there were Humans around him. They looked at him, sat with him sometimes, but did not touch him. For some time he did not know who they were—or where he was. Later, he compared this period with his earliest infancy. It was a time he remembered but took no part in. But even as an infant, he had been fed and washed and held. Now no hand touched him.

He slowly became aware that two people did talk to him. Two females, both Human, one small and yellow-haired and pale. One slightly larger, dark-haired, and sun-browned.

He was glad when they were with him.

He dreaded their coming.

They aroused him. Their scents reached deep into him and drew him to them. Yet he could not move. He lay, being drawn and drawn and utterly still. It was torment, but he preferred it to solitude.

The females talked to him. After a while, he came to know that they were Tate and Yori. And he remembered all that he knew of Tate and Yori.

Tate sat close to him and said his name. She told him how well she felt and how her crops were growing and what different people in the settlement were doing. She did her sewing and her writing while sitting with Akin. She kept a journal.

Yori kept one, too. Yori's became a study of him. She told him so. He was in metamorphosis, she said. She had never seen metamorphosis before, but she had heard it described. Already there were small, new sensory tentacles on his back, on his head, on his legs. His skin was gray now, and he was losing his hair. She said he must find a way to tell them if he wished to be touched. She said Tate was all right, and Akin must find a way to communicate. She said anything he asked would be done for him. She would see to it. She said he must not worry about being alone because she would see that someone was always with him.

This comforted him more than she could know. People in metamorphosis had little tolerance for solitude.

Gabe sat with him. Gabe and the two women had lifted the bench he lay on and carried it and him into a small sunlit room.

Sometimes Gabe tempted him with food or water. He could not know that the scent of the women tempted Akin more strongly than anything Gabe could place near him. He would have wanted food before he fell asleep if he had gone into metamorphosis normally. He would have eaten, then slept. He had heard that ooloi did not sleep straight through much of their second metamorphosis. Lilith had told him that Nikanj slept most of the time, but woke up now and then to eat and talk. Eventually it would fall into another deep sleep. Males and females slept through most of their one metamorphosis. They did not eat, drink, urinate, or defecate. The women stirred Akin, focused his attention, but the smells of food and water did not interest him. He noticed them because they were intermittent. They were environmental changes that he could not fail to notice.

Gabe brought him plants, and he realized after a while that the plants were some of those that he had enjoyed eating when he was younger, upon which Gabe had seen him grazing. The man remembered. That pleased him and eased the sudden shock when, one day, Gabe touched him.

There was no warning. As Gabe had decided to come into

the room and separate Akin and Tate, he now decided to do one of the things Yori had told him and Tate not to do.

He simply placed his hand on Akin's back and shook Akin.

After a moment, Akin shuddered. His small, new sensory tentacles moved for the first time, elongating reflexively toward the touching hand.

Gabe jerked his hand away. He would not have been hurt, but he did not know that, and Akin could not tell him. Gabe did not touch him again.

Pilar and Mateo Leal took their turns sitting with Akin. Tino's parents. Mateo had killed people Akin had cared for very much. For a time, his presence made Akin intensely uncomfortable. Then, because he had no choice, Akin adjusted.

Kolina Wilton sat with him sometimes but never spoke to him. One day, to his surprise, Macy Wilton sat with him. So the man was not always lying drunk in the street.

Macy came back several times. He carved things of wood while he sat with Akin, and the smells of his woods were an announcement of his coming. He began to talk to Akin—to speculate about what had happened to Amma and Shkaht, to speculate about children he might someday father, to speculate about Mars.

This told Akin for the first time that Gabe and Tate had spread the story, the hope that he had brought.

Mars.

"Not everyone wants to go," Macy said. "I think they're crazy if they stay here. I'd give anything to see homo sap have another chance. Lina and I will go. And don't you worry about those others!"

At once, Akin began to worry. There was no way to hurry metamorphosis. Bringing it on so traumatically had nearly killed him. Now there was nothing to do but wait. Wait and know that when Humans disagreed, they sometimes fought, and when they fought, all too often they killed one another.

= 5 =

Akin's metamorphosis dragged on. He was silent and motionless for months as his body reshaped itself inside and out. He heard and automatically remembered argument after argument over his mission, his right to be in Phoenix, the Human right to Earth. There was no resolution. There was cursing, shouting, threats, fighting, but no resolution. Then, on the day his silence ended, there was a raid. There was shooting. One man was killed. One woman was carried off.

Akin heard the noise but did not know what was happening. Pilar Leal was with him. She stayed with him until the shooting was over. Then she left him for a few moments to see that her husband was all right. When she returned, he was trying desperately to speak.

Pilar gave a short, startled scream, and he knew he must be doing something that she could see. He could see her, hear her, smell her, but he was somehow distant from himself. He had no image of himself and was not sure whether he was causing any part of his body to move. Pilar's reaction said he was.

He managed to make a sound and know that he had made it. It was nothing more than a hoarse croak, but he had done it deliberately.

256

Pilar crept toward him, stared at him, "*Está despierto?*" she demanded. Was he awake?

"Sí," he said, and gasped and coughed. He had no strength. He could hear himself, but he still felt distanced from his body. He tried to straighten it and could not.

"Do you have pain?" she asked.

"No. Weak. Weak."

"What can I do? What can I get for you?"

He could not answer for several seconds. "Shooting," he said finally. "Why?"

"Raiders. Dirty bastards! They took Rudra. They killed her husband. We killed two of them."

Akin wanted to slip back into the refuge of unconsciousness. They were not killing each other over the Mars decision, but they were killing each other. There always seemed to be reason for Humans to kill each other. He would give them a new world—a hard world that would demand cooperation and intelligence. Without either, it would surely kill them. Could even Mars distract them long enough for them to breed their way out of their Contradiction?

He felt stronger and tried to speak to Pilar again. He discovered she was gone. Yori was with him now. He had slept. Yes, he had a stored memory of Yori coming in, Pilar reporting that he had spoken, Pilar going out. Yori speaking to him, then understanding that he was asleep.

"Yori?"

She jumped, and he realized she had fallen asleep herself. "So you are awake," she said.

He took a deep breath. "It isn't over. I can't move much yet."

"Should you try?"

He attempted a smile. "I am trying." And a moment later, "Did they get Rudra back?" He had not known the woman, though he remembered seeing her during his stay in Phoenix. She was a tiny brown woman with straight black hair that would have swept the ground if she had not bound it up. She and her husband were Asians from a place called South Africa.

"Men went after her. I don't think they're back yet."

"Are there many raids?"

"Too many. More all the time."

"Why?"

"Why? Well, because we're flawed. Your people said so."

He had not heard her speak so bitterly before.

"There were not so many raids before."

"People had hope here when you were a baby. We were more formidable. And . . . our men had not begun raiding then."

"Phoenix men raiding?"

"Humanity extinguishing itself in boredom, hopelessness, bitterness . . . I'm surprised we've lasted this long."

"Will you go to Mars, Yori?"

She looked at him for several seconds. "It's true?"

"Yes. I have to prepare the way. After that, Humanity will have a place of its own."

"What will we do with it, I wonder?"

"Work hard to keep it from killing you. You'll be able to live there when I've prepared it, but your lives will be hard. If you're careless or can't work together, you'll die."

"We can have children?"

"I can't arrange that. You'll have to let an ooloi do it."

"But it will be done!"

"Yes."

She sighed. "Then I'm going." She watched him for a moment. "When?"

"Years from now. Some of you will go early, though. Some of you must see and understand what I do so that you'll understand from the beginning how your new world works."

She sat watching him silently.

"And I need help with other resisters," he said. He strained for a moment, trying to lift a hand, trying to unknot his body. It was as though he had forgotten how to move. Yet this did not concern him. He knew he was simply trying to rush things that could not be rushed. He could talk. That had to be enough.

"I probably look a lot less Human than I did," he continued. "I won't be able to approach people who used to know me. I don't like being shot or having to threaten people. I need Humans to talk to other Humans and gather them in."

"You're wrong."

"What?"

"You need mostly Oankali for that. Or adult constructs."

"But—"

"You need people who won't be shot on sight. Sane people only shoot Oankali by accident. You need people who won't be taken prisoner and everything they say ignored. That's the way Human beings are now. Shoot the men. Steal the women. If you have nothing better to do, go raid your neighbors."

"That bad?"

"Worse."

He sighed. "Will you help me, Yori?"

"What shall I do?"

"Advise me. I'll need Human advisors."

"From what I've heard, your mother should be one of them."

He tried to read her still face. "I didn't realize you knew who she was."

"People tell me things."

"I've chosen a good advisor, then."

"I don't know. I don't think I can leave Phoenix except with the group that goes to Mars. I've trained others, but I'm the only formally trained doctor. That's a joke, really. I was a psychiatrist. But at least I have formal training."

"What's a psychiatrist?"

"A doctor who specializes in the treatment of mental illness." She gave a bitter laugh. "The Oankali say people like me dealt with far more physical disorders than we were capable of recognizing."

Akin said nothing. He needed someone like Yori who knew the resisters and who seemed not to be afraid of the Oankali. But she must convince herself. She must see that helping Humanity move to its new world was more important than setting broken bones and treating bullet wounds. She probably already knew this, but it would take time for her to accept it. He changed the subject.

"How do I look, Yori? How much have I changed?"

"Completely."

"What?"

"You look like an Oankali. You don't sound like one, but if I didn't know who you were, I would assume you were a small Oankali. Perhaps a child."

"Shit!"

"Will you change any more?"

"No." He closed his eyes. "My senses aren't as sharp as they will be. But the shape I have is the shape I will have."

"Do you mind, really?"

"Of course I mind. Oh, god. How many resisters will trust me now? How many will even believe I'm a construct?"

"It doesn't matter. How many of them trust each other? And they know they're Human."

"It's not like that everywhere. There are resister settlements closes to Lo that don't fight so much."

"You might have to take them, then, and give up on some of the people here."

"I don't know if I can do that."

"I can."

He looked at her. She had placed herself so that he could see her with his eyes even though he could not move. She would go back to Lo with him. She would advise him and observe the metamorphosis of Mars.

"Do you need food yet?" she asked.

The idea disgusted him. "No. Soon, perhaps, but not now."

"Do you need anything?"

"No. But thank you for seeing that I was never left alone."

"I had heard it was important."

"Very. I should begin to move in a few more days. I'll still need people around."

"Anyone in particular?"

"Did you choose the people who've been sitting with me—other than the Rinaldis, I mean?"

"Tate and I did."

"You did a good job. Will they all immigrate to Mars, do you think?"

"That's not why we chose them."

"Will they immigrate?"

After a while she nodded. "They will. So will a few others."

"Send me the others—if you don't think my looks now will scare them."

"They've all seen Oankali before."

Did she mean to insult him? he wondered. She spoke in

such a strange tone. Bitterness and something else. She stood up.

"Wait," he said.

She paused, not changing expression.

"My perception isn't what it will be eventually. I don't know what's wrong."

She stared at him with unmistakable hostility. "I was thinking that so many people have suffered and died," she said. "So many have become... unsalvageable. So many more will be lost." She stopped, breathed deeply. "Why did the Oankali cause this? Why didn't they offer us Mars years ago?"

"They would never offer you Mars. I offer you Mars."

"Why?"

"Because I'm part of you. Because I say you should have one more chance to breed yourselves out of your genetic Contradiction."

"And what do the Oankali say?"

"That you can't grow out of it, can't resolve it in favor of intelligence. That hierarchical behavior selects for hierarchical behavior, whether it should or not. That not even Mars will be enough of a challenge to change you." He paused. "That to give you a new world and let you procreate again would... would be like breeding intelligent beings for the sole purpose of having them kill one another."

"That wouldn't be our purpose," she protested.

He thought about that for a moment, wondered what he should say. The truth or nothing. The truth. "Yori, Human purpose isn't what you say it is or what I say it is. It's what your biology says it is—what your genes say it is."

"Do you believe that?"

"... yes."

"Then why—"

"Chance exists. Mutation. Unexpected effects of the new environment. Things no one has thought of. The Oankali can make mistakes."

"Can we?"

He only looked at her.

"Why are the Oankali letting you do this?"

"I want to do it. Other constructs think I should. Some will help me. Even those who don't think I should understand why I want to. The Oankali accept this. There was a consensus. The Oankali won't help, except to teach. They won't set foot on Mars once we've begun. They won't transport you." He tried to think of a way to make her understand. "To them, what I'm doing is terrible. The only thing that would be more terrible would be to murder you all with my own hands."

"Not reasonable," she whispered.

"You can't see and read genetic structure the way they do. It isn't like reading words on a page. They feel it and know it. They... There's no English word for what they do. To say they know is completely inadequate. I was made to perceive this before I was ready. I understand it now as I couldn't then."

"And you'll still help us."

"I'll still help. I have to."

She left him. The expression of hostility was gone from her face when she looked back at him before closing the wooden door. She looked confused, yet hopeful.

"I'll send someone to you," she said, and closed the door.

6

$\mathbf{A}$kin slept and knew only peripherally that Gabe came in to sit with him. The man spoke to him for the first time, but he did not awaken to answer. "I'm sorry," Gabe said once he was certain Akin was asleep. He did not repeat the words or explain them.

Gabe was still there some time later when the noise began outside. It wasn't loud or threatening, but Gabe went out to see what had happened. Akin awoke and listened.

Rudra had been rescued, but she was dead. Her captors had beaten and raped her until she was so badly hurt that her rescuers could not get her home alive. They had not even been able to catch or kill any of her captors. They were tired and angry. They had brought back Rudra's body to be buried with her husband. Two more people lost. The men cursed all raiders and tried to figure out where this group had come from. Where should the reprisal raid take place?

Someone—not Gabe—brought up Mars.

Someone else told him to shut up.

A third person asked how Akin was.

"Fine," Gabe said. There was something wrong with the way he said it, but Akin could not tell what it was.

The men were silent for a while.

"Let's have a look at him," one of them said suddenly.

difficult it was for him to draw his sensory tentacles back, to break the deep, frustrating contact.

"What was that all about?" she asked when she had her hand back.

He was not quick enough to think of an innocuous answer before she began to laugh.

"I thought so," she said. "We should definitely get you home. Do you have mates waiting?"

Chagrined, he said nothing.

"I'm sorry. I didn't mean to embarrass you. It's been a long time since I was an adolescent."

"Humans called me that before I changed."

"Young adult, then."

"How can you condescend to me and still follow me?"

She smiled. "I don't know. I haven't worked out my feelings toward the new you yet."

Something about her manner was a lie. Nothing she said was a direct lie, but there was something wrong.

"Will you go to Mars, Tate, or stay on Earth?" he asked.

She seemed to pull back from him without moving.

"You'll be as free to stay as you will be to go." She had Oankali mates who would be overjoyed to have her stay. If she did not, they might never settle on Earth.

"Truce," Tate said quietly.

He wished she were Oankali so that he could show her he meant what he was saying. He had not spoken in response to her condescension, as she clearly believed. He had responded instead to the falseness of her manner. But communication with Humans was always incomplete.

"Goddamn you," Tate said softly.

"What?"

She looked away from him. She stood up, paced across to a window, and stared out. She stood to one side, making it difficult for anyone outside to see her. But there was no one outside that window. She paced around the room, restless, grim.

"I thought I'd made my decision," she said. "I thought leaving here would be enough for now."

"It is," Akin said. "There's no hurry. You don't have to make any other decisions yet."

"Who's patronizing whom?" she said bitterly.

More misunderstanding. "Take me literally," Akin said. "Assume that I mean exactly what I say."

She looked at him with disbelief and distrust.

"You *can* decide later," he insisted.

After a while she sighed. "No," she said, "I can't."

He did not understand, so he said nothing.

"That's my problem, really," she continued. "I don't have a choice anymore. I have to go."

"You don't."

She shook her head. "I made my choice a long time ago—the way Lilith made hers. I chose Gabe and Phoenix and Humanity. My own people disgust me sometimes, but they're still my people. I have to go with them."

"Do you?"

"Yes."

She sat down again after a while and put the gun on her lap and closed her eyes.

"Tate?" he said, when she seemed calm.

She opened her eyes but said nothing.

"Does the way I look now bother you?"

The question seemed to annoy her at first. Then she shrugged. "If anyone had asked me how I would feel if you changed so completely, I would have said it would upset me, at least. It doesn't. I don't think it bothers the others either. We all watched you change."

"What about those who didn't watch?"

"To them you'll be an Oankali, I think."

He sighed. "There'll be fewer immigrants because of me."

"Because of us," she said.

Because of Gabe, she meant.

"He thought I was dead, Akin. He panicked."

"I know."

"I've talked to him. We'll help you gather people. We'll go to the villages—alone, with you, or with other constructs. Just tell us what you want us to do."

His sensory tentacles smoothed again with pleasure. "Will you let me improve your ability to survive injuries and heal?" he asked. "Will you let someone correct your Huntington's disease genetically?"

She hesitated. "The Huntington's?"

"You don't want to pass that on to your children."

"But genetic changes... That will mean time with an ooloi. A lot of time."

"The disease had become active, Tate. It was active when I healed you. I thought perhaps... you had noticed."

"You mean I'm going to get sick with it? Crazy?"

"No. I fixed it again. A temporary fix. The deactivation of a gene that should have been replaced long ago."

"I... couldn't have gone through that."

"The disease may be the reason you fell."

"Oh my god," she whispered. "That's the way it happened with my mother. She kept falling. And she had... personality changes. And I read that the disease causes brain damage—irreversible..."

"An ooloi can reverse it. It isn't serious yet, anyway."

"Any brain damage is serious!"

"It can be repaired."

She looked at him, clearly wanting to believe.

"You can't introduce this to the Mars colony. You know you can't. It would spread through the population in a few generations."

"I know."

"You'll let it be corrected, then?"

"Yes." The word was hardly more than a moving of her lips, but Akin saw it and believed her.

Relieved and surprisingly tired, he drifted off to sleep. With her help and the help of others in Phoenix, he had a chance of making the Mars colony work.

7

When he awoke, the house was aflame.

He thought at first that the sound he heard was rain. The smoke scent forced him to recognize it as fire. There was no one with him. The room was dark, and he had only a stored memory of Macy Wilton sitting beside him, a short, thick gun across his knees. A double-barreled gun of a type Akin had not seen before. He had gotten up and gone to investigate a strange noise just outside the house. Akin replayed his memory of the noise. Even asleep, he had heard what Macy probably had not.

People whispering.

"Don't pour that there. Throw it against the wall where it will do some good. And throw it on the porch."

"Shut up. They're not deaf in there."

Footsteps, oddly unsteady.

"Go pour some under the mongrel's window, Babe."

Footsteps coming closer to Akin's window—almost stumbling closer. And someone fell. That was the sound Macy heard: a grunt of pain and a body landing heavily.

Akin knew all this as soon as he was fully awake. And he knew the people outside had been drinking. One of them was the man who had wanted to get past Gabe to see Akin.

The other was Neci. She had graduated from attempting mutilation to attempting murder.

What had happened to Macy? Where were Tate and Gabe? How could the fire make so much noise and light and not awaken everyone? It had crept up outside one window now. The windows were high off the ground. The fire he could see must already be eating its way through the wall and floor.

He began to shout Tate's name, Gabe's name. He could move a little now, but not enough to make a difference.

No one came.

The fire ate its way into the room, making choking smoke that Akin discovered he could breathe easier if he did not breathe through his mouth. He had a sair at his throat now, surrounded by large and strong sensory tentacles. These moved automatically to filter the smoke from the air he breathed.

But, still, no one had come to help him. He would burn. He had no protection against fire.

He would die. Neci and her friend would destroy Human chances at a new world because they were drunk and out of their minds.

He would end.

He shouted and choked because he did not quite understand yet how to talk through a familiar orifice and breathe through an unfamiliar one.

Why was he being left to burn? People heard him. They must have heard! He could hear them now—running, shouting, their sounds blending into the snapping and roaring of the fire.

He managed to fall off the bed.

Landing was only a small shock. His sensory tentacles automatically protected themselves by flattening into his body. Once he was on the wood floor, he tried to roll toward the door.

Then he stopped, trying to understand what his senses were telling him. Vibrations. Someone coming.

Someone running toward the room he was in. Gabe's footsteps.

He shouted, hoping to guide the man in the smoke. He saw the door open, felt hands on him.

With an effort that was almost painful, Akin managed not to sink his sensory tentacles into the man's flesh. The man's touch was like an invitation to investigate him with enhanced adult senses. But now was not the time for such things. He must do all he could not to hinder Gabe.

He let himself become a thing—a sack of vegetables to be thrown over someone's shoulder. For once, he was glad to be small.

Gabe fell once, coughing, seared by the heat. He dropped Akin, picked him up, and again threw him over one shoulder.

The front door was blocked by sheets of fire. The back would be blocked in a moment. Gabe kicked it open and ran down the steps, for a moment actually plunging through flames. His hair caught fire, and Akin shouted at him to put it out.

Gabe stopped once he was clear of the house, dropped Akin into the dirt, and collapsed, beating at himself and coughing.

The tree they had stopped under had caught fire from the house. They had to move again, quickly, to avoid burning branches. Once Gabe had put out his own fire, he picked Akin up and staggered farther away toward the forest.

"Where are you going?" Akin asked him.

He did not answer. It seemed all he could do to breathe and move.

Behind them, the house was totally engulfed. Nothing could be alive in there now.

"Tate!" Akin said suddenly. Where was she? Gabe would never save him and leave Tate to burn.

"Ahead," Gabe wheezed.

She was all right, then.

Gabe fell again, this time half-atop Akin. Hurt, Akin locked into him in helpless reflex. He immediately paralyzed the man, stopping significant messages of movement between the brain and the rest of the body.

"Lie still," he said, hoping to give Gabe the illusion of choice. "Just lie there and let me help you."

"You can't help yourself," Gabe whispered, struggling to breathe, to move.

"I can help myself by healing you! If you fall on me again, I might sting you. Now shut up and stop trying to move. Your lungs are damaged and you're burned." The lung damage was serious and could kill him. The burns were only very painful. Yet Gabe would not be quiet.

"The town . . . Can they see us?"

"No. There's a cornfield between us and Phoenix now. The fire is still visible, though. And it's spreading." At least one other house was burning now. Perhaps it had caught from the burning tree.

"If it doesn't rain, half the town might burn. Fools."

"It isn't going to rain. Now be quiet, Gabe."

"If they catch us, they'll probably kill us!"

"What? Who?"

"People from town. Not everybody. Just troublemakers."

"They'll be too busy trying to put out the fire. It hasn't rained for days. They chose the wrong season for all this. Just be quiet and let me help you. I won't make you sleep, so you might feel something. But I won't hurt you."

"I hurt so bad already, I probably wouldn't know if you did."

Akin interrupted the messages of pain that Gabe's nerves were sending to his brain and encouraged his brain to secrete specific endorphins.

"Jesus Christ!" the man said, gasping, coughing. For him the pain had abruptly ceased. He felt nothing. It was less confusing for him that way. For Akin, it meant sudden, terrible pain, then slow alleviation. Not euphoria. He did not want Gabe drunk on his own endorphins. But the man could be made to feel good and alert. It was almost like making music— balancing endorphins, silencing pain, maintaining sobriety. He made simple music. Ooloi made great harmonies, interweaving people and sharing pleasure. And ooloi contributed substances of their own to the union. Akin would feel that soon when Dehkiaht changed. For now, there was the pleasure of healing.

Gabe began to breathe easier as his lungs improved. He did not notice when his flesh began to heal. Akin let the useless burned flesh slough off. Gabe would need water and food soon. Akin would finish by stimulating feelings of hunger and thirst in the man so that he would be willing to eat or drink whatever Akin could spot for him. It was especially important that he drink soon.

"Someone's coming," Gabe whispered.

"Gilbert Senn," Akin said into his ear. "He's been searching for some time. If we're still, he may not find us."

"How do you know it's—?"

"Footsteps. He still sounds the same as he did when I was here before. He's alone."

Silently Akin finished his work and withdrew the filaments of his sensory tentacles from Gabe. "You can move now," he whispered. "But don't."

Akin could move too, a little more, although he doubted that he could walk.

Abruptly Gilbert Senn found them—all but stumbled over them in the moonlight and the firelight. He leaped back, his rifle aimed at them.

Gabe sat up. Akin used Gabe to pull himself up and managed not to fall when he let go. He could hurry everyone's bodily processes but his own. Gilbert Senn looked at him, then carefully avoided looking at him. He lowered the rifle.

"Are you all right, Gabe?" he asked.

"I'm fine."

"You're burned."

"I was." Gabe glanced at Akin.

Gilbert Senn carefully did not look at Akin. "I see." He turned toward the fire. "I wish that hadn't happened. We would never have burned your home."

"For all I know, you did," Gabe muttered.

"Neci did," Akin said quickly. "She and the man who wanted to get into the house to see me. I heard them."

The rifle came up again, aimed only at Akin this time. "You will be quiet," he said.

"If he dies, we all die," Gabe said softly.

"We all die no matter what. Some of us choose to die free!"

"There will be freedom on Mars, Gil."

The corners of Gilbert Senn's mouth turned down. Gabe shook his head. To Akin he said, "He believes your Mars idea is a trick. A way of gathering in the resisters easily to use them on the ship or in the Oankali villages on Earth. A lot of people feel that way."

"*This* is my world," Gilbert Senn said. "I was born here, and I'll die here. And if I can't have Human children—fully Human children—I'll have no children at all."

This was a man who would have helped cut sensory

tentacles from Amma and Shkaht. He had not wanted to do such things to children, to females, but he honestly believed it was the right thing to do.

"Mars is not for you," Akin told him.

The gun wavered. "What?"

"Mars isn't for anyone who doesn't want it. It will be hard work, risk, and challenge. It will be a Human world someday. But it will never be Earth. You need Earth."

"You think your childish psychology will influence me?"

"No," Akin said.

"I don't want to hear it from you or from Yori."

"If you kill me now, no Humans will go to Mars."

"None will go anyway."

"Humanity will live or die by what you do now."

"No!"

The man wanted to shoot Akin. Perhaps he had never wanted anything as much. He might even have come into the field hoping to find Akin and shoot him. Now he could not shoot Akin because Akin might possibly somehow be telling the truth.

After a long time, Gilbert Senn turned and went back toward the fire.

After a moment, Gabe stood up and shook himself. "If that was psychology, it was damn good," he said.

"It was literal truth," Akin told him.

"I was afraid it might be. Gil almost shot you."

"I thought he might."

"Could he have killed you?"

"Yes, with enough ammunition and enough persistence. Or perhaps he could have made me kill him."

He bent to pick Akin up. "You've made yourself too valuable to take risks like that. I know guys who wouldn't have hesitated." He shook himself again, shaking Akin. "God, what's this stuff you've smeared me with? Goddamn slimy shit!"

Akin did not answer.

"What is it?" Gabe insisted. "It stinks."

"Cooked flesh."

Gabe shuddered and said nothing.

═ 8 ═

Tate waited at the edge of the forest amid a cluster of other people. Mateo and Pilar Leal were there. How would Tino take seeing them again? How would they take seeing him with Nikanj? Would he stay with his mates and his children or go with his parents' people? It was not likely that Nikanj could let him go or that he could survive long without Nikanj. Mars might even make Tino's choice of the Oankali more acceptable to Tino. He would no longer be helping Humanity breed itself out of existence. But he would not be helping it shape its new world either.

Yori was there, standing with Kolina Wilton and Stancio Roybal. Sober now, Stancio looked tired and ill. There were people Akin did not recognize—new people. There was Abira— an arm reaching out of a hammock, lifting him in.

"Where's Macy?" Gabe asked as he put Akin down.

"He hasn't come," Kolina answered. "We hoped he was helping you with Akin."

"He went out when he heard Neci and her friend setting the fire," Akin said. "I lost track of him after that."

"Was he hurt?" Kolina demanded.

"I don't know. I'm sorry."

She thought about this for a moment. "We have to wait for him!"

"We'll wait," Tate said. "He knows where to meet us."

They moved deeper into the forest as the light from the fire grew brighter.

"My home is burning," Abira said as everyone watched. "I didn't think I would have to watch my home burn again."

"Just be glad you aren't in it," one of the strangers said. Akin knew at once that this man disliked Abira. Humans would carry their dislikes with them to be shut up together on Mars.

The fire burned through the night, but Macy did not come. A few other people arrived. Yori had asked most of them to come. It was she who kept others from shooting them as they were spotted. If they shot anyone, they would have to leave quickly before the sound drew enemies.

"I have to go back," Kolina said finally.

No one said anything. Perhaps they had been waiting for this.

"They could be holding him," Tate said finally. "They could be waiting for you."

"No. Not with the fire. They wouldn't think about me."

"There are those who would. The kind who would hold you and sell you if they thought they could get away with it."

"I'll go," Stancio said. "Probably no one's even noticed that I've left town. I'll find him."

"I can't leave without him," she said.

"But we have to leave soon," Gabe said. "Gil Senn nearly killed Akin back there in the field. If he gets another chance, he might pull the trigger. I know there are others who wouldn't hesitate, and they'll be out hunting as soon as it's light."

"Someone give me a gun," Stancio said.

One of the strangers handed him one.

"I want one, too," Kolina said. She was staring at the fire, and when Yori thrust a rifle at her, she took it without turning her head. "Keep Akin safe," she said.

Yori hugged her. "Keep yourself safe. Bring Macy to us. You can find the way."

"North to the big river, then east along the river. I know."

No one said anything to Stancio, so Akin called him over. Gabe had propped Akin against a tree, and now Stancio squatted before him, clearly not bothered by his appearance.

"Would you let me check you?" Akin asked. "You don't look well, and for this you may need to be... very healthy."

Stancio shrugged. "I don't have anything you can cure."

"Let me have a look. It won't hurt."

Stancio stood up. "Is this Mars thing real?"

"It's real. Another chance for Humanity."

"You see to that, then. Don't worry about me." He put his gun on his shoulder and walked with Kolina back toward the fire.

Akin watched them until they disappeared around the edge of the cornfield. He never saw either of them again.

After a while, Gabe lifted him, hung him over one shoulder, and began to walk. Akin would be able to walk himself tomorrow or the day after. For now, he watched from Gabe's shoulder as the others fell in, single file. They headed north toward the river. There, they would turn east toward Lo. In less time than they probably realized, some of them would be aboard shuttles headed for Mars, there to watch the changes begin and be witnesses for their people.

He was perhaps the last to see the smoke cloud behind them and Phoenix still burning.

ABOUT THE AUTHOR

I'm a 48-year-old writer who can remember being a 10-year-old writer and who expects someday to be an 80-year-old writer. I'm also comfortably asocial—a hermit in the middle of Los Angeles—a pessimist if I'm not careful, a feminist, a Black, a former Baptist, an oil-and-water combination of ambition, laziness, insecurity, certainty, and drive.

I've had ten novels published so far: *Patternmaster, Mind of my Mind, Survivor, Kindred, Wild Seed, Clay's Ark, Dawn, Adulthood Rites, Imago,* and *Parable of the Sower,* as well as a collection of my shorter work, entitled *Bloodchild.* I've also had short stories published in anthologies and magazines. One, "Speech Sounds," won a Hugo Award as best short story of 1984. Another, "Bloodchild," won both the 1985 Hugo and the 1984 Nebula awards as best novelette.

—**Octavia E. Butler**

In 1995 Octavia E. Butler was awarded a MacArthur Grant. In what is popularly called the genius program, the John D. and Catherine T. MacArthur Foundation rewards creative people who push the boundaries of their fields.

DON'T MISS THESE SCIENCE FICTION MASTERPIECES FROM HUGO AND NEBULA AWARD-WINNER
OCTAVIA E. BUTLER

☐ **ADULTHOOD RITES**
(0-445-20-903-8, $5.99 USA) ($6.99 Can.)
☐ **DAWN**
(0-445-20-779-5, $5.50 USA) ($6.99 Can.)
☐ **IMAGO**
(0-445-36-454-1, $5.50 USA) ($6.99 Can.)
☐ **MIND OF MY MIND**
(0-446-36-188-7, $5.50 USA) ($6.99 Can.)
☐ **PARABLE OF THE SOWER**
(0-446-60-157-7, $5.99 USA) ($6.99 Can.)
☐ **PATTERNMASTER**
(0-446-36-281-6, $5.50 USA) ($6.99 Can.)
☐ **WILD SEED**
(0-445-20-537-7, $5.99 USA) ($6.99 Can.)

AVAILABLE AT A BOOKSTORE NEAR YOU FROM

 **WARNER BOOKS**

622-c

TURN THE PAGE FOR
A SPECIAL BONUS CHAPTER OF

IMAGO

by Octavia E. Butler

1

I slipped into my first met-
amorphosis so quietly that no one noticed. Metamorphoses were not supposed to begin that way. Most people
begin with small, obvious, physical changes—the loss
of fingers and toes, for instance, or the budding of new
fingers and toes of a different design.

I wish my experience had been that normal, that safe.

For several days, I changed without attracting attention. Early stages of metamorphosis didn't normally last
for days without bringing on deep sleep, but mine did.
My first changes were sensory. Tastes, scents, all sensations suddenly became complex, confusing, yet unexpectedly seductive.

I had to relearn everything. River water, for instance:
when I swam in it, I noticed it had two distinctive major

flavors—hydrogen and oxygen?—and many minor flavors. I could separate out and savor each one individually. In fact, I couldn't help separating them. But I learned them quickly and accepted them in their new complexity so that only occasional changes in minor flavors demanded my attention.

Our river water at Lo always came to us clouded with sediment. "Rich," the Oankali called it. "Muddy," the Humans said, and filtered it or let the silt settle to the bottom before they drank it. "Just water," we constructs said, and shrugged. We had never known any other water.

As quickly as I could, I learned again to understand and accept my sensory impressions of the people and things around me. The experience absorbed so much of my attention that I didn't understand how my family could fail to see that something unusual was happening to me. But beyond mentioning that I was daydreaming too much, even my parents missed the signs.

They were, after all, the wrong signs. No one was expecting them, so no one noticed when they appeared.

All five of my parents were old when I was born. They didn't look any older than my adult sisters and brothers, but they had helped with the founding of Lo. They had grandchildren who were old. I don't think I had ever surprised them before. I wasn't sure I liked surprising them now. I didn't want to tell them. I especially didn't want to tell Tino, my Human father. He was supposed to stay with me through my metamorphosis—since he was my same-sex Human parent. But I did not feel drawn to him as I should have. Nor did I feel drawn to Lilith, my birth mother. She was Human, too, and what was happening to me was definitely not a Human thing. Strangely I didn't want to go to my Oankali father, Dichaan, either, and he was my logical choice after Tino. My Oankali mother, Ahajas, would have talked to one of my fathers for me. She had done that for two of my brothers who had been afraid of metamorphosis—afraid they would change too much, lose all signs of their Humanity. That could happen to me, though I had never worried about it. Ahajas would have talked to me and for me, no matter what my problem was. Of all my parents, she was the easiest to talk to. I would have gone to her if the thought of doing so had been more appealing—or if I had understood why it was so unappealing. What was wrong with me? I wasn't shy or afraid, but when I thought of going to her, I felt first drawn, then . . . almost repelled.

Finally there was my ooloi parent, Nikanj.

It would tell me to go to one of my same-sex parents—one of my fathers. What else could it say? I knew well enough that I was in metamorphosis, and that that was one of the few things ooloi parents could not help with. There were still some Humans who insisted on seeing the ooloi as some kind of male-female combination, but the ooloi were no such thing. They were themselves—a different sex altogether.

So I went to Nikanj only hoping to enjoy its company for a while. Eventually it would notice what was happening to me and send me to my fathers. Until it did, I would rest near it. I was tired, sleepy. Metamorphosis was mostly sleep.

I found Nikanj inside the family house, talking to a

pair of human strangers. The Humans were standing back from Nikanj. The female was almost sheltering behind the male, and the male was making a painful effort to appear courageous. Both looked alarmed when they saw me open a wall and step through into the room. Then, as they got a look at me, they seemed to relax a little. I looked very Human—especially if they compared me to Nikanj, who wasn't Human at all.

The Humans smelled most obviously of sweat and adrenaline, food and sex. I sat down on the floor and let myself work out the complex combinations of scents. My new awareness wouldn't allow me to do anything else. By the time I was finished, I thought I would be able to track those two Humans through anything.

Nikanj paid no attention to me except to notice me when I came in. It was used to its children coming and going as they chose, used to all of us spending time with it, learning whatever it was willing to teach us.

It had an incredibly complex scent because it was ooloi. It had collected within itself not only the reproductive material of other members of the family but cells of other plant and animal species that it had dealt with recently. These it would study, memorize, then either consume or store. It consumed the ones it knew it could re-create from memory, using its own DNA. It kept the others alive in a kind of stasis until they were needed.

Its most noticeable underscent was Kaal, the kin group it was born into. I had never met its parents, but I knew the Kaal scent from other members of the Kaal kin group. Somehow, though, I had never noticed that scent on Nikanj, never separated it out this way.

The main scent was Lo, of course. It had mated with Oankali of the Lo kin group, and on mating, it had altered its own scent as an ooloi must. The word "ooloi" could not be translated directly into English because its meaning was as complex as Nikanj's scent. "Treasured stranger." "Bridge." "Life trader." "Weaver." "Magnet."

Magnet, my birth mother says. People are drawn to ooloi and can't escape. She couldn't, certainly. But then, neither could Nikanj escape her or any of its mates. The Oankali said the chemical bonds of mating were as difficult to break as the habit of breathing.

Scents . . . The two visiting Humans were longtime mates and smelled of each other.

"We don't know yet whether we want to emigrate," the female was saying. "We've come to see for ourselves and for our people."

"You'll be shown everything," Nikanj told them. "There are no secrets about the Mars colony or travel to it. But right now the shuttles allotted to emigration are all in use. We have a guest area where Humans can wait."

The two Humans looked at one another. They still smelled frightened, but now both were making an effort to look brave. Their faces were almost expressionless.

"We don't want to stay here," the male said. "We'll come back when there's a ship."

Nikanj stood up—unfolded, as Humans say. "I can't tell you when there'll be a ship," it said. "They arrive when they arrive. Let me show you the guest area. It isn't like this house. Humans built it from cut wood."

The pair stumbled back from Nikanj.

Nikanj's sensory tentacles flattened against its body in

amusement. It sat down again. "There are other Humans waiting in the guest area," it told them gently. "They're like you. They want their own all-Human world. They'll be traveling with you when you go." It paused, looked at me. "Eka, why don't you show them?"

I wanted to stay with it now more than ever, but I could see that the two Humans were relieved to be turned over to someone who at least looked Human. I stood up and faced them.

"This is Jodahs," Nikanj told them, "one of my younger children."

The female gave me a look that I had seen too often not to recognize. She said, "But I thought . . ."

"No," I said to her, and smiled. "I'm not Human. I'm a Human-born construct. Come out this way. The guest area isn't far away."

They did not want to follow me through the wall I opened until it was fully open—as though they thought the wall might close on them, as though it would hurt them if it did.

"It would be like being grasped gently by a big hand," I told them when we were all outside.

"What?" the male asked.

"If the wall shut on you. It couldn't hurt you because you're alive. It might eat your clothing, though."

"No, thanks!"

I laughed. "I've never seen that happen, but I've heard it can."

"What's your name?" the female asked.

"All of it?" She looked interested in me—smelled sexually attracted, which made her interesting to me. Human females did tend to like me as long as I kept my few body tentacles covered by clothing and my few head tentacles hidden in my hair. The sensory spots on my face and arms looked like ordinary skin, though they didn't feel ordinary.

"Your Human name," the female said. "I already know . . . Eka and Jodahs, but I'm not sure which to call you."

"Eka is just a term of endearment for young children," I told her, "like lelka for married children and Chka between mates. Jodahs is my personal name. The Human version of my whole name is Jodahs Iyapo Leal Kaalnikanjlo. My name, the surnames of my birth mother and Human father, and Nikanj's name beginning with the kin group it was born into and ending with the kin group of its Oankali mates. If I were Oankali-born or if I gave you the Oankali version of my name, it would be a lot longer and more complicated."

"I've heard some of them," the female said. "You'll probably drop them eventually."

"No. We'll change them to suit our needs, but we won't drop them. They give very useful information, especially when people are looking for mates."

"Jodahs doesn't sound like any name I've heard before," the male said.

"Oankali name. An Oankali named Jodahs died helping with the emigration. My birth mother said he should be remembered. The Oankali don't have a tradition of remembering people by naming kids after them, but my birth mother insisted. She does that sometimes—insists on keeping Human customs."

"You look very Human," the female said softly.

I smiled. "I'm a child. I just look unfinished."

"How old are you?"

"Twenty-nine."

"Good god! When will you be considered an adult?"

"After metamorphosis." I smiled to myself. Soon. "I have a brother who went through it at twenty-one, and a sister who didn't reach it until she was thirty-three. People change when their bodies are ready, not at some specific age."

She was silent for some time. We reached the last of the true houses of Lo—the houses that had been grown from the living substance of the Lo entity. Humans without Oankali mates could not open walls or raise table, bed, or chair platforms in such houses. Left alone in our houses, these Humans were prisoners until some construct, Oankali, or mated Human freed them. Thus, they had been given first a guest house, then a guest area. In that area they had built their dead houses of cut wood and woven thatch. They used fire for light and cooking and occasionally they burned down one of their houses. Houses that did not burn became infested with rodents and insects which ate the Humans' food and bit or stung the Humans themselves. Periodically Oankali went in and drove the non-Human life out. It always came back. It had been feeding on Humans, eating their food, and living in their buildings since long before the Oankali arrived. Still the guest area was reasonably comfortable. Guests ate from trees and plants that were not what they appeared to be. They were extensions of the Lo entity. They had been induced to synthesize fruits and vegetables in shapes, flowers, and textures that Humans recognized. The foods grew from what appeared to be their proper trees and plants. Lo took care of the Humans' wastes, keeping their area clean, though they tended to be careless about where they threw or dumped things in this temporary place.

"There's an empty house there," I said, pointing.

The female stared at my hand rather than at where I pointed. I had, from a Human point of view, too many fingers and toes. Seven per. Since they were part of distinctly Human-looking hands and feet, Humans didn't usually notice them at once.

I held my hand open, palm up so that she could see it, and her expression flickered from curiosity and surprise through embarrassment back to curiosity.

"Will you change much in metamorphosis?" she asked.

"Probably. The Human-born get more Oankali and the Oankali-born get more Human. I'm first-generation. If you want to see the future, take a look at some of the third- and fourth-generation constructs. They're a lot more uniform from start to finish."

"That's not our future," the male said.

"Your choice," I said.

The male walked away toward the empty house. The female hesitated. "What do you think of our emigration?" she asked.

I looked at her, liking her, not wanting to answer. But such questions should be answered. Why, though, were the Human females who insisted on asking them so often small, weak people? The Martian environment they were headed for was harsher than any they had known. We would see that they had the best possible chance to survive. Many would live to bear children on their new world. But they would suffer so. And in the end, it would all be for nothing. Their own genetic conflict had betrayed and destroyed them once. It would do so again.

"You should stay," I told the female. "You should join us."

"Why?"

I wanted very much not to look at her, to go away from her. Instead I continued to face her. "I understand that Humans must be free to go," I said softly. "I'm Human enough for my body to understand that. But I'm Oankali enough to know that you will eventually destroy yourselves again."

She frowned, marring her smooth forehead. "You mean another war?"

"Perhaps. Or maybe you'll find some other way to do it. You were working on several ways before your war."

"You don't know anything about it. You're too young."

"You should stay and mate with constructs or with Oankali," I said. "The children we construct are free of inherent flaws. What we build will last."

"You're just a child, repeating what you've been told!"

I shook my head. "I perceive what I perceive. No one had to tell me how to use my senses any more than they had to tell you how to see or hear. There is a lethal genetic conflict in Humanity, and you know it."

"All we know is what the Oankali have told us." The male had come back. He put his arm around the female, drawing her away from me as though I had offered some threat. "They could be lying for their own reasons."

I shifted my attention to him. "You know they're not," I said softly. "Your own history tells you. Your people are intelligent, and that's good. The Oankali say you're potentially one of the most intelligent species they've found. But you're also hierarchical—you and your nearest animal relatives and your most distant animal ancestors. Intelligence is relatively new to life on Earth, but your hierarchical tendencies are ancient. The new was too often put at the service of the old. It will be again. You're bright enough to learn to live on your new world, but you're so hierarchical you'll destroy yourselves trying to dominate it and each other. You might last a long time, but in the end, you'll destroy yourselves."

"We could last a thousand years," the male said. "We did all right on Earth until the war."

"You could. Your new world will be difficult. It will demand most of your attention, perhaps occupy your hierarchical tendencies safely for a while."

"We'll be free—us, our children, their children."

"Perhaps."

"We'll be fully Human and free. That's enough. We might even get into space again on our own someday. Your people might be dead wrong about us."

"No." He couldn't read the gene combinations as I could. It was as though he were about to walk off a cliff simply because he could not see it—or because he, or rather his descendants, would not hit the rocks below for a long time. And what were we doing, we who knew the truth? Helping him reach the cliff. Ferrying him to it.

"We might outlast your people here on Earth," he said.

13

"I hope so," I told him. His expression said he didn't believe me, but I meant it. We would not be here—the Earth he knew would not be here—for more than a few centuries. We, Oankali and construct, were space-going people, as curious about other life and as acquisitive of it as Humans were hierarchical. Eventually we would have to begin the long, long search for a new species to combine with to construct new life-forms. Much of Oankali existence was spent in such searches. We would leave this solar system in perhaps three centuries. I would live to see the leave-taking myself. And when we broke and scattered, we would leave behind a lump of stripped rock more like the moon than like his blue Earth. He did not know that. He would never know it. To tell him would be a cruelty.

"Do you ever think of yourself or your kind as Human?" the female asked. "Some of you look so Human."

"We feel our Humanity. It helps us to understand both you and the Oankali. Oankali alone could never have let you have your Mars colony."

"I heard they were helping!" the male said. "Your . . . your parent said they were helping!"

"They help because of what we constructs tell them: that you should be allowed to go even though you'll eventually destroy yourselves. The Oankali believe . . . the Oankali *know to the bone* that it's wrong to help the Human species regenerate unchanged because it *will* destroy itself again. To them it's like deliberately causing the conception of a child who is so defective that it must die in infancy."

"They're wrong. Someday we'll show them how wrong."

It was a threat. It was meaningless, but it gave him some slight satisfaction. "The other Humans here will show you where to gather food," I said. "If you need anything else, ask one of us." I turned to go.

"So goddamn patronizing," the male muttered.

I turned back without thinking. "Am I really?"

The male frowned, muttered a curse, and went back into the house. I understood then that he was just angry. It bothered me that I sometimes made them angry. I never intended to.

The female stepped to me, touched my face, examined a little of my hair. Humans who hadn't mated among us never really learned to touch us. At best, they annoyed us by rubbing their hands over sensory spots, and once their hands found the spots they never liked them.

The female jerked her hand back when her fingers discovered the one below my left ear.

"They're a little like eyes that can't close to protect themselves," I said. "It doesn't exactly hurt us when you touch them, but we don't like you to."

"So what? You have to teach people how to touch you?"

I smiled and took her hand between my own. "Hands are always safe," I said. I left her standing there, watching me. I could see her through sensory tentacles in my hair. She stood there until the male came out and drew her inside.